THE
FOREVER FAE
SERIES

REIGN OF
ICE

L.P. DOVER

Reign of Ice

By:

L.P. Dover

All rights reserved. No part of this book may be reproduced or transmitted in any form by any means, electronic or mechanical, including photocopying, recording, or by any information storage and retrieval system, without written consent from the author.

Reign of Ice
L.P. Dover
Copyright 2013 by L.P. Dover
Editor: Melissa Ringsted
Cover Artist: Regina Wamba
www.maeidesign.com
Formatting: Amanda Heath
https://www.facebook.com/LittleDoveFormatting

This is to everyone who has believed in me and has given my faeries a chance. The end has come, but it's also the beginning to something new. I want to thank you all for your undying support and your kind words. I know my faeries appreciate it as well. I also want to say that it's been an amazing journey in the Land of the Fae and I look forward to writing more in this wonderful realm.

Table of Contents

The Prophecy

Summer, Fall, Winter, Spring
two Courts to Four is what it will bring.
Without the Four the evil will spread,
the Land of the Fae will fall into dread.
The next generation will provide the Four,
the maiden souls and nothing more.
The Power of Four will start with the first,
if he gets the power, only then will you be
cursed.
The Power of Four will be drawn to the
others,
their power is strong, the power of lovers.
The moment they become one,
only then will the change have begun.
Two Courts to Four is what needs to be,
to save the Land, so shall we see.

Prologue

Ariella

A Few Days Ago

THERE WAS A stirring in the air that reeked of menace and death, and as my fingers touched the land below me it felt as if it was weeping. I could sense the sadness all around me as I looked out over the horizon. Drake and Sorcha left a while ago to rescue her guardian, Oren, and her friend, Sarette, from the dark sorcerer's army. Knowing my brother they would surely succeed, but something just wasn't right. I was training alone in the Spring Court garden, practicing my new sword techniques, when I heard the stampede of hooves trembling on the ground beneath me. The sound of horns bellowed out from a distance, signaling a cry for help, and with that sound my blood ran cold.

Racing toward the front of the palace, my eyes went wide at the sight before me, my heart plummeting in my chest. Warriors from Summer, Spring, and Winter were headed toward the palace, most of which were in varied states of injury. Some were bleeding or slumped over their horses, while some I could tell would soon be piles of ash.

Kalen and Meliantha both charged out of the palace, along with dozens of their Spring Court warriors, as they rushed to the gates. Sheathing my sword, I ran up to my sister and faltered when I saw her weary gaze.

"Meliantha?"

"It's bad," she whispered, turning a tear-streaked face my way. "I can feel it in my blood."

My sister had healing capabilities, but even I didn't know how much of her power she could give until it drained her. "Will you be able to save them?" I asked.

She kept her gaze on the warriors as they approached the gate. "Yes, I'll be able to, but it doesn't change the fact that we've lost so many. So many are … gone."

As soon as the warriors entered through the gate, we all rushed to help them. The warrior I approached first had an arrow sticking out of his chest and was about to fall off his horse, his face pale and drawn. Luckily, I caught him in my arms before he hit the ground.

"Thank you," he wheezed, coughing and sputtering.

Holding him in my arms, I half carried and half dragged him up the steps, trying my best not to jostle him. "It's okay, I got you," I murmured soothingly.

Before I could carry the warrior into the palace, my blood froze in my veins when I heard Kalen's roar; it echoed loudly in my ear. When I turned to see the slumped figure in his arms I knew exactly who it was going to be. From the short, brown hair, creamy pale skin, and the black and silver warrior gear I knew without a doubt that it was Brayden in his arms.

"Oh no," I cried, wishing I could go to him. There was a reason I had that unnerving feeling and it wasn't because of the war, it was because of him. He was hurt and deep down I knew it. *Please, let him be all right.*

Kalen rushed inside, carrying an unconscious Brayden in his arms, while Meliantha followed, casting me a worried glance before she too disappeared inside the palace. Quickly, I draped the warrior's arm around my neck and put my hand around his waist, trying my best not to touch the arrow. As soon as I got him helped and healed, I was going to find out how Brayden was.

"Come on, warrior, let's get you fixed up and healed," I grunted, trying to hold as much of his weight as I could.

"Kamden," he whispered, lifting up his head. His soft hazel eyes were full of pain, but his lip pulled up at the side in a sad smile. "My name is Kamden, Your Highness. I trained with you the other day."

Forcing a smile on my face, I blew out a shaky breath and said, "That's right, Kamden, you did. I'm sorry I didn't catch your name during that time. You can call me Ariella." Worry for Brayden plagued my mind, but the warrior in my arms needed help just as badly. Carrying him inside, I was directed to a room by one of the servants who had a bed already for Kamden. I placed him on the soft sheets, and as he lay down he hissed when the arrow jostled in his chest. It was slowly moving out on its own, but I knew he would heal quicker if I pulled it out.

"This is going to hurt, but you'll heal a lot faster if I pull it out. Is that okay?" I asked hesitantly.

He nodded quickly and groaned, "I trust you, Princess. Just take it out." His forehead was covered in sweat and he took short, shallow breaths as I prepared to remove the arrow.

Taking a deep breath, I grasped onto the wooden arrow and pulled it out quickly, cringing when the sound of ripping flesh echoed throughout the room. Kamden growled with the pain and lifted off the bed as a spurt of blood gushed out of his wound. Immediately, I ran to the bathroom and grabbed a few towels, placing one over his chest and applying pressure to it.

"You'll be okay, now," I promised. "All we have to do is wait on the wound to heal and you'll be just as good as new."

Kamden clasped my hand and held it to his heart. "Thank you for tending to me, Your Highness. I promise to repay you in any way I can."

Smiling, I wiped the sweat away from his forehead with one of the other towels. As his eyes fluttered shut, I murmured softly, "No payment necessary, warrior. You healing is all the payment I need."

❄❄❄

I waited for Kamden to fall asleep completely, and when I knew he would be okay, I ran out of the room in search of Meliantha. I had no clue where they would have taken Brayden, but when I finally found her, she was leaning against Kalen looking drawn and pale. The healing must've gotten to her and worn her down.

"Ariella," she whispered, blinking her eyes slowly with a tiny smile on her face. "I did it."

Kalen held her tighter and lifted her into his arms. "I'm going to take her to lie down. She needs her rest after all she's done." His long, black hair hung in his face and his shirt was stained with ungodly amounts of blood; Brayden's blood.

"Is your brother all right?" I whispered, staring horrifically at the red stains spattered across his shirt.

Kalen nodded and blew out a heavy breath. "He will be, but if he would have been a few minutes later probably not."

With that, Kalen left with my sister in his arms and disappeared around the corner. The door to the room in front of me was closed, but I knew without a doubt that Brayden was behind it. There was something in me that could sense him every time he was near. Slowly, I opened the door and snuck inside, hoping to not wake him if he was sleeping.

Something in my soul wanted me to see him, to make sure he was all right. The shades were drawn, making the room appear ominous and dark, just like Brayden and his broody ways. He was standoffish at times, but there were also times when I would catch him staring curiously at me. It made me wonder if I wasn't the only one who had mixed feelings about the other.

Slowly, I approached his frozen form where he lay motionless in the bed. He was cast in shadows, but with my fae sight I could tell—even from this distance—that his eyes were closed. *What was I even doing in here?* I wondered. If he woke up he would probably tell me to get out.

Blood covered his clothing, which was discarded on the floor, and the primal urge to run to him and take care of him pushed me closer to the bed. I had never really spoken to him before, but I knew without a doubt that there was something happening between us. I could feel it. It wasn't the usual flirty feelings I got when I joked around with the warriors, but something deeper … something real.

Sitting on the edge of the bed, I watched Brayden as he took slow breaths in and out, his chest rising and falling easily with each turn. For the rest of the day and the day after that, I sat with him and watched over him, only leaving every now and again to relieve myself and stretch. Meliantha checked on him occasionally and couldn't understand why he wouldn't wake up. He should have already woken up. I sang to him periodically, songs of love and adventure, and most importantly songs of winter and going home, hoping it would bring him back. His lips twitched every once in a while during my songs, and it would always make me falter.

I wanted to kiss those lips, and run my hands through his tousled brown hair to make him wake up so I'd know he was truly all right. I couldn't rest until I knew he was going to wake up. As I leaned over to touch his lips with my fingers, the door flew open, startling me, and in strode Kalen and Meliantha with smirks on their faces. I immediately pulled back and smiled at them as they approached the bed, ignoring their amused expressions, and put distance between me and the Winter prince.

Kalen's grin grew bigger as his gaze landed on his brother and I froze in place with his next words. "Well, it's about time you woke up, little brother," he teased. "I was starting to think you were pretending so you could keep Ariella all to yourself."

My breath hitched in my chest. When I summoned the courage to look over at the bed, Brayden's eyes were indeed wide open, staring daggers at Kalen. Suddenly, he turned those deep brown eyes to me and all I could do was stare back, completely motionless. *Oh yeah, I think I'm definitely going to be in trouble,* I thought to myself.

✳✳✳

The day we found out Sorcha was safe and with my brother, Drake, the whole Spring Court rejoiced in celebration. Kalen put together the best party ever and broke out his reserves of faerie wine, which quickly began to diminish. The sparkly blue liquid glistened in my cup as I downed the first glass, letting it fizzle all the way down into my belly. I poured myself another, and then another. Swaying to the music, I closed my eyes and smiled, thinking about how happy my brother and Sorcha must be now that they were together. He had his princess and soon to be queen in his arms.

As I was about to take another sip of my wine, a set of arms wrapped around my waist and twirled me around, making me spill the whole glass of wine I just poured onto the floor. Kamden's laugh sounded in my ear along with Zanna's. Thankfully, none spilled all over the sleeveless midnight blue gown I chose to wear for the occasion.

"Now look what you did," I grumbled halfheartedly—teasing—as Kamden set me back on my feet. I smacked his arm and placed my hands on my hips. "That was a perfectly good glass of faerie wine, Kam. Now what am I going to do?"

"Uh … pour another glass," he suggested mockingly. I set my glass down and sighed. It was probably best I didn't drink more. One glass of faerie wine was potent enough to get anyone drunk, and I was already feeling way more than tipsy as it was.

I'd grown really close to Kamden and Zanna while being in the Spring Court and I just realized how much I was going to miss them when I left to go back to Summer. They were both originally from the Winter, but they chose to follow Kalen when he became king of the Spring Court. Kamden's rich, black hair matched Zanna's perfectly along with their shimmery golden skin of the Spring. It was amazing how their skin glittered under the light, but that was one of the perks about being a Spring Fae.

Kamden held out his hand for me to take and asked sweetly, "Will you dance with me, Princess?"

I raised a brow at Zanna who in turn rolled her eyes and pushed me into his arms. "Stop looking at me like that. I'm not going to get mad if you dance with him. I know who his heart belongs to, not to mention I know where yours belongs as well." I lifted a brow and rolled my eyes. I asked her a few questions about Brayden just to get an insight on who he was since she lived in the Winter Court before, and ever since then she claimed that I was in love with him.

Smiling, she winked and waved at us before disappearing into the crowd. I gazed up at Kamden. "You are one lucky man, Kam. Maybe one day I'll be able to find someone who can put up with me."

He chortled and pulled me close, placing a hand on my waist while holding my hand in the other.

"It'll happen one day, but this person Zanna speaks of … is she talking about Prince Brayden?"

Biting my lip, I averted my gaze from his hazel eyes and smiled. "Maybe," I began. "All I know is there's something about him. It's a feeling I get when he's close. I can feel it even now."

"That's because he's headed this way," he remarked. "And let me tell you … he looks pissed as hell that you're dancing with me."

Kamden turned me around, but kept his hand on my waist with a glint in his eye. "What are you doing?" I whispered incredulously.

He leaned down to whisper in my ear, "Just trust me. I'm a guy, I know how this works."

Brayden's glare hardened as he approached us, darting his eyes back and forth from me to him. Whatever was going on, he didn't look happy. Could it really be that I was with Kamden? The second he stopped in front of me, I blurted out the first thing that came to mind, "Good evening, Brayden. Are you enjoying the party?"

He scoffed and looked down at Kamden's hand on my waist, gritting his teeth. "Not really, which is why I'm heading back to the Winter Court. Would you mind if I spoke to you?" he said, directing the question to me. His eyes lifted and met Kamden's before adding, "In private."

Kamden bowed his head graciously and winked at me quickly before Brayden could notice. "As you wish, Your Highness. It was a pleasure seeing you again."

L. P. DOVER

"Likewise," Brayden retorted dryly.

After Kamden left to join Zanna, Brayden and I stood there in awkward silence. "So ..." I stated nervously. "What did you need to speak to me about?"

My heart thundered in my chest as I took all of him in. He was tall with short chocolate brown hair that matched his chocolate brown eyes, and creamy pale skin that I knew would be cold to the touch. His hand rested on the sword that was inside the sheath attached to his armor belt while the other was clenched in a tight fist. He definitely wasn't a jokester like Kalen or passionate like Ryder, but there was something mysterious about him that intrigued me. He was so unlike anyone I had ever met. He needed someone to loosen him up, to show him how to have fun and not be serious all the time. For once, I had a challenge and I actually looked forward to it.

Brayden finally opened his mouth to speak, "I wanted to say thank you for tending to me when I was injured. Kalen told me you never left my side."

Nonchalantly, I smiled and shrugged a shoulder. "I didn't, but I know how important you are to Kalen and to the Winter Court. I had to make sure you were going to be all right."

"Is that the only reason?" he asked curiously, his eyes roaming over my face. His gaze landed on my lips, but quickly averted them back to my eyes in all seriousness; it only made me smile more.

"What other reason would there be, Prince Brayden?" I inquired teasingly. I hoped to get a rise out of him, but of course, being the closed off prince that he was I failed miserably.

He stiffened and looked away while saying, "No reason, Princess. Enjoy the rest of your night." He turned to walk away, but something in me just couldn't let him leave. That driving force within my body urged me to follow him, to not let him go.

"Brayden, wait," I shouted, moving through the crowd. The second I caught up to him and grabbed his hand to make him stop, the whole room and everyone in it disappeared. The last thing I saw before the vision took me away was Brayden's intense gaze staring into mine, freezing me into place, and a million emotions swirling uncontrollably through my body.

The Vision

The air was cold and fresh with the smell of winter snow and ice. The land sparkled with each glittery flake that fell from the gray sky above, but then magically disappeared before hitting the ground. It reminded me of silver faerie dust. It was magical in every way possible, but what made it more magical was that it was my court ... my Winter.

I knew my heart belonged in Winter, but I could feel it even more now as the man behind me wrapped his arms around my waist, pulling me to him and away from the window in our room. His hands deftly untied the sash to my robe, slipping his hands inside and across my stomach. The flames in the fireplace

L. P. DOVER

flickered, giving the room a sensual glow, but the heat had no effect whatsoever on our haven of ice. Brayden turned me around and as I did, the robe fell to the floor and he scooped me up into his arms.

He laid me down on the bundle of blankets splayed out in front of the fireplace and settled himself between my legs. As he entered me gently, he smoothed the hair from my face and opened my lips with his kiss. The taste and smell of him was crisp, clean, and everything Winter. Everything felt right and whole, like the weight of the Land of the Fae had been lifted. However, what made it even more complete was the man above me, peering down at me with a love I never thought possible.

Our bodies moved as one, and as the tears from my eyes froze into crystals, they slowly melted when Brayden's hands wiped them away with his fire. He may be the Winter King, but underneath all that fierceness and ice lay a heart of flame. I was where I belonged ... I was where I was destined to be.

The second the vision disappeared, Brayden abruptly let go of my hand and stumbled back as if I'd burned him. Everyone around us stared and whispered amongst themselves, looking delighted and joyful, knowing very well what just happened between us. I felt the same way in my heart, but my smile quickly vanished when Brayden turned on his heel and walked away with not so much as a word to me. We'd just had a vision of our destiny and of us making love to each other, and he up and walked away from me.

I don't think so.

Clenching my hands into tight fists at my side, my blood boiled and ignited in my veins as I watched his retreating form head for the door. "Seriously?" I shouted.

I was mortified and completely embarrassed as everyone in the room witnessed my rejection. Their pitying looks were too much to bear. Before he disappeared out the door, I yelled one last thing to him, "Don't slip on the ice you cold-hearted bastard!"

Gasps erupted throughout the room, but I was too pissed to care. Marching out of the chamber, I kept my head held high and sucked back the angry tears that trembled behind my eyes. I should've known from my sisters' experiences that what I felt before was the connection calling to my soul. Of all the princes I was to be bound to ... why did it have to be the one that knew nothing about love, or even how to smile for that matter?

The Land of the Fae was doomed.

L. P. DOVER

Chapter One

ALASDAIR

"I BELIEVE MY time here in the mortal realm is over for the time being, Gothin."

Gothin nodded and slowly backed out of the mortal woman's bedroom. His troll characteristics had to be hidden in the mortal realm while I procured my army ... among other things. The naked woman on the bed was just one of many of my delights during my time here, and one that would ensure my future. The spell I put on her would keep her incapacitated until my presence was long gone. Mortal women were so weak and vulnerable I almost had to second guess my plan, but if things worked out the way I wanted them to then my legacy would never die. They all served a purpose and one day that purpose would be revealed.

"What shall we do now, Master?" Gothin asked. "Now that Sorcha has been rescued, what are the next steps to capturing the last of the Four? You already told her in her dream what you've been doing here. Do you think they are making plans to attack?"

I scoffed and threw on my clothes quickly; we slipped out of the house undetected. Once we were outside, I summoned my magic and made a portal back to the Black Forest. When the veil shimmered, we walked through the opening and were right back in the darkness I called home … for now.

Once we were safely back in the forest, I turned to Gothin and laughed incredulously. "They can't possibly be making plans any of attack. I told Sorcha about the mortal army so they would know what they were up against. The fae can't compete with the mortals' iron weapons. If they decide to attack, I'll summon them, but for now I'm going to have them sit tight."

"And the next princess?"

I sighed. "She has one more day before she turns twenty-one. She won't come into her full power until then. The good thing is that the scroll is hidden and the danger to me is gone for now. However, I do fear that taking Ariella is going to be the hardest of all. I have a plan, but it's going to take time to get it in motion. In the meantime, though, I think Ariella and I need to have a little chat."

"Will that not be risky, Master?"

I cackled sinisterly and slapped him on the shoulder. "Yes, it will, but I think it's time I had a little bit of fun."

Chapter Two

Ariella

SORCHA AND DRAKE'S Summer Court had been formed and everything was right in the Land of the Fae, except one thing. I had the vision with Brayden, but instead of him talking to me and figuring things out, he up and left me standing alone in the middle of the dance floor in the Spring Court.

Two days had passed since then, and instead of being in the Spring Court I was now standing in the new Summer Court palace. It was completely different from my home in the other Summer Court. This one looked more like a tropical paradise with its sandy beaches and palm trees. It was beautiful.

Sorcha had tricked the dark sorcerer when he demanded to have the scroll back. Instead of giving him the scroll, she handed him a letter that she had written to my brother stating how much of a jackass he was when he blew her off a while back. The expression on his face if he ever found out would be priceless.

Only my family and the Winter Court family were in the room to discuss the meaning of the scroll. I thought maybe Brayden would come around once he spent a couple of days away, but I was wrong. Staring at him from across the room, as he avoided my gaze, only fueled the fire more. As Elvena deciphered the meaning of the scroll, she had all of us hold hands: Calista, Meliantha, Sorcha, and I. The magic between the four of us was the most raw and powerful force I'd ever felt flow through my veins. However, that feeling did not compare to the panic I felt after hearing Elvena explain the rest of the scroll in full detail. Surely, I wasn't hearing her right.

Elvena began, "To defeat the dark sorcerer we need the blood of the Four … the *bonded* blood of the Four. Which means Ariella will need to be bonded to Brayden for this to work."

Squeezing my eyes shut, I inwardly groaned and then glanced at Brayden, who stood motionless by his father, King Madoc. I glared at him, waiting on him to look at me, but nothing … it was always nothing with him. *You have got to be kidding me. Why won't he acknowledge me?* All I knew was that my heart was racing and I wanted to scream. I wanted to punch

Brayden in the face so hard and see what he'd do. *Would he just stand there and take it or would he actually say something?* Maybe I should try.

Sorcha squeezed my hand and leaned over to whisper in my ear, "It's going to be okay. Brayden isn't the type to express his feelings, and neither am I really, but Drake has helped with that. I know he's feeling the connection, but he probably just needs more time to process everything. He'll come around."

"I guess we'll see," I whispered back through gritted teeth. I needed more answers than just the vague explanation Elvena spouted off. "Does it say why the blood has to be bonded?" I asked Elvena. "My blood should still be the same, bonded or not."

Elvena shook her head. "No, my child, it won't. Right now we have Calista with Fall blood, Meliantha with Spring, Sorcha with Summer, and you. As of right now you're Summer, but we need you to be the Winter."

Lowering my head, I closed my eyes and sighed, clenching my jaw. "Thank you. Unfortunately, I get it now." I let go of Sorcha and Calista's hands and backed away, determined to get out of there. They all had pitying looks on their faces and I couldn't stand to see them directed toward me. My sisters looked as if they wanted to follow me, but I held up my hands, stopping them. "If you'll excuse me, I need to get some fresh air ... alone."

Hastily, I retreated from the room and out of the palace onto the sandy beach, breathing in the salty sea air. The sound of the water was soothing—almost

L. P. DOVER

hypnotic—as I gazed out at it. However, its lulling magic wasn't working on me at the moment.

"This is ridiculous," I snapped out loud. "Talking to someone should not be this complicated. I'm going to go right back in there and *make* him talk to me." Taking a deep breath, I turned away from the magical blue water and marched right up the steps of the palace and down to the main hall. I was disappointed when I approached the room and found that everyone was already gone except Elvena, Calista, Meliantha, and Sorcha.

I was about to go in there when their words made me halt at the door.

"What aren't you telling us?" Calista demanded. "You may be able to fool everyone else, but you can't fool me."

What was going on? I wondered. I sidled closer to the door and closed my eyes, trying hard to concentrate on what they were saying.

Elvena sighed. "It's not something to worry about right now. There's still plenty of time ahead of us until we can even think about making the weapon, since the current state of Ariella and Brayden's union is complicated."

This time it was Sorcha who snapped, "I saw your face, Elvena, and it sure as hell appeared to be a look that it was something we needed to worry about. If I have to take the scroll away from you and decipher it myself I will."

"All right, child, I'll tell you," Elvena whispered regretfully.

"Do I need to fetch Ariella?" Meliantha asked, cutting in. I was about to walk in when Elvena's panicked voice rang out.

"No," Elvena cried. "I don't want her in here. She has so much to worry about right now. I can't put this burden on her."

What the hell! *What burden?* I wondered, breathlessly. The whole world felt like it was closing in all around me and there was no way out. I could barely hear from the pounding in my heart vibrating in my ears.

"Did the scroll mention something having to do with Ariella?" Sorcha questioned curiously.

"That's the thing," Elvena whispered sadly. "You all have sacrificed so much, and now one of you might have to sacrifice it all. If what the scroll says is true, I fear it's going to have to be Ariella that kills him, and I just don't know what the outcome of that will be."

I'm the one who has to kill him? I screamed in my mind.

Meliantha's voice was laced in fury. "Please don't tell me she's going to die if she kills that son of a bitch. You're not saying that, right?" The pounding in my chest grew louder … harder.

Elvena replied. "To be honest, I'm not sure. The scroll states that the only one with the ability to kill the dark sorcerer will be the one who can earn his trust. We all know he's not going to trust any of you, which leaves only one left. Since Ariella hasn't fully come into her power, we need to wait and see what

L. P. DOVER

happens before we tell her. I don't want her knowing yet. We'll cross that bridge when the time comes."

More words were mumbled between them, but I couldn't focus on them. They were deliberately trying to keep this from me, and for what, to protect me? What was I ... three years old? Out of all the years of being tormented by the dark sorcerer, who would have thought it would all came down to me? Now no one knew if I'd live through it or not. I knew he needed my power, but knowing the fate of my land depended on me to end it ...

How the hell am I going to defeat him when it depended on me bonding to a complete asshole?

Slowly, I backed away from the door, hoping they couldn't hear my steps, and ran as fast as I could toward the stables to fetch Lennox, my white stallion. I couldn't stay there a moment longer, not when I was being deceived and lied to by those I loved.

As my feet pounded against the sand, I could hear someone behind me, chasing me, but I didn't slow down. I pushed harder but it didn't matter because a set of strong hands caught my arms in an instant and whirled me around. I was not expecting it to be the man it was, the one who hadn't cared to acknowledge me from the very beginning.

My breath came out raspy from running, but I immediately pulled out of his grasp and glared at him. "What do you want?" I hissed.

He clenched his jaw and sighed. If I was reading his gaze correctly he almost looked worried for me, but that definitely couldn't be right ... right?

"I saw you run out of the palace and I wanted to make sure you were all right. Are you leaving?" he asked.

I snorted and rolled my eyes incredulously. "Yes, I am. So if you'll excuse me I need to saddle my horse and get the hell out of here." I turned to walk away, making sure to keep my chin in the air with dignity after being humiliated by him on numerous occasions. I groaned when I looked over and noticed he was keeping his pace beside me.

"I'll accompany you," he insisted. "It's the least I can do."

I didn't know what came over me, but I burst out laughing. I whirled on him and placed my hands on my hips, narrowing my eyes at him. "The least you can do?" I muttered sardonically. "I'm sorry, Prince Brayden, but the least you can do is leave me alone. I think you've done enough. I hate that talking to me is such an inconvenience to you."

Brayden closed his eyes and lowered his head. He ran his hands over his face and groaned before lifting his chocolate brown gaze to mine. "Talking to you is not an inconvenience, Princess. You need to understand that this is all new to me. Your ways are very different from mine."

That was definitely true, I thought to myself.

"That may be the case," I snapped, "but it doesn't give you the right to be an ass to me. You humiliated me in front of everyone in the Spring Court, and today you refused to talk to me or even look at me. I stayed with you day and night when you were injured because *I* wanted to. You fascinated me, and I thought there was more to you than what you let on, but I was wrong."

Even saying those words felt wrong. My heart was warring with me to take them back, but I couldn't. When Brayden tried to reach for my hand, I backed away and swallowed hard, shaking my head against the tears that stung behind my eyes. *You cannot fall,* I repeated over and over in my mind. I did not want to cry in front of him or show him any weakness whatsoever.

My gaze never faltering, I looked straight at him and said, "We'll figure out another way to save our land. There has to be another way. I may be young, but I'm not going to put up with your bullshit, even if we are destined to be together."

His mouth flew open and he looked at a loss for words. It didn't matter anyway because we were interrupted by someone hollering my name. "Ariella," a voice called out. Kamden approached me warily while furrowing a questioning brow. "Are you okay?"

Averting my gaze from Brayden, I nodded at Kamden and smiled. "Everything will be fine as soon as I get home."

Entering the stables, they both followed me in. I found Lennox, my white stallion, bucking against the stall and whinnying. "Shh … calm down boy, I'm okay. We're going home," I cooed, running my fingers through his mane.

He could feel my distress as I secured my saddle onto his back while Brayden stood off to the side and watched. With the reins in my hand, I pulled Lennox out of the stall and waited on Kamden.

Hitching up his own saddle, Kamden secured it down and came to my side. "I'll make sure you get there safely. I don't want you going alone."

Brayden scoffed and had the gall to look offended. "That won't be necessary, warrior. I'll accompany her home."

"Like hell you will," I argued, climbing onto Lennox's back. "Trust me, Prince Brayden, the last place you want to be right now is around me. I'm too angry, and when I'm angry I want to hit things. You need to stay out of my way."

"She's right," Kamden admitted. "I've trained with her."

Brayden's lip tilted up in a slight smirk and his eyes glinted with humor, almost mockingly. He didn't even acknowledge Kamden but kept his gaze on me the entire time. "In a way, I want to call your bluff, Princess. I do like a good challenge and a fierce female is something I have longed to behold. I'll grant your wish and stay out of your way … this time. However, next time you're going to face me."

Curling my lip, I glared down at him and said, "And I'll be ready, although, I don't think you will be."

I nodded toward Kamden and he sped out of the stables onto the white sand and stopped, waiting for me to follow. Brayden stepped out of the way so I could have a clear path, but before I could speed past him he placed his hand on my knee, halting me. My heart jumped at his touch and I couldn't deny that it actually felt right.

"I'm sorry if I caused you pain. It was never my intention," he admitted, his brown eyes softening.

I sighed and held onto the reins tighter, nodding my head because I had no clue what to say or do. "Good-bye, Brayden. I wish you a safe journey back to the Winter Court."

It was lame but that was all I could come up with. Nudging Lennox with the heel of my feet, he slowly bounded out of the stables and out onto the powdery white sand. I caught up to Kamden, and against my better judgment I looked back to take one last glance at Brayden. The emotion on his face was one of the last ones I had expected to see … sadness.

As much as I wanted to deny it, I felt the same way.

Chapter Three

Brayden

"I CAN'T BELIEVE you let her go," Sorcha scolded, approaching me from behind. I couldn't believe it either.

Without turning around, I kept my gaze on Ariella's retreating form as she rode off down the beach with Kamden by her side. As much as I wanted to hate the warrior with her, I couldn't. He used to be one of my warriors in the Winter Court until he decided to follow Kalen to Spring. He was a strong fighter and I knew he'd keep Ariella safe.

"You know as well as I do that she wouldn't have listened to me. It would only push her away even more. I am not stupid, Sorcha."

Sorcha scoffed. "Umm … I hate to break it to you, dear brother, but I think you've already pushed her away. It took all I had not to kick your ass inside." She came around to stand before me with her arms crossed over her chest and with a scowl on her face. "Do you want to know something, Brayden?"

Even if I said no she was going to tell me anyway so I said, "Yes."

"Loving someone doesn't make you a weak person. I know you're the leader of the Winter Army. You're strong, extremely stubborn, and closed off. A lot of us Winter Fae are like that. I tried to be an ice cold bitch like mother, but it wasn't in me to be like that. It's not easy to tell someone how you feel and believe me, I know. Drake isn't exactly passionate like Ryder, or a complete moron like Kalen, but we all know what love is and we feel it. Stop fighting it and go to her. I can see it in your eyes that you feel something for her. You're only fooling yourself if you think otherwise."

She turned on her heel to walk away, but then stopped and her lips tilted up in an evil smirk when she said, "Oh yeah, by the way, you better be glad it was me who came out here to talk to you and not Drake. He's really fond of Ariella and he isn't too happy with you right now. So do me a favor and make things right with your princess. You don't have to profess your feelings to the whole world if that's what you're worried about. Only Ariella needs to know how you truly feel." And that was where I had my problem. There was never a time when I needed to express how I felt with words. It wasn't something I did … ever.

"When does she have her guardian ceremony?" I asked curiously. I had an idea brewing in my mind, except I wondered if it would even be possible. There was only one way to find out.

A glint sparkled in Sorcha's eyes and she smiled. "Tomorrow, why?"

"You'll see," I remarked slyly. "I have an idea, but I'm sure it's going to anger Ariella more."

Throwing her hands in the air, Sorcha groaned and mumbled to herself as she walked away. Ariella said she'd be ready to face me, and I was going to make tomorrow be that day. I just needed to talk to her father first and prayed that he would approve of my request.

Chapter Four

Ariella

KAMDEN RODE WITH me the whole way back, which only took less than an hour. Since my family was all still in the other Summer Court, he decided to stay for a while. The mischievous smile on his face as he got off his horse grated on my nerves, though.

"What is that look for, Kam? Tell me."

He chuckled and put his arm around my shoulders as we walked up the steps to the palace. "Brayden has it bad for you, Princess. I have never heard or seen him look at a female the way he did you."

I snorted in disbelief. "It still doesn't change the fact that he's an ass," I remarked. "Was he always so closed off when you were his friend?"

Kamden shrugged and pursed his lips. "I wouldn't say we were friends per se. Kalen was the one who was my friend and that's why I chose to follow him to Spring along with Zanna. But yes, he was always quiet but fierce when he fought. Most of the warriors hated fighting with him because he could be lethal."

When we got inside and settled in one of the sitting rooms, one of the servants brought us a tray filled with fruits and berries along with some sparkling water. My nerves were frazzled from everything going on, but I managed to eat a handful of berries and drink all of my water. Not knowing if I was going to live to see our land saved had me feeling in despair, and lost. My guardian ceremony was tomorrow, but what good would a guardian do if I was destined to die?

Kamden gazed warily at me. "What's on your mind, Princess? You shut off on me there for a second."

I wanted to talk to someone about what I heard, but I knew I couldn't and that it had to remain a secret in case there were traitors in our midst or ears lurking around every corner. I didn't like feeling alone. Exhausted, I released a heavy sigh and smiled. "I'm sorry, I was just thinking. So tell me about Brayden. Did he have a lot of women in the Winter Court?"

Kamden groaned and tilted his head back in the chair, avoiding my gaze. That groan could only mean one thing …

"He did, didn't he?" I questioned through clenched teeth.

He threw his hands in the air, keeping his head tilted back. "What does it matter anyway? I'm sure you had your fair share of men. I mean, come on, Ariella, you're hot as hell and you're one of the funniest women I know. I keep waiting on you to play one of your sick jokes on me like you do the other warriors."

I stared at him for the longest time before we both laughed and let the tension ease. He lifted his head and hunched over, resting his elbows on his thighs. "Look, Brayden's a guy and guys have needs sometimes. Especially when we're fighting and training. We have to let out some of that tension before we kill each other. So yes, he had lots of women, but like I said he's never looked at them the way he does you. I don't think he even talked to the women he slept with."

"Well that's comforting," I quipped sarcastically, rolling my eyes. "It makes me wonder if he'll be that way with me. I have no clue what's going to happen with us now. Tomorrow I turn twenty-one and I don't know what's going to happen with my powers or who's going to be my guardian. I don't even see the point in having a guardian."

Scoffing, Kamden shook his head and grabbed my hands that were in my lap. Kneeling down on the floor, he clasped our hands together and gazed up at me with his exotic hazel eyes. "No matter how many people are in yours and Brayden's past that's where they're at … the past. I have women in mine and Zanna has men in hers, but we both love each other no matter what. As far as your guardian ceremony goes, I have a question I wanted to ask you."

"What is it?" I asked, squeezing his hands. "Are you going to come to it?"

He smirked and squeezed my hands back. "Actually, I wanted to see if you'd let me fight in it."

My eyes went wide and I gasped. Was he serious? "You mean you want to fight for me? Really? What does Zanna think about it?" I asked excitedly.

Letting go of my hands, he laughed and sat back in his chair. "We were talking about it right before I found you in the stables. I was looking for you so I could ask you what you thought about it."

I studied him, trying hard to keep from smiling. If there was anyone I wanted to be my guardian it would be him. I hadn't known him for long, but he and Zanna had become family to me over the past couple of weeks and I honestly loved them both.

I lifted a curious brow and crossed my arms over my chest. "Do you think you can handle me, Kam? I mean, think about it … you're going to be in my head every single day and listening to my crazy thoughts. I want you to understand what you're getting yourself into."

"The same goes to you, Princess. You're going to hear all my thoughts as well. Do you think you can handle *me*?" he asked teasingly.

I chuckled. "I have no doubt. Okay, you can compete, but I'm warning you … my Summer warriors are fierce. You might regret it."

He rolled his eyes. "Yeah right. I have complete faith in myself."

We sat there and talked and laughed for hours until my mother and father arrived back from Drake and Sorcha's Summer. After showing Kamden to a spare bedroom he could sleep in for the night, I retired to my room and shut the door, leaning heavily against it as all my thoughts bombarded me at once.

I am the one to end the evil and I don't know how. I am most likely going to die in the process as well. I turn twenty-one tomorrow and gain my powers, the same powers the dark sorcerer wants. I had the prophetic vision with Brayden, who acts like I'm not worthy of his time, not to mention we have to be bonded before the weapon of mass destruction can be made. I'm not supposed to know what's going on, but I do and the weight of it lies heavily on my chest. I have to figure out how to save the land, and the last thing I want to do is let my people down.

Before lying down on my bed, I changed out of my clothes and put on a simple gray T-shirt that I got from the mortal realm. I never travelled there much since I was basically forbidden to until I had procured a guardian. Tomorrow was going to be a busy day and I had a strange feeling that Brayden was going to make sure he was there.

The room was quiet and dark, but I could see the twinkling lights of the sprites out by my window. I knew I should be terrified of my fate, and in a way I was, but there was nothing I could do about it. I knew my time was coming.

I never thought my life would end so soon, but what my sisters failed to realize was that I valued our world and our land above anything else, including my own existence. I would save them … I just needed to figure out how.

❄❄❄

The sunlight beaming in through the window shone bright, but that wasn't what had awoken me. Someone was sitting on the bed with me; I could feel the bed jostle and hear their breath as they sat quietly. Groaning, I turned over and was met with the beaming smile of my friend, Zanna, with her wide blue eyes jumping with excitement. "Happy birthday," she cheered. "Do you feel any different?"

"What are you doing here?" I asked groggily, having endured the worst night sleep ever. "It's kind of early don't you think, Zanna?"

"Yeah, if you consider mid-day to be early. Everyone's waiting on you to get ready for the ceremony. Kamden wanted to come in here and wake you up hours ago, but I told him no."

So that's why she looks immaculate. Her raven colored hair was pulled up and away from her face in a bundle of curls, and her silky emerald colored gown made her skin sparkle like golden glitter. It was amazing how our bodies changed with our chosen courts.

"So what did he say when he saw you looking like that?" I asked, grinning at her. "You look amazing. I'm sorry he didn't make it back to you last night. He stayed here and talked to me for a while."

"It's okay, Ariella, I promise. Kamden didn't exactly say anything when he saw me. He pulled me into his room and, well … you get the picture, right?" She averted her gaze shyly but I couldn't resist, I burst out laughing.

"I completely understand. So when are you both going to take that final step? You two have been together for ages."

She sighed. "Yes, we have, but there's still plenty of time for that. He's excited about fighting today. Will your mother and father approve of him since he's not of your court?"

With a shrug of my shoulders, I got out of bed and started for the bathroom. I had no idea if they would approve. My father would most likely accept, but my mother was the one who was the stickler with following the traditions.

"It's never been done before," I called out over my shoulder, "but I don't see why they would have a problem with it. The only concern I have is that he will be with me in the Summer Court if he wins. Not to mention that if and when I bond with Brayden I'll be a Winter Fae, which means I'll be living in the Winter Court. Is that really what you want?"

Zanna stopped in the doorway to the bathroom, her lips set in a firm line as she peered at me with a serious glare. "Yes, it's what we want. I'll admit, I love Spring, but Kamden wants to do this for you and wherever he goes I follow. I think we make a nice trio, don't you think? And besides, our mission is to get some sense knocked into the hard headed Winter prince for you."

I scoffed and rolled my eyes, while taking off my clothes. "Good luck with that, but be my guest to try. I'm going to take a quick shower so I can get ready for the ceremony. Do you mind getting my dress out of the closet for me?"

"Of course," she said, turning around to walk back into my room. I turned on the water and waited for it to get steamy before stepping in.

"Which dress is it, Ariella? You have a ton in your closet," she shouted so I could hear her over the running water. I washed quickly since I was already running out of time.

"It's the silver one with the thin straps," I called out. "It should be right there in front."

"You mean the one with the plunging neckline. Seriously, Ariella, your warriors aren't going to be able to concentrate with you wearing this. I'm going to have to keep Kamden away from you."

I could hear her laughing and fumbling around in my room. Zanna was such a fun loving spirit and always understanding, not to mention beautiful with a big heart. I didn't know any of the Winter Fae could be as sweet as her, but I guess the changeover to

Spring might have had an influence. All I knew was that I felt closer to her than any of my other friends in the Summer Court.

Slipping into my robe, I tied it at the waist and joined Zanna in my bedroom. She already had my shoes picked out and was searching through my jewelry with her brows furrowed. "I absolutely love this necklace you have, Ariella. It's just so …"

When she turned to acknowledge me, her mouth flew open and she dropped the necklace on the floor, covering her mouth with a shaky hand. Immediately, I flew around thinking there was someone behind me, but when I looked there was no one there. What was going on? *Is she looking at me like that?* I wondered.

"What is wrong with you?" I asked, picking up my dress. "I don't look that bad, do I? I know I didn't get much sleep, but I actually feel fine now that I took a shower."

"Ariella?" she whispered, gazing at me like she'd never seen me before.

"Yes, it's me. Who else would it be? Seriously, Zanna, what is with you?"

Not taking her stunned gaze from me she pointed to the bathroom with a shaky hand and muttered anxiously, "You might want to go look at yourself in the mirror. Something's wrong."

Dropping my dress, I ran to the bathroom and ran a hand frantically over the fogged mirror, scared to see what Zanna saw but curious to know what was going on. The second my reflection came into view I stumbled back into the wall and screamed.

Chapter Five

Brayden

I ARRIVED TO the Summer Court early for Ariella's guardian ceremony alongside my mother and father, Queen Mab and King Madoc. I had hoped to see her around before the ceremony, but no one had seen or heard from her all morning.

"Are you sure you want to do this?" King Oberon asked, smirking at me. "I know my daughter and it's not just you she's going to be furious at. She's going to be angry at me as well. This sort of thing has never been done before."

I nodded. "I understand, and I'm willing to accept the consequences of my actions, but this is something I know I need to do."

L. P. DOVER

King Oberon sighed. "Very well, Prince Brayden. I grant you permission, but if we're going to do this there needs to be some kind of compromise. I can't have Ariella causing a big scene and walking away."

And that's precisely what she would do. "What exactly would this compromise entail?" I questioned curiously.

King Oberon smiled and put his arm around me, steering me down the massive golden halls of his palace. "I have an idea, but it's going to require you to put aside your pride. Can you do that just once … for Ariella's sake?"

I would do anything for her, whatever it took.

We continued down the desolate hallway until we came upon a door King Oberon stopped in front of. With his hand on the latch, he raised a brow and repeated again, "Can you do that?"

Without finding out what was at stake, I nodded my head and agreed, "Yes, I'll do it for her. I owe her my life for the way I treated her."

"Good," King Oberon said, turning the latch on the door with a smirk on his face. As soon as the light filtered into the room I took a look around and groaned at the sight before me.

"Oh hell," I mumbled. "If this doesn't show her how serious I am then I don't think anything will."

The king clapped a hand on my shoulder and guffawed. "She won't see it that way at first, but if you give her time she'll come around. I heard how you left her at the Spring Court after you had the vision. She doesn't forgive very easily, and I can honestly say she got that from her mother. I think a little humility is good for the soul."

There was definitely going to be some humiliation tonight … mine. I was doing it all for Ariella even though she hated me for what I'd done. It was the first step to redeeming myself.

Chapter Six

Ariella

MY BEDROOM DOOR burst open just as I collapsed on the floor away from the mirror, away from the sight of someone else's eyes staring back at me. *What the hell is going on?* That wasn't me in the mirror … it was Zanna looking back at me.

Kamden stormed in the room all dressed in his Spring Court warrior gear and his sword drawn, ready for action. He ran to Zanna and searched over her, but then his gaze landed on me when she pointed in my direction. "What the …" he began. He approached me warily and tilted his head to the side, narrowing his gaze unsurely. "What's going on? Who are you?"

"It's me, Kam. Now stop talking so I can concentrate," I demanded impatiently.

Marching over to the bed, I collapsed onto it and took some deep breaths. I twirled the dark hair in between my fingers that was all Zanna's and immediately thought of my own, concentrating as hard as I could. And just as if I willed it, the hair between my fingers began to change colors; it was slowly going from black to blonde again. Kamden and Zanna both gasped as I ran to the bathroom and gazed hesitantly at myself in the mirror.

I was me again, but how?

"Ariella?" Kamden muttered, coming to the door. "How did you do that? How did you make yourself look like Zanna?"

Touching my face, I leaned closer to the mirror to inspect myself. Everything was back to normal. "I don't know how I did it. All I know is that I was thinking about Zanna and how amazing she was and then I changed. And just now when I was looking at my hair I was thinking about how mine was blonde and then it came back."

Kamden's eyes grew wide and he bellowed, "Well, happy birthday, Princess. It looks like you've come into your new powers. I must say I'm a bit jealous. Just think of all the jokes you can play on people now. Are you going to tell everyone at the ceremony?"

Thoughts of what Elvena and the others discussed came back at me full force. They were waiting to see how my powers progressed before they told me about what the scroll actually said. For some reason, I had the sinking suspicion that this gift needed to stay hidden.

Gazing back and forth from Kamden to Zanna, I sighed and said, "No, I'm not going to tell anyone and neither are you two. Promise me you won't say anything. I know it's an amazing gift, but it's something I don't want anyone knowing just yet. Promise me."

Zanna nodded. "I promise, but what are you going to tell everyone when they ask what special powers came to you? You know they're going to ask," she responded incredulously. "The others had some pretty amazing abilities come to them and I know they will be anxious to hear what happened with you."

I waved her off and grabbed my dress. "I'll come up with something, but this is important. I can't let anyone know that I can do this other than you two. Kamden, you need to promise me."

Kamden smiled and shook his head. "I promise, Princess, but you know I would've figured it out once I became your guardian. I don't think you could've hidden that from me."

Sadly, I smiled and said, "You'd be surprised, Kam. I'm pretty good at keeping secrets. But you seem pretty confident that you're going to win. Arrogance can lead to mistakes if you're not careful."

"Don't you worry about me. I'll be fine. You are the one who needs to concentrate on staying you so you can keep your secret. Now hurry up or we'll be late. You still need to ask your father if I can compete."

That's right, I do, but I know he'll say yes.

Rushing into the bathroom, I removed my robe and slid on my silver gown. My ice blue eyes stared back at me in the mirror, and I could feel the extra power flowing through my veins like a jolt of energy. Staring into the mirror, I called on my magic to make my eyes purple like Meliantha's. Immediately they turned and I squealed in excitement.

"This is amazing," I breathed.

I experimented with my hair color, my facial features, and even my dress. It wasn't just my face I could change, it was my whole body including my clothes. I could be anyone I wanted to be and change at will. It was all starting to become clear to me as I stared at my changing form in the mirror. *This is how I'm going to trick the dark sorcerer.* I guess it was a good thing I was great at tricking people.

❋ ❋ ❋

I experimented with my shifting way longer than I should have because I was already late for the ceremony. Kamden and Zanna waited on me to finish because they were both going to walk me down to the Great Room where the fighting would begin. Before I could open my bedroom door, Drake barged in looking annoyed and agitated.

"It's taking you long enough," he snapped. "Everyone's waiting on you. We need to go." He glanced back at Kamden and Zanna and said, "You two can go ahead and make your way down there. I'm going to escort Ariella myself."

I held out my arm when they were about to pass me to stop them. "Wait, Drake. I need to ask father if Kamden can compete with the other warriors for the right to be my guardian."

Drake sighed and waved his hand impatiently for me to hurry. "I'm sure that won't be a problem. It seems this ceremony has taken on new rules." To Kamden he said, "Just go down there and join the other warriors. If this is what you truly want and Ariella wishes it then so be it. Good luck to you."

Kamden grabbed Zanna's hand and pulled her out of my room. He turned around once and winked. "I'll see you down there, Princess." Zanna waved at me and smiled before they both disappeared down the hall.

"What do you mean by the new rules?" I asked, taking hold of his arm.

Drake chuckled lightly and patted my arm. "Oh, you'll see when we get down there. It's going to be very interesting." My heart pounded harder with each step we took. If Drake said it was interesting then there was something going on that I didn't know about.

As we approached the closed doors of the Great Room, I stopped mid-stride and took a deep breath. I didn't want to ask my next question, but I had to know. "Is Brayden in there?" I asked, tilting my head toward the room.

Drake pursed his lips and narrowed his eyes. "You know, I don't think I saw him out in the audience. I saw Queen Mab and King Madoc earlier, but I never saw Brayden."

If I thought his absence wouldn't bother me I was sorely mistaken. With such an important event in my life, I figured he'd want to be a part of it since he we was bound to me … but I guess not.

Forcing a smile, I turned toward the door and said, "It doesn't matter anyway. I'm sure I'll be just fine without him. Let's go."

Drake chuckled. "Whatever you say, Ariella. Tell that lie to someone who believes you."

I scoffed, but before I could say anything in my defense the doors to the Great Room opened. Drake took my hand and linked our arms together so he could walk me inside. With each passing step, my heart thundered in my chest. There were so many people here, much more than what I had anticipated.

My mother and father were waiting for me on the dais, both with smiles on their faces, but their presence didn't help my frazzled nerves at all. What made it even more peculiar was that the warriors all had their armor and gear on, but they also had their helmets on as well. I looked up at Drake questioningly, but he just smiled and elbowed me in the side. I wasn't going to be able to tell who was who in the fight.

When I reached my father, Drake let me go. My father took my hands and kissed my cheek before escorting me to the chair beside his. When I sat down, I leaned over to whisper in his ear, "What's going on with the helmets? Why are they wearing them now when they've never had to wear them before?"

"No, they didn't have to before. However, if you would've graced us with your presence earlier, and on time like you were supposed to, then you would have heard the story King Madoc told all of us about Sorcha's ceremony. It appears someone lost an ear during that fight, so we wanted to avoid that and any other facial injuries that could occur. I'm sure you understand."

My eyes went wide and I grabbed his hand. "Oh, of course I do. I was just curious. I would never want our warriors to get hurt like that."

"I know, little one. Well, are you ready?" he asked. "I think our warriors are getting a little restless. I also see that we have an extra one competing with us today." He glanced over at Kamden in his Spring Court armor and smiled.

"Yes, Father, we do. Kamden wanted to fight and I agreed. Is that all right?"

His smile grew wider and he nodded his head, except it seemed like he found something else humorous as well. "Of course, it's all right. However, he's got some pretty strong competition out there. I'm curious to see who wins."

Me too, I said to myself. It was going to be interesting.

My father stood up from his throne and walked to the edge of the dais so he could address the crowd. Everyone was there, including: Calista and Ryder, Meliantha and Kalen, Sorcha and Drake, Durin, the leader of the dwarves, Queen Mab and King Madoc, and also Aelfric and Rhoswen of the Elvish kingdom. I glanced quickly at them, acknowledging them with a nod of my head before focusing back on my father.

"Good evening all honored guests and friends. Tonight we celebrate my youngest daughter's twenty-first birthday along with her guardian ceremony. I wanted to thank you all for coming and to also wish our warriors the best of luck. Afterwards, we will have an amazing celebration to honor both Ariella and her guardian."

My father raised his arms toward the warriors and motioned for them to get in position. The only person I knew in the crowd was Kamden because his armor was different from everyone else's. It was a good thing, because now I would be able to spot him in the fray.

The warriors took up their stances; their swords poised in the air and their muscles ready. My father's booming voice echoed across the room, "Warriors, you may begin!"

Chapter Seven

Ariella

THE SOUND OF metal clanging and clashing against each other was piercingly loud as the warriors fought. There were so many good fighters and I was beginning to recognize some of them by their movements. I trained with these men so I knew how our techniques worked and what our style was, especially those I fought with on a regular basis. As I searched through the crowd, hoping that I would find Brayden, there was something inside me that told me he was there … somewhere. I could feel the pull on my soul like I did every time he was near.

"Father?" I whispered, tilting my head in his direction. "Have you seen Prince Brayden? Is he here? I can feel him, but I don't see him out in the crowd."

"He probably just arrived and hasn't made it in here yet," he said quietly. "I'm sure you will see him later, little one. I know things are hard between you two, but it will all work out. Just have faith in your heart."

My mother scoffed and leaned forward so she could see past my father to me. "Of course things are hard after what he did," she said, looking from me to my father. "He deserves every ounce of wrath you can give him after he left you in the Spring Court the way he did. He's just a typical Winter Fae."

My father whirled on her and hissed, "That's enough, Tatiana. Our daughter has been through a lot over the past couple of days and she can make her own decisions concerning the matters of *her* heart. The young man deserves a chance to prove that he is worthy."

"He has a lot of proving to do if that's the case," I mumbled to myself.

Over time, the amount of warriors on the floor started diminishing rapidly as more and more of them became injured. The fighting had been brutal with many limping away and bleeding, but there were still four fighters going strong, Kamden being one of them. Once the wounded warriors took off their helmets, I was shocked to see Riddik as one of them. He happened to be the same warrior I used my wind magic on six years ago when I blew him across the Summer Court because he refused to be my date to Calista's guardian ceremony. That incident earned me a night of solitude in my room while everyone else enjoyed the party. Lowering my head, I couldn't stop the smile from spreading across my face at the thought. It was amazing how much things had changed since then, especially me.

By the time my gaze found the warriors again, there were only two left. Kamden and one of my Summer warriors. They mirrored each other exactly, their swords drawn and angled perfectly in the striking position. I edged closer in my seat to get a better look, but the Summer warrior's back was to me so I couldn't get a glimpse of who he was.

The more I watched them fight, the more confused I became. I had never seen two fighters move with the same grace and efficiency and block each other as if they knew their next steps. We didn't fight like that in the Summer Court at all. It was almost like …

"Oh, no," I groaned quietly, placing a hand over my mouth. It couldn't be, could it?

Frozen, I watched as Kamden's moves slowly began to falter and grow tired, weary. When the other warrior knocked him on his knees and kicked his sword away, I saw the defeat in Kamden's eyes and I knew it was over. He lost.

The Summer warrior backed up and sheathed his sword before turning around and strolling up to the dais; his walk and stance very familiar. My father immediately stood and clapped his hands; the whole room exploded into applause. My guardian had been chosen.

"Well done, warrior," my father announced. The warrior bowed his head, but made no move to take off his helmet. My heart was pounding out of control, and it wasn't going to stop until I saw the face of my guardian. I had to see him with my own eyes, because my soul was screaming at me it could only be one person, except that couldn't be possible. There was no way it could be him.

Standing from my chair, I started to take a step forward to approach the warrior, but my father's large hand grasped my elbow, halting me in place. "Wait," he insisted quickly.

Before I could protest, his voice rose above the crowd, but the grip he had on my arm was one I knew very well; it was the same one he would use on me as a child when he wanted me to stay quiet. It wasn't until his next words that I understood why he didn't want me to make a scene.

"Due to the intimate circumstances of the Blood Ritual, it has been decided that it will be done in private this time. I know it hasn't been done like this in the past, but I must respect these wishes. If you would, I ask that you please enjoy all the food and wine to your heart's content while Ariella and her guardian take a short intermission. We have much to celebrate when they return."

My father nodded to the warrior and he slowly retreated out of the room, and out the door. Gritting my teeth and trying to keep my calm, I hissed quietly, "Father, let me go. I have to know who he is if I am to be bound to him. Why do we have to do the Blood Ritual in private?"

He sighed and let my arm go. "You'll find out very soon, little one. But for now I need you to calm down and come with me."

Reluctantly, I nodded and said, "Fine, but give me one minute with Kamden." I rushed down to the floor. Zanna was already there at Kamden's side, helping him to his feet.

When I got there, he took off his helmet and grabbed my hands. "Please forgive me, Ariella. I'm so sorry I didn't win for you." His whole body was drenched in sweat and the look of defeat in his eyes made my heart break.

I squeezed his arm and shook my head, smiling warmly. "You did fantastic, Kam. There's nothing to be sorry for. Your fighting was amazing."

Pulling me closer, his eyes went wide and he searched all around us to make sure no one could hear him. Quickly, he started to whisper, "Ariella, there's something you need to know."

"What is it?" I asked hesitantly.

He closed his eyes and blew out a sigh. "Your guardian is—" That was as far as he could get before my father interrupted us.

"Ariella," my father commanded, sending Kamden a warning glare. "I need you to come with me. Now."

Kamden sighed and stepped away from me. Calista and Meliantha came to my side and took my hands, tugging me with them. "We have to go,"

Calista said. "You can talk to your friends when you get done with the Blood Ritual."

"Do you know what's going on?" I demanded, following them out of the Great Room and into the hallway.

"Not exactly," Meliantha admitted truthfully, "but we have an idea."

We were headed toward my father's study and behind us Ryder and Kalen followed close by, along with Sorcha and Drake.

When we approached the door to the study, my mother and father were there along with Queen Mab, King Madoc, Elvena, and Durin holding a box in his hands. I stopped mid-step and jerked my hands away from Calista and Meliantha. "Okay, this is it. What's going on? I'm getting sick and tired of being left in the dark about everything. I want answers right now."

"Ooh, she is feisty," Queen Mab acknowledged with a huge grin on her face. "She will do well in the Winter Court. My son is a lucky man."

My mother rolled her eyes and scoffed, earning an even bigger grin from Queen Mab. Durin, the leader of the dwarves, approached me warily and handed me the long wooden box that I was for certain had my guardian dagger in it. Durin was short, reaching about four foot tall, and his warm hazel colored eyes were always soft and genuine when he'd talk to me. I'd seen him at his fiercest and there was nothing soft about him when he was like that. His short brown hair and closely shaven beard was not something you would see on a dwarf, but Durin was different … he was separate from all the rest.

"I brought the dagger for you, Princess. I incorporated your Summer heritage along with the Winter since you'll soon be one of them. However, given all the gloomy faces here I don't know if that was such a good idea on my part, but hopefully, it'll be what you want."

Taking a deep breath, I slowly opened the box, and when the dagger came into view I gasped, "Oh my."

The weapon was exquisitely beautiful, and with it coming from Durin I knew there was no way it wouldn't be. I could feel the power in the blade as I touched it. The handle was wrapped in vines representing the Summer Court, but what made it even more beautiful was that the vines were covered in ice, or at least that's what it looked like. There was a crystal coating around the vines that gave off a blue hue and it sparkled like snow, glittering just like my skin did in the vision.

I leaned down and kissed Durin on the cheek, completely in awe with his masterpiece. "It's beautiful, Durin. Thank you."

He bowed his head. "You're welcome, Your Highness. However, I think I will leave you all and get back to the celebration. Good luck with the Blood Ritual and make sure you don't kill your guardian with that," he teased, glancing down at the dagger with a smirk on his face. He bowed one more time before disappearing down the hall.

The tension in the hallway was awkward, and much to everyone's disbelief I wasn't stupid. I knew who was waiting for me and I wanted to know why he and everyone else decided to trick me. I may have been fooled at first, but my heart knew who was in that room.

Clutching the box in my hand, I started for the door, but paused when my father placed a reassuring hand on my shoulder. "I know you know, Ariella, and I know you are angry. I'm sorry I kept it from you, but it was all his idea and I agreed to it. He's trying hard to win your trust, little one." He paused for a second and hesitated before asking, "Are you going to accept him as your guardian?"

Did I even have a choice? I wondered.

"I don't know what I'm going to do," I said softly. "But I do know that I need to talk to him in private. He tends to not speak when others are around."

Ryder and Kalen both chuckled in the background and Sorcha nodded in agreement when I glanced at her. They knew their brother well. If I was going to get any headway with him it needed to be without everyone's prying eyes and ears. Surely, they all agreed and left me to myself, except Elvena who pulled me away from the door with a determined gleam in her eye.

"What's wrong, Elvena?"

She put a finger to her lips and whispered, "Shh … I don't want Brayden to hear us out here." I nodded my head in understanding, but I was intrigued

L. P. DOVER

as to what was on her mind. She continued, "None of us know what's going to happen if you bond with Brayden in the guardian bond. This sort of thing has never happened before."

"What do you think I should do?" I asked nervously. "What do you think will happen?"

Elvena shrugged. "I'm not sure, Princess, but if what I think might happen happens then it could be the key to saving our land."

"How so?" I asked, wide-eyed.

She smiled and took my hand, turning my palm up. "When you and Brayden join hands, blood to blood, your essence will mingle with his. His blood will flow through your body and it'll no longer be purely Summer ... but Winter. Do you understand what I'm saying, child? Do you realize what this could mean for us?"

Slowly, I nodded as everything became clear. Could it really all be that simple? With Brayden's blood intertwined with mine I would complete the circle and Durin could forge the weapon we needed to defeat the dark sorcerer. I wouldn't have to complete the marriage bond with Brayden to save our land just like we first thought.

The only problem was that I would be consenting to a bond that was just as deep as the marriage bond. Brayden would be able to feel and hear my thoughts unless I purposefully shielded them. It wasn't going to be easy, especially with what I already knew my future was going to entail. Keeping that from him was going to be hard, but I had no choice, not if this was the key to saving our land. If bonding with him right now would ensure everyone's survival then I was going to do it.

Lifting a brow, I crossed my arms over my chest and said, "You do realize how hard this is going to be for me to be bonded with him right now, don't you? We don't exactly have the best relationship. I might end up killing him before we can even complete the bond."

Elvena giggled and patted me on the cheek. "I highly doubt that. Even though you two are at odds right now, he is still the one for you. Who knows, this might be what you both need. Now go in there and claim your guardian, child."

She looked back at me once and winked before turning the corner and heading out of sight. I walked slowly to the door to my father's study and paused, placing my hand on the handle.

Taking a deep breath, I opened the door. Once I was inside, I slammed it shut behind me. I couldn't back down now, but the moment he came into vision, my knees almost buckled at the sight before me. It was not what I expected to see.

Brayden stood there, not in his armor, but in a simple black button down shirt and dark denim jeans. I just realized I had never seen him in plain clothes, and for once he almost looked normal. My heart raced just staring at him and I almost forgot why I was standing there. As he moved closer, I had nowhere to go but toward the door. I moved back until I could move no further. His lips tilted up in the corner as he gazed down at my mouth and then into my blue eyes.

"Are you ready to face me yet?" he asked.

I stood up straighter and pushed off the door thinking he'd step back, but he didn't. All it did was put me flush with his body where I couldn't help but breathe him in. However, I wasn't going to let it distract me. Smirking, I replied, "I think the real question here is if *you* are ready to face *me*. I guess we'll see, won't we?"

Chapter Eight

Ariella

"WHEN DID YOU realize it was me?" Brayden asked. He was so close I could smell his Winter scent and feel the coldness of his skin through my dress. It sent chills down my body, and made more than my skin shudder at the close contact.

I shrugged my shoulders. "I didn't realize it was you until the very end. I could feel you near, but with you dressed in the Summer armor I didn't think it could possibly be you. I have to say, it was the first time I've been tricked by someone. Whose idea was it to dress you in the Summer armor?" I asked. "I figured someone like you would have despised giving up the Winter crest during a fight."

He licked his lips and sighed. "It wasn't easy, Princess, but it was something I had to do. Pride and loyalty to my court has always been my top priority." He paused and took a deep breath, closing his eyes with his next words. "If you must know, Ariella, I did it all for you."

"Why, Brayden? Why did you do it for me?" I challenged. Pushing away from the door and from him, I went to stand in front of my father's desk, crossing my arms over my chest. We stared at each other for what felt like an eternity. When he didn't respond, I opened my arms wide and gazed around the empty room. Exasperated, I snapped, "There's no one in here for you to be embarrassed about hearing you. What is so hard about answering a simple question?"

"It's because it is not a simple question," he retorted. "Nothing about you is simple, Ariella. You're very ... complicated."

I scoffed. "*I'm* complicated? What about you? Why do you even bother with me if I'm so complicated? You could easily go back to your Winter Court and have uncomplicated relationships with whoever you fill your bed with."

Brayden groaned and ran his hands over his face. It was the first real emotion I'd seen from him and with it I saw the fire ... literally. His ability was for fire and his hands blazed with it. He stalked toward me with nothing but heat in his gaze until I backed up against the desk; it made me tremble, and for the first time ever being around him I saw the spark.

"First off, Princess, I may be complicated but I'm not the type of man to spill out my feelings like a damn female, especially in front of others. And about the women you speak of, I haven't indulged in a woman's touch since before I met you at the Winter palace. I know I walked away from you after the vision and I apologized for that. It was a mistake on my part and I asked for your forgiveness. I did what I did tonight to win back your trust and mend what I had broken."

He smiled sadly and continued, "If you bond with me tonight you will know exactly how I feel about you, and I offer those feelings freely. Only you are the important one to know how I feel. I may not speak them openly and I will most likely infuriate you more because I keep them hidden inside, but *you* will be able to feel them." He grabbed my hand and placed it over his heart. "In here," he added.

I didn't know I was holding my breath until I had the sudden urge to release it. The anger I felt before had diminished with each word that came out of his mouth, and all I felt was … excitement, love. I was shocked and completely taken aback. He spoke the truth and I didn't need to have the guardian bond to know that he was genuine. We were both so different, yet so much alike in ways. The last thing I wanted was to attach myself to him knowing I had a dark fate ahead of me.

Unfortunately, I had no choice.

Was I selfish that I wanted to bond to him even though I was going to leave him? Yes, I was selfish, but in a way I wanted to experience what it was like to be bonded before my life ended. I wanted to know what it was like to be my sisters and have someone love me unconditionally.

A tear escaped the corner of my eye, and when I turned my head, Brayden took my chin and gently pulled me back while wiping the tear away with the pad of his thumb. He lowered down on his knees and muttered softly, "Will you accept me as your guardian, Ariella? I don't know what this is going to mean for you, but for me it'll be a great honor to protect you … to protect the woman that completes my soul."

I knew what I had to do. I was scared as hell, and even if I was ready or not it was something that had to be done.

"Yes," I breathed. "I accept you as my guardian."

Chapter Nine

Ariella

INSTEAD OF DOING the Blood Ritual in my father's study, I decided it would be best to finish it in my bedroom. If things were going to change, I wanted to be able to be away from the eyes of others if we had to leave. Brayden and I snuck through the hallways until we reached my bedroom. When I opened the door, he smirked and lifted a questioning brow.

Sighing, I rolled my eyes and waited for him to enter. "I didn't bring you here for *that,* Brayden. I just wanted to make sure we had some privacy."

He walked past me into my room and gazed around. My room was filled with shades of blue and silver, and now that I thought about it, it reminded me of the Winter Court. Subconsciously, I guess I was always thinking of Winter without ever knowing it. Brayden strolled around my room and spent a lot of extra time on the paintings I had hung on my walls. I didn't visit the mortal realm much, but when I did I always brought back a piece from my favorite artists.

"Did you paint these?" he asked, sounding amazed. "If you did, they're amazing."

When he turned back to me I shook my head and laughed incredulously. "Oh, no. I wish I could paint like that, but I don't have the skills. When I go to the mortal realm I always find a new piece to bring home."

He furrowed his brows. "Do you go to the mortal realm a lot?"

I shook my head. "No, not often. Maybe a couple of times a month to find some new paintings. I never ventured off like Calista did. Her and her friends loved to go there all the time. Why, do you go out there a lot?"

His answer was immediate, "No, I prefer the magic and beauty of our land. There's too much suffering in the mortal realm."

I crossed the floor to stand beside him, suddenly feeling nervous and hopeful, as we stood there staring at the paintings. I prayed to the heavens that this bonding would be what we needed to defeat the dark sorcerer.

"Are you ready to do this, Princess?"

I'm ready to end the evil at whatever cost, I thought. Gazing up into his chocolate brown eyes, I nodded my head and sighed. "I'm ready."

I walked over to my bed and sat down, setting the box with the dagger in it on my lap. Brayden came and stood in front of me as I pulled it out. With his arms crossed at the chest, he gave me an accusatory glare.

"Why are you giving in so easily? I can see it in your eyes that there's more to this bonding than you're letting on. There's an ulterior motive here and I want to know what it is. You may be able to trick your friends and your warriors, but I can see right through it. Tell me," he demanded.

"And if I don't tell you?" I countered, just trying to gauge his reaction.

The energy in the room spiked hotter than Hell as Brayden unleashed his fire along with his anger. My body grew flush with sweat and the heat actually made me begin to feel dizzy. How could that be? I was Summer. I could withstand countless amounts of heat.

"Trust me, Princess. You want to tell me," he warned with a glint in his eye.

"Fine," I gave in, standing up to hand him the dagger. "Just dial down the heat, will you?"

Instantly, the room went back to normal and it was as if the temperature hadn't been changed at all. If Brayden wanted to know the truth there was no reason not to tell him, so I explained, "Once we bond tonight, Elvena thinks that it'll be enough of a change for us to forge the weapon to defeat the dark sorcerer. So instead of us having to consummate the relationship we can do the guardian bond and everything will be right in the world. There's no rush or even a reason for us to have to complete the marriage bond now. This should be enough to save our land without having to wait on us."

Brayden moved closer, the dagger in hand. "Is that what you want? What if the guardian bond isn't enough? What if we *need* to consummate the relationship and be bonded fully?"

I held out my hand, palm up, ready for him to slice open my skin and get the bond started. "I just hope it doesn't come to that. This *has* to be enough," I whispered.

He winced at my words but stayed silent; even I caught myself wincing at my words as they came out of my mouth. They were harsh and cruel, and he didn't deserve it after all he'd done. The last thing I wanted to do was hurt him when he was being nothing but sincere to me, but I didn't know what else to do or how to feel.

Taking my hand, he held it gently in his, rubbing his thumb along my palm. "I'm sorry you feel that way," he said sadly. My gaze immediately shot to his just as he sliced the dagger across my skin. I hissed at the pain and took a deep breath while I watched the blood absorb into my dagger.

Why was he being this way? It would be a lot easier if he didn't say things like that. "I didn't mean for it to come out like that, it's just—"

"There's no need to explain," he murmured, handing me the glowing blade that just absorbed my Summer blood. He held out his palm and finished, "It's probably easier this way."

"Yeah," I agreed, grasping his cold hand. "It is." *But I don't think either one of us believes that.*

The dagger felt warm in my hands, but when I grazed Brayden's palm with the blade the vines on the handle started to change; they turned cold and began to ice over … literally. "Wow," I breathed. "That's amazing."

Staring at each other, with bloodied palms, we both took a step forward. Breathing hard, Brayden wrapped his arm around my waist and pulled me closer, never taking his gaze from mine. "What are you doing?" I asked nervously. "I don't think we need to be this close for it to work."

Clasping his fingers with mine, there was only a breath of space keeping his palm from connecting and completing the bond. "No, we don't," he replied, "but I think it'll make it more enjoyable." The look in his eyes was heated, full of hundreds of emotions that I thought he would never open up and let me see. I was so enamored by his gaze that I didn't even stop him when he lowered his lips to mine.

Groaning, he pulled me closer, and even though he was a Winter Fae, he had me melting in his arms. He deepened the kiss at the same time he closed our palms together, sealing our minds as one. My mind flooded with images and feelings, all of which were from Brayden. However, what overtook them all was the growing need I felt coming from him, from within his heart.

He grasped me tighter. I could feel my feet moving closer to the bed; being that I secretly craved his touch, I didn't protest. Slowly, I sat down on the edge of the bed and Brayden followed by lightly covering my body with his, leaning us back across the mattress. His hunger fueled my own and it was hard to tell who was feeling what with my own warring emotions mingling with his. I could feel him growing harder between his legs, and if things weren't so difficult I'd demand he take me. Unfortunately, it was too soon to let it go that far.

"Look inside," Brayden insisted in my mind, as he grazed my lips with his teeth. *"You are the only one who will ever know me like this."*

Closing my eyes, I pressed my forehead to his and concentrated on the images he replayed in his mind. It was like I could see myself through his eyes. They were all images of how he saw me from his past and how he felt during those times. The first one was of me at Calista and Ryder's marriage ceremony and how he wished he could dance with me, but he also thought I was immature and young. The second one was at the Winter Solstice Ball and how he was amazed at how much I'd changed from the years prior. I could actually feel the anger flowing through his veins when he saw me dancing with another Winter Fae at the ball.

I laughed, but Brayden squeezed my hand and growled. *"It's not funny, Princess. I could see the lust in my warrior's eyes and I didn't like it. I didn't want him taking advantage of you."*

I scoffed. *"Please, give me a break. I'm not exactly the type of girl guy's take advantage of. You obviously don't know of my experience with men."*

"How can I when you have your mind blocked? I think it's only fair that you let me in. Do you have things to hide, Princess?" Actually, I did, but I couldn't tell him that.

I sighed. *"Soon, Brayden. Right now you owe me this."*

I couldn't let him in fully, but if I played it just right I wouldn't have to; I could give him bits and pieces of my life. It was already a hardship for me knowing I didn't have much time, and the last thing I wanted to do was burden him.

The next image that came through our bond was of me sitting beside his bed when he was injured. He loved the way I sang to him and …

"You mean to tell me you were awake during that time? I sat there and sang to you for hours hoping you'd wake up," I scolded him. *"For hours I sat there!"*

Sheepishly, he muttered, *"I know and I'm thankful that you did. For the first time in my life I was selfish. I wanted you there with me and not with Kamden. I heard you were staying with him while he healed, but I wanted you with me."*

"Kamden is just my friend. He and Zanna are very special to me."

"I know that. He was one of the Winter Court's finest warriors. I hated to see him go, but he was closer to Kalen than anyone. I wasn't surprised when he chose to switch allegiances."

With my eyes still closed and his body so close as he lay against me, I asked the one question that hung thick in the air. "Where do we go from here?" Opening my eyes as Brayden lifted up on his elbows and released my hand, I watched as he ran his thumb over the wound that was slowly healing already from the feel of it.

"I'm not sure," he said, gazing down at me. Out of nowhere, his eyes went wide and a slow smile spread across his face.

"What's wrong?" I asked nervously. "Why are you looking at me like that?"

"Well … I think we just got that question answered and it's pretty obvious where we go from here."

"Which is?" I prodded.

He ran a finger down my cheek all the way down to my hand, where he clasped it and brought it up to my face so I could see. I gasped, looking down at my arms and touching my face. "Oh wow," I breathed. "I'm pale."

"And completely Winter," he added. "I don't see a trace of Summer in you at all. We might need to tell our families. They're probably afraid you killed me." He slid off of me and grabbed my hand to pull me up from the bed. His touch was gentle as he led me to the door, but I squeezed his hand and anchored my feet to the floor.

"Wait," I said. "I don't want to go out there right now. I'm not ready to face them all. I need some time to process this, and the last thing I want is a bunch of questions directed at me. It's all happening so fast, and now that this has happened …" I said, gesturing to my creamy, pale skin, "… I know there's no way I can stay here in the Summer Court anymore. I'm not going to belong here."

Brayden took my face in his hands, and I noticed that his skin felt the same on mine, there was no difference. They weren't cold like they used to be … but perfect.

"Do you want to stay hidden away until the morning?"

"Yes," I said, nodding my head.

"Do you want me to stay in here with you?" he asked. He bit his lip and added quickly but silently, *"I'll keep my distance from you if that's what you want, but I know it'll be easier to explain things with you by my side."*

"I know," I assured him. "We can talk to them tomorrow. And yes, you can stay in here with me. I know how you are in a crowd, so sending you out there would be like torture. However, I am kind of tired. We both have a busy day tomorrow."

I was a little nervous to see myself in the mirror, but I grabbed a nightgown and robe to sleep in before going into the bathroom and shutting the door behind me. Taking a deep breath, I blew it out slowly and lifted my eyes to the reflection in the mirror. I gasped at the sight before me. My hair was still the same platinum blonde, almost white, and my eyes were still the same color of blue ice. My skin, however, was completely different. The once golden hue signifying my birth as a Summer princess was now gone and replaced with the paleness of the Winter.

Brayden's blood made me change, the guardian bond made me change … we were both connected. It made me wonder if it had changed my magic. I guess it was time to find out. Concentrating on myself in the mirror, I willed my body to change, to make me look like someone else. I thought about Calista and her golden blonde hair and bright green eyes with the subtle golden skin of the Fall Fae. The magic swirled inside my body and I could actually feel the change happening as I was thinking about it. Calista's form slowly morphed into being as I watched it progress in front of the mirror.

I still have it, I thought excitedly.

Briskly, I changed into my short, silky red nightgown and put on my robe, leaving it open in the front. Before I left the bathroom, I made sure to shift back into myself. The second I saw Brayden my mouth dropped open. He was lounging in one of my chairs with a book in his hands, his shirt completely off, exposing every hard plane of his abs and chest. All I wanted was to feel his bare body on mine, to taste every square inch of him with my tongue.

He slowly closed the book and lifted those hooded chocolate brown eyes up my body until he met my gaze with a devilish smirk on his face. "You were saying, angel?"

My mouth gaped open. *Shit, I forgot to shield my thoughts!* I could feel my cheeks flush with all the blood rushing to them, and if there was any way a Winter Fae could turn bright red I was sure I was flaming. And what's worse was that hearing him call me angel in that deep husky voice of his made the spot between my legs clench and tighten. I could imagine him calling me that while we made love.

Stop it, Ariella! I screamed at myself.

I was beginning to think bonding with him was a mistake. I was definitely going to be in some deep shit.

Standing up straight, I sauntered over to the bed and buried myself underneath the covers, feigning indifference. "I have no clue what you're talking about," I lied, hoping I could play it off.

Brayden stood and approached the bed, his stride graceful yet determined. "Ariella," he whispered gruffly. "You need to let me in. The tension between us will only get worse if you don't."

Softly, I sighed and said, "I know, but I'm not ready."

He narrowed his eyes and climbed up on the bed. "You lie. I know you're ready, but you're scared of something. What is it?"

I stared at him for a long while, wondering if I should just come right out and tell him the truth. In the end, I balked and turned away, putting my back to him as I lay on my side. He huffed and I could feel his annoyance as he also lay down on the bed.

"I'm sorry, Brayden. Goodnight."

"Goodnight, angel."

Without moving a muscle, I tried desperately to fall asleep. However, it wasn't until Brayden's arm snaked around my waist that I was finally able to relax. His warm breath on my neck and the protective hold he had, trapping me against his body, made me shiver … and it wasn't because I was cold.

Chapter Ten

Ariella

THE SECOND I entered into my dream I could tell I wasn't going to be alone. I knew that because I was standing on the beach in Sorcha and Drake's Summer Court, still in my nightgown, peering out at the setting sun on the horizon of the crystal blue sea.

"So how did it go with you and my brother? You didn't kill him, did you?" Sorcha teased, her voice coming from behind me.

When I turned around to face her with my arms crossed, she gasped and covered her mouth with her hand. She was dressed in a simple blue gown that billowed out in the wind as she walked toward me as if she floated on the sand. However, there was nothing gentle about her. She was a dragon just like my brother and one of the smartest and fiercest females in all the land. She approached me and slowly took in my newly changed skin and smiled.

"You and Brayden completed the bond already? I thought you hated him?"

I gasped and quickly shook my head, laughing. "Oh no, we didn't complete it in the way you think. We did bond, but only the guardian bond. When our blood mixed this happened to me. I don't even feel like a Summer Fae anymore."

"Well you definitely don't look it. Where is Brayden now?" She walked up to me and touched my skin. "Oh yeah, you're definitely Winter."

I rolled my eyes. "He's with me in my room. I didn't want to complete the Blood Ritual in my father's study and then have to face everyone like this."

Studying me, she narrowed her eyes and pursed her lips. "You don't seem surprised that this happened. Did you know fulfilling the guardian bond would change you?"

"Elvena told me it was a possibility," I confided honestly. "And that it could be the key to getting my blood bonded to form the weapon we need to defeat the dark sorcerer."

Sorcha's eyes immediately filled with worry and concern. "I thought there would be more time. We were all hoping that you and Brayden would come to your senses and one day form your own court. He's stubborn and can be a complete pain in the ass, but I *was just like him until I met your brother. I know you hate him now, but he'll come around. I know he cares for you."*

I smiled and waved my hand for her to stop. "I know he does, Sorcha. I could feel it through the guardian bond."

"Do you still hate him then?" she asked curiously.

Warily, I responded, "No, I don't hate him. After seeing myself through his eyes and how he truly is on the inside there's no way I can hate him. He's so different than what I thought he would be."

Surprised, Sorcha's mouth flew open and she snickered. "Don't let him hear you say that to anyone."

"I don't plan on it," I remarked in all seriousness. "And neither will you. This is as far as it goes." She lost her smile and watched me intently as I paced up and down the shore.

"You are going to complete the bond with my brother, aren't you?"

I stopped mid-stride and glanced sheepishly at her before turning away and saying, "No, I'm not."

"Why not?" she snapped incredulously, pulling on my arm and whirling me around to face her. "Has he not proven himself worthy of you yet? What more do you want from him? I thought this was what you wanted."

"It is." I sighed. "But unfortunately, a happy ending is not in my future."

L. P. DOVER

"And why would you say that ..." Her voice trailed off, but when I pierced her with a firm, hard glare she balked and bit her lip, looking unsure of what to say.

"I know everything, Sorcha. I was there when you and the others were discussing the scroll," I told her. *"And that I'm most likely not going to live through it."*

Her lip trembled slightly and she closed her eyes, taking in a deep breath. *"We've been trying to figure out other ways to get through this without putting you in harm's way. I'm sorry it was kept from you. Now that your blood is Winter we can get Durin to make the weapon and then we can all discuss our plans of attack."*

"No," I shouted. *"You're not going to tell anyone I know. If you do then they will keep me back from doing what I'm supposed to do, especially Brayden. You know this, Sorcha."*

Sorcha scoffed and threw her hands in the air, exasperated. *"Well, then what are you going to do? Did your new powers magically enhance you to become invincible?"*

"No, not exactly, but I do have a way I can defeat him. I need you to trust me on this. Think of all the lives that could be saved if I get in there undetected and put an end to this. You would do the same thing, wouldn't you ... take the risk for everyone you love?"

She groaned. *"Yes, but we're going to come up with a plan. I'll keep your secret for now. However, if you do something stupid I'm not going to have a choice but to tell everyone. It's up to you, Ariella. I know how you are and I know what you're capable of as far as running head first into trouble. This isn't one of those times. Be smart about this and let us help you."*

"Thank you," I muttered, grateful. "I know I can do this. No one knows the true outcome of what will happen. I could still have a chance." I said it, but I didn't believe it. Going into the Black Forest alone was a death wish in itself.

The dream world started to fade, but Sorcha grabbed onto my hands and held them tight. Quickly, she asked, "If things weren't the way they are right now, would you be happy about completing the final bond with Brayden?"

As everything around me started to disappear, I looked into her emerald green eyes and smiled. "Yes, Sorcha, I would be happy. He's a pain in the ass, but I would be happy. I can't see how it would be fair to him to get attached when I know I'm not going to survive the ending."

Sorcha's grip on my hands lessened and we both began to disappear. Before my eyes opened to the new dawn I heard a final whisper escape Sorcha's lips ... it was a promise.

"You will live, Ariella. I promise you that."

L. P. DOVER

Chapter Eleven

Ariella

WHEN I AWOKE, I was alone in my bed, with the low sun trickling in through the window with the coming dawn. My first thought was that everything had just been a dream, but it all became clear again when I looked down at my pale, creamy skin. *Nope, it all happened.*

"*Brayden?*" I sent out through our bond.

"*Yes, angel.*"

"*Where are you?*"

"*Why, do you miss me already?*"

I rolled my eyes. "*I swear I never would've thought you could joke around. In a way, I think I miss the brooding and silent Brayden.*" He was easier to hate and stay away from when he was like that. I could hear his chuckle through my mind, and as much as I didn't want it to it made a smile spread across my face.

Getting out of bed, I removed my robe and my nightgown, and fetched a towel from my closet. *"Seriously, Brayden, where are you? I want to know if you've seen anyone yet."*

Padding across the room on my bare feet with my towel in hand, I opened up the bathroom door and immediately froze, dropping the towel on the floor. "Holy hell," I gasped, unable to take my eyes away from the man in front of me. Brayden stepped out of the shower as if nothing was amiss, gloriously naked and covered in droplets of water, with steam swirling around his Winter skin. He smiled at me, but not before raking an appreciative gaze down my own naked form.

"Good morning, angel. I see you found me, and to answer your question, no I haven't seen anyone yet. I've been with you all morning, which is going to get everyone asking questions the moment they look at you."

Picking up my towel, I wrapped it around my body and held it tight while Brayden chose to stand there with his draped over his shoulder. I tried my best to keep my eyes focused on his face, but my traitorous gaze kept lowering until it found the one thing my body desired to feel between my legs. *Oh my.*

I tried to open my mouth to speak, but all I could do was stutter, "I'll … I'll go wait out in the bedroom until you get done in here." When I turned to walk out, Brayden gently grabbed my arm and pulled me back into the bathroom.

Grinning, he turned on the shower water and put the towel around his waist. "Take your shower and meet me downstairs. I'll get everyone together so we can tell them you're coming home with me this evening. That is what you still want, right?"

Biting my lip, I nodded quickly. "Yes," I replied, my heart sputtering in my chest. "I don't belong here anymore. I'll be down there as soon as I can."

He released my arm, slowly sliding his fingers down my skin before turning his back and closing the door as he left. I showered hastily because I wanted to be down there when he told my family what had happened. As I laced up my brown warrior leathers, I realized how out of place it looked on my pale skin. I would soon have to trade out my brown and gold armor of the Summer Court and replace them with the black and silver of the Winter.

I pulled my hair back in a tight braid, just like Meliantha always did, and started for the door. However, a feeling in my gut made me freeze where I stood. A loud knock echoed through my room, and before I could open the door, Kamden took the liberty of opening it himself and strolled in like it was his right. *What the hell?*

"Just come on in, Kam," I muttered sarcastically. "I know we're friends, but you can't just walk in like that. If Brayden was in here you'd probably have your ass kicked."

His stance was rigid, his eyes dark and menacing, and so unlike the sweet Kamden I grew to care for. Chuckling, he prowled toward me and said, "I'd like to see him try. You know, I heard that your precious prince is your guardian now. I honestly didn't think you would complete the bond with him after he left you standing in the middle of the dance floor looking all pathetic and alone in the Spring Court. I must say that it was a shame I wasn't there to see it."

Something was wrong and I knew it from the dread building up in the pit of my stomach. All I could sense around me was darkness. My insides screamed at me to run, to fight, but I had nowhere else to go. Kamden had me cornered against the wall, trapped. Unfortunately, my instincts told me it wasn't Kamden gazing back at me through those evil, malicious eyes. It was someone else, someone I was going to have to face and destroy all on my own.

"Alasdair," I growled. His lip quirked into a smile, but then disappeared with my next words. "The only pathetic one here is you. You have to hide behind a disguise to get to me. I would say that makes you a spineless coward and definitely not what I expected from an all mighty sorcerer."

Taking my chin in his strong grasp, he slammed my head against the wall and held me firm so I couldn't turn away. He looked straight into my eyes and hissed, "Is this better?"

I could feel his dark magic spreading its evil tentacles across my skin as the form of one of my best friends slowly disappeared and was replaced with someone else. Instead of the short, black hair and hazel eyes of my friend it was interchanged with shoulder-length brown hair and the evil looking gray eyes of the sorcerer.

I could feel the power in his strength and in his body as he pressed it against mine, leaning close to breathe me in. I knew there was no way I could fight him off without a weapon. It angered me to know that I was caught off guard by his intrusion and that I was defenseless.

Groaning in my ear and still holding my face in his firm grasp, he used his other hand to glide his fingers down my body. First, he trailed a finger down my neck to my breasts, and then down my stomach to my waist where he squeezed tightly, digging his fingers in sharply. I hissed with the pain as his fingertips cut into my skin, drawing blood.

"Brayden! The dark sorcerer is in my room!" I screamed in his mind. I felt his panic almost immediately.

"What! No!" he yelled in reply. *"Dammit, I'll be right there. Stay calm, angel."*

Through gritted teeth, I spat angrily, "You better be glad I don't have a weapon right now or I would've already chopped off your hands. And possibly other protruding parts if you don't back off."

He laughed, a loud noise that grated my already raw nerves. "Ah, there is still hope for you yet,

Princess," he chided with a smirk on his face. "You may be bonded to the Winter prince, but your body still doesn't belong to him. From what I've heard he discards more women than me on a daily basis. That's pretty impressive. He'll get tired of you like he does everyone else." He tilted his head to the side and bit his lip. "I think I may need to get pointers from him on how to fuck women since he obviously has so many. Then again, you will see that for yourself soon."

"Screw you," I sneered. "Your words mean nothing to me."

"Ah … that's where you're wrong, Princess. You can't lie to me. I can see the doubt in your eyes."

Footsteps thundered from beneath us and I knew it would only be a matter of seconds before Brayden stormed through the door. Alasdair clucked his tongue and scolded me like a child, narrowing those evil gray eyes of his, "Now, now, Ariella that wasn't nice using your bond to get your prince in here. I see we will have to delay this visit for another time." He released my chin and flashed to the door in a matter of seconds, morphing back into Kamden in the process.

"There's not going to be another time," I growled, rubbing my aching chin.

He glanced over his shoulder at me and smiled. "Yes there will be, Your Highness. I can promise you that. It's not going to matter where you are or what you're doing. I will always have a way to get to you."

L. P. DOVER

And I will soon have a way to get to you, I thought to myself, and with that last thought, he disappeared.

❄ ❄ ❄

When Brayden stormed through the door to my room, his body shook with pent up rage and worry as he scooped me up into his arms. Ryder and Kalen burst through the door behind him, swords drawn and ready for battle, but when they saw Brayden holding me their mouths flew open in surprise and they lowered their blades.

"Are you okay? There were so many things going through my head on the way up here. I didn't know if he was going to take you, or try to kill you. All I knew was that if he did take you I would hunt him down until the end of time to find you. I would've failed you not only as your guardian, but as—"

"Brayden, I'm all right," I interrupted him, pulling out of his arms to get some distance.

His closeness confused me because I wanted it; I wanted him near. However, I couldn't stop the ping of jealousy in my gut after what the dark sorcerer said about the many women Brayden had occupied his time with. It was basically the same thing Kamden told me before about him as well. Was I going to have to deal with other women falling at his feet, wanting him to have sex with them?

Deep down I knew Alasdair wanted to plant the seed of doubt, but it still didn't change the fact that

Kamden said the same thing. He wouldn't lie to me. My sisters' never had to worry about other women with their men, well … except Meliantha when Kalen was about to bond with Breena when he thought she didn't want him. From what I heard he had his fair share of women also, but I saw the way he looked at my sister at the Winter Solstice Ball. It was the same way Ryder would watch Calista. Why did I have to get the one who screwed around all the time and liked to keep his emotions hidden? Granted he was getting better at it, but still …

"I can feel your tension and anger, angel. As much as you try to shield that I can still feel it, which means it's of copious proportions. Talk to me," he pleaded.

"We can talk later," I remarked verbally, heading out my bedroom door. "Right now I need to talk to the others. This needs to end." Brayden followed quickly on my heels, along with his brothers and several of his Winter warriors. Their armor made clanking sounds as we briskly walked down the golden halls toward the Great Room where I knew everyone would be.

I could hear Ryder whispering to Brayden behind me. "Don't worry, brother. She's exactly like Calista. When she's pissed or worried just leave her be. The more you provoke her, the angrier she gets."

Brayden grunted in reply while Ryder and Kalen chuckled. I sent them both a quick glance over my shoulder and said, "I guess you learned pretty quickly, huh, Ryder?"

Kalen spoke up, "I think we both had to learn. You Summer girls aren't exactly easy to deal with."

"Please," I remarked incredulously. "I don't think you Winter men are easy to deal with either. It definitely hasn't been a walk in the park."

"Well, technically Ryder and I are no longer Winter so you can't include us in that," Kalen said with a sly smile. "So that jab can only be directed at my little brother."

Brayden scowled and clenched his jaw while gripping onto the handle of his sword. Rolling my eyes, I shook my head and kept walking. *"Calm down, oh silent one. Your brother is just picking on you. Loosen up a bit and get that scowl off your face."*

"Right now is not a time of joking, angel. My brother has failed to realize what could've happened just now. The time for laughter has ended. We have bigger problems on our hands."

"Yes, we do," I agreed. *"But we can't let Alasdair suck the life out of us. I still plan on living mine just as I've always had. Soon it'll all be over."*

We finally made it to the Great Room, and once the doors opened Calista and Meliantha both ran up to me while Sorcha acknowledged me with a thoughtful nod. They didn't look surprised to see my changed skin so Brayden must've already had the chance to tell them before I called him up to my room.

"Did he take your power?" Calista asked quickly, embracing me tight.

I shook my head. "No, he didn't, but he said he'd be back for me."

She sighed and hung her head, gritting her teeth with a low sounding growl. "And unfortunately he will. So is it true that you'll be leaving with Brayden for the Winter Court today?"

"Yes, it's true," I replied.

She smiled and grabbed my hand, turning it over and to the side so she could inspect my skin. "It's so weird seeing you like this. Meliantha and I only have subtle changes, but you—"

"Yeah, I know it's strange," I interrupted her, spotting Durin over her shoulder. I grabbed her hand and pulled her with me toward our parents. I regretted that decision as soon as we came to my mother.

My mother gasped and tears flew out of her eyes as she ran to me. "Oh my heavens, look at you. You don't even look like my daughter anymore."

I rolled my eyes and bit my tongue from the comment I wanted to say. "Thanks, Mother. As if the circumstances aren't already complicated enough," I spouted sarcastically. "We have bigger problems to worry about and the fact that I'm a Winter Fae now can be discussed later." Turning my head, I decided to ignore her and focus on Durin who already knew what I was going to ask.

He acknowledged me with a nod and glanced at everyone in the room before announcing, "I am assuming now that the bonding has been completed that you wish for me to forge the final weapon?"

"Yes," I spoke up hastily over the crowd. "It needs to be done as soon as possible."

Calista, Meliantha, and Sorcha all three joined my side as Durin came toward us. "I will get it done, Your Highnesses. What type of blade would you prefer?" he asked us all. "It needs to be something you all can wield."

We all four studied each other, but it was clear what the weapon of choice needed to be. I would've suggested a sword since that was what I was good at, but a dagger would suffice. I knew for a fact that the others knew how to wield one along with their other talents. A dagger would be the easiest to drive through the dark sorcerer's heart, if that's what you wanted to call it. I didn't think he'd have one, but obviously he did.

"A dagger," I suggested to Durin. "That's what we need."

Elvena joined us and said, "That's not all he will need."

She left the room, and came back moments later with a vial in one hand and a knife in the other. "He needs your blood, children. I want you all to cut your palms and let your blood flow into the vial." She handed Calista the knife first, who sliced her palm and clenched her fist to squeeze the blood out faster. Once she completed her part she passed the knife to Meliantha, then to Sorcha, and then to me.

I sliced the palm of my other hand, the one opposite to the one I bonded with Brayden with, and let my newly bonded essence fill up the rest of the glass vial. Once the first drop touched the others' blood, the whole vial exploded with a burst of bright light that was stronger than the summer sun. The magic swirled around the tube and grew stronger the more blood I added to it.

"What's happening to it?" I asked, shielding my eyes.

Elvena's lip tilted up in a smile, but it was a sad kind of smile. Softly, she said, "It's the power of the Four combined, child. What more can I say other than it's the most potent and raw power this land has ever seen."

When the vial was completely filled up with our blood, I sealed it and handed it to Durin. He wrapped the vial in a black cloth so that we wouldn't be blinded anymore and packed it away in his bag. "I will get the dagger made as fast as I can. It's going to take some time, but as soon as it's finished I will deliver it myself."

With those final words he bowed to us all and hastily retreated out of the Great Room. I could only pray to the heavens that he hurried. Now it was time to say good-bye to my parents before I had to leave and travel to my new home … the Winter Court.

Chapter Twelve

Ariella

SAYING GOOD-BYE TO my family wasn't as hard as I thought it was going to be, but it still wasn't easy. My mother was a blubbering mess, repeating over and over how she didn't have any daughters left. I loved her, but she could be overdramatic at times and it was frustrating. The hardest farewell I had to make was to my father. His warm, loving smile was going to be the one thing I missed most about being at home ... except Summer was no longer my home.

I could feel the effects of my change when I stepped out into the Summer sun. It no longer soaked into my skin, making me feel refreshed, but burned and pierced through my flesh like hot coals. *No wonder the Winter Fae never stay long when they visit.* Even if I wanted to stay here and defy Brayden's demand that I live with him in the Winter Court there was no way I could. I wouldn't be able to stand the heat of the Summer for the rest of my life. The blood flowing through my veins knew where it belonged, and it wasn't with the green meadows, waterfalls, and beaches. It was with the gray clouds, snow, and ice.

Instead of riding to Winter on my horse, Lennox, I chose to ride in the carriage with Queen Mab, who was Brayden's mother, and my mother's archenemy. I had never really gotten the chance to talk to her, and I figured it would be a good time to find out more personal things about her son and why he was the way he was.

Queen Mab twirled a lock of her long, black hair between her fingers as she studied me from across the carriage. Between her and my mother, Queen Mab was the only one who was happy about the change to my body. However, in a way I couldn't tell if that was because she was truly happy about my change, or if it was because it caused my mother heartache. Their feud was a mystery to us all.

"When do you think you'll complete the bond with my son, Ariella?" she asked curiously. I averted my gaze to peer out the window in order to avoid her curious stare. I didn't know how to answer her. When I turned back to her I could see it in her eyes that she understood my wariness to the question. Her gaze could freeze anyone where they stood, literally, but what she showed me was warmth and compassion.

Leaning my head against the carriage wall, I sighed and regretfully answered, "To be honest, Queen Mab, I'm not sure when we will complete it. Brayden and I are complete opposites in every way imaginable. We have nothing in common, except a faraway attraction to each other that we can't deny. I think we've only had one real verbal conversation the whole time I've known him."

The queen smiled and let out a sad sigh. "Oh, Princess, you couldn't be more wrong. Not every relationship is based on how much you talk, but how your souls connect. I've watched my sons grow and turn into the men they are today, and since Brayden has always been a Winter Fae at heart, I've spent most of my time with him. He's extremely gifted, and once he gets you home I'm sure you will find out for yourself. If you give him time I know things will change between you two. Your and Brayden's relationship reminds me so much of a couple I used to know. They were very different, but their love was what they had in common."

"Really ... so what happened to them? Did they live happily ever after?" I asked.

She winced and bit her lip, her eyes closing as if in pain. When she opened them, a lone tear escaped the corner of her eye and froze on her skin before it could run down her cheek. She wiped it off and I could hear the clinking sound of it as it hit the carriage floor.

Sadly, she explained, "No, darling, they didn't. However, that's not the point I wanted to make. You and Brayden won't end up like them because your love isn't forbidden, although you both have the same qualities and differences like they had. A long time ago when I was younger things weren't like they are now. I don't know how much of our history you are aware of, but there was a time when the Summer and Winter Courts were enemies. It was unheard of for a Winter Fae and a Summer Fae to fall in love. It just wasn't the way things worked."

Intrigued by her story, I sat up and moved closer, wanting to hear more. "So I'm assuming this couple you knew of was a Winter Fae and a Summer Fae?"

She nodded and smiled, but her eyes showed nothing except sorrow. "Yes, and I haven't spoken of them in over a century."

My eyes went wide. "Wow, that's a long time. I would love to hear the story if you want to tell it to me."

Queen Mab gazed out the window to the tall, plush trees of the Mystical Forest. The wind that blew through the carriage smelled of fall and changing leaves, signaling our approach to the Fall Court ... Ryder and Calista's court. I thought maybe she didn't want to tell me the story since it was obviously hard for her. I could feel the sorrow pouring out of her mixed with the undertone of resentment, but it wasn't directed at me. It was coming from deep within her soul as if ...

"It was you, wasn't it?" I acknowledged softly. "You were the Winter Fae in the story you speak of."

With a heavy heart, she nodded and finally revealed the story of forbidden love, "Yes, it was me, Ariella. Sometimes it feels as if it was just a bad dream, but there are times when I can't help but remember. When I see the one responsible for all the heartache, it all comes back to me. I'm sure you know of whom I speak. It's not exactly a secret that I loathe her. To this day, she still refuses to accept the blame."

Her admission caught me off guard and I gasped, holding my hand over my mouth and shaking my head. She couldn't be talking about my mother, could she? What had my mother done to earn that level of hatred?

"Tell me what happened," I demanded. "I have to know."

The queen closed her eyes and smiled as if remembering those times long ago, of a time when she was just a princess and in love with someone she could never be with. With tear filled eyes, Queen Mab began, "It all started about a hundred and thirty years ago. Going to the mortal realm was frowned upon, but I loved to sneak away and watch how the humans interacted with each other. I stayed away during the times they were at war, but when they weren't I was there. I don't know if you go there often, but when you spend a lot of time there our fae magic calls to each other. Faeries will always find other faeries no matter what, especially in a place where no other magic exists. Do you go there frequently?"

I shrugged. "Not really. I only go there to procure paintings. I really love their art. I left all my pieces in my room back home. I didn't see the point in packing them all."

A mischievous gleam sparkled in Queen Mab's eyes when she said, "Oh, I don't think you have anything to worry about with that."

"What do you mean?" I asked.

She waved her hand in the air dismissively and snickered. "You'll find out later, my dear. It just goes with the theory that no matter how different you and my son are, there will always be something that ties you together. Okay, now back to the story. I was in the mortal realm and I had just gotten through walking across the Brooklyn Bridge when I spotted him. He was peering out over the bridge to the city, leaning over on his elbows on the railing. His golden skin stood out among the mortals, and even though he was dressed in mortal clothes I could tell underneath all of that that he was a warrior. I remembered just standing there, staring at him like I had never seen a Summer Fae before."

"What did he do when he saw you?" I wondered.

Queen Mab laughed and shook her head. "He knew I was there the whole time watching him. After a while, without turning around to look at me, he finally asked me to join him. He also promised he wasn't going to throw me over the bridge. I knew we were supposed to be enemies, but I didn't feel any animosity coming off of him at all."

I chuckled along with her and sat on the edge of my seat, dying to hear more. She wiped her eyes that were misty with tears and continued, "I had no clue what to expect from him. He was so full of life, just like you, and he brought me out of the shell I was in, made me feel things I never thought possible. I guess you could say Brayden is like me in that instance. He's reserved, but he has a passion inside of him that's stronger than any of my other sons. He likes to keep to himself, but even in the last day or two I could see a change in him. He just needs the right person to show him the way. *You* are that person to help him find that way."

I knew Brayden had started to change, especially since he became my guardian. He kept his emotions open to me fully, which I knew couldn't be easy for someone who had kept them hidden all his life.

Knowing Queen Mab's story didn't have a happy ending and that my mother was the cause of it, I had to know what happened. "What was his name?" I asked.

"Alaric," she whispered. "His name was Alaric."

I could feel her pain like a knife in the gut. She must've really loved him to have that kind of anguish inside her soul. "What did my mother do? How did she tear you and Alaric apart?"

Queen Mab scoffed and shook her head. "What didn't she do is the question. Alaric and I knew our relationship was forbidden, so we kept our love hidden from our world. We would meet on the Brooklyn Bridge at sunset, even if it was just for a moment. Staying apart made it hard to breathe and during the day I could barely think of anything else other than being in his arms and making love to him. He was my first love and I thought maybe ... just maybe things would change in the Land of the Fae to where we could be together. It just so happens that your mother put a stop to it."

Closing her eyes, she huffed and tightened her hands into fists beside her. "I don't hate anyone as much as I hate your mother. I didn't know that she fancied Alaric and that they had once been lovers. When he met me, their relationship had ended and she had moved on to another warrior. However, when she noticed him not panting along after her she got suspicious and decided to follow him to the mortal realm."

"So she saw you two together," I cut in, ashamed that my mother could be so cruel. I knew where this story was going and I didn't like it one bit.

Queen Mab nodded. "Yes, she saw us together and turned us in. I never got to say good-bye to him."

My heart broke for her because I couldn't imagine falling in love with someone only to have them ripped away and not be able to say good-bye. Although, most of all, I felt anger. How could my mother do that? How could she be so damn selfish and vindictive?

My voice shook when I responded, "Where is he now? Did my mother have him killed?"

"She might as well have," she remarked. "He was banished to the mortal realm and I was banished *from* the mortal realm. I don't know if he's alive or dead. All I know is that I've hated your mother ever since and I will hate her to the end of my time."

"Angel, are you all right?" Brayden inquired through our bond. *"I can feel your anger and despair."*

He rode up beside the carriage and I peered out the window at him. I nodded my head and answered, trying to smile, *"I'm fine, Brayden. You're mother and I were talking and she told me some things that—"*

"What did she say to upset you?" he interrupted, a scowl on his face. When I glanced over at Queen Mab she lifted a brow in question, but then realized what we were doing. She then smirked and sat there, watching us in amusement.

I huffed and rolled my eyes at Brayden, except a part of me couldn't help but notice how sexy he looked riding on his horse. His muscles bulged in his arms as he held onto the reins and his body also moved gracefully along with his horse's as they galloped along beside us. *Stop it, Ariella*, I chided myself.

Through the bond, I groaned. *"Calm down, caveman. She didn't say anything ill toward me. She told me something about my mother, something that made me realize how happy I am to be away from her."*

"I'm sorry," he said. *"Would you like to talk to me about it later?"*

"Are you going to actually talk to me or are we going to stare at each other and do this mind to mind mojo shit?" I asked, a hint of a smile tilting the corner of my lips.

"As soon as we get to our place I'm all yours. You can talk to me as long as you want, angel."

"Our place? What do you mean our place?" I shrieked.

Brayden winked at me and rode off, leaving me hanging. *"You'll like it when you see it, Princess. Don't worry ... I'm not going to ravish you against your will. I'm going to wait until you beg for it."*

"Not going to happen," I muttered quickly, watching his backside as he left.

"We'll see," he teased in his deep, seductive voice. *"We will see ..."*

Queen Mab spoke up, taking my mind off of Brayden's wayward thoughts. "So what is my son saying to you?"

I rolled my eyes and sighed, hoping to keep the blush from spreading to my cheeks. "Oh just the usual caveman stuff that he's been known to spout out."

Queen Mab doubled over, laughing. "I do believe you two are going to be a great match for each other. You are certainly going to keep him on his toes."

"Yes, I am," I agreed wholeheartedly, and then to myself I mumbled, "And he's going to keep me on mine."

Chapter Thirteen

Ariella

WHEN WE ARRIVED in the Winter Court, I was expecting to feel the bite of the cold breeze against my skin, but it never came. I bent down to grab a handful of snow, and smiled when it didn't freeze my fingers or turn them blue. No wonder the Winter Fae could walk around in just their bare skin. I gazed around in awe at the white covered terrain and the gray clouds above dropping thousands of giant-sized snowflakes. I caught one in my hand, expecting it to melt, but it sat there, whole and still together.

"This is fascinating," I breathed, filling my lungs with everything Winter. "It feels like …"

L. P. DOVER

"Home?" Brayden finished, sidling up beside me.

I looked over at him. "Yes, it does. It feels like I've always belonged to the Winter."

His brown eyes softened as he moved closer. "It's because you have, angel." I searched around quickly and noticed that we were alone on the palace steps. How could that be? There were people out here just a few seconds ago.

"Wait! Where did everyone go?" I asked. "They were just out here not too long ago."

Brayden chuckled and shook his head. "Yes, they were, but that was about an hour ago."

"Oh, wow," I laughed. "I guess I got carried away with being here."

I gazed up at him, our eyes locking with mutual desire. I wanted him to kiss me—hell, I wanted him to do more than kiss me—but I knew it would be selfish to do so. He looked down at my lips and started to lower his head. My heart thumped wildly in my chest and all I wanted was to take what was mine. Even though we hadn't known each other long, he was mine … if only for a short while.

Giving in to my selfish desires, I let Brayden close the distance. His lips hovered over mine for an instant before they claimed me. He pulled me closer against his body as he deepened the kiss, and opened up the connection to his soul.

"I will prove to you that I'm worthy," he whispered in my head. His fingers ran circles over

my back, making my skin tremble and shake under his touch.

My hands went straight to his short brown hair, which had grown a little longer over the past few days, and then down along the roughness of the stubble along his chin. I could just picture myself running my hands through his dark tresses while we made love, and feel the hair across his face rubbing along the tender flesh of my breasts. I shuddered just thinking about it before I remembered where we were. We were in front of the palace where anyone could see. If the dark sorcerer saw then everything could be in jeopardy. If he keeps thinking I hate Brayden then that should definitely buy me some time.

Pulling away abruptly, I took a couple of steps back and said, "We have to be careful, Brayden. We can't do this out in the open."

He lifted his eyebrows slyly and smirked. "Yeah, I don't think we should either, considering what you had going through your mind. I see you aren't going to make things easy for me, are you? If you didn't want to be with me then why were you thinking about—"

I slapped a hand to his mouth to keep him from saying it out loud. "First, I don't do anything easy," I challenged. "Second, you can't just expect me to fall into your arms anytime you want like I'm sure you're used to with other women." His smile disappeared but I continued, "Third, if Alasdair can get to me easily like he claims then that could mean he's watching us. If he thinks we are getting close to finishing the bond then he's going to come for me. He could tell we weren't fully bonded when he sniffed me out. We have to watch ourselves and not get carried away."

Taking my hand, he pulled me up the steps to the palace entrance and I followed. We walked through the foyer and out the back to where I could see the separate dwellings that Brayden, Ryder, and Kalen all lived in when they were here. "I don't like this, Ariella. We are supposed to be a united front here and you're asking me to stay away from you. How can I do that when I'm your guardian? Each second I'm near you it takes every single ounce of control I have to keep my distance."

"I'm sorry, Brayden, but that's the way it has to be. Right now, Alasdair thinks we hate each other. He's trying to turn me against you by telling me all the women you've been with, and to be honest he's not the only one who's told me." Brayden's eyes went wide, but before he could speak I held up my hand to stop him and continued, "We can talk about that later, and believe me I'm not happy with what I heard. Anyway, like I said, if he thinks we are getting too close then he's going to come for me. Is that what you want?"

Brayden abruptly let go of my hand, throwing his hands in the air and through his hair, while trudging up the front steps to his cabin, our home. His strides were angry and hard; I flinched with each step he took away from me. When he opened the door to his cabin, he paused and huffed loudly. Without turning to look at me, I could tell he was close to losing control by the anger in his voice when he spoke, "Do you want to know what I want, Ariella? Do you even care?"

I couldn't form the words to speak because insisting that I didn't care infuriated me, and of course with my hot temper I couldn't let it slide. I screamed my next words in his mind, *"Yes, I care! Look at me and tell me what you want!"*

He finally turned around to pierce me with his anger-filled eyes. "I am sick and tired of having to worry about if my people will be safe when we leave the palace walls. I've lost too many good men to the sorcerer's evil and I've had enough. This is *our* land, not his. He's dictating what we do and how we live our lives, and I'm done with it. You told me yourself that you want me to prove how sorry I am. How can I do that if you want me to stay away from you? Have you forgotten that without you and me together our courts won't stand a chance against Alasdair if he takes your power? We're trailing on thin ice right now until our court is formed."

"I haven't forgotten," I whispered, turning away from his gaze. If we completed the bond now there was no way Alasdair could defeat us. We would be stronger than him, but bonding with Brayden through marriage and making love to him was a huge decision … and one I knew I wanted to make. However, I knew we couldn't take that step.

"Why are you closing yourself off from me?" Brayden hissed. "I know you have to be feeling something in that body of yours, but all I get is nothing. If distance is what you want, then distance is what you'll get, Princess. From now on, my thoughts are mine. When you're ready you can come to me, and I'll let you back in. However, until you open yourself up to me I'm done."

I gasped as the inner connection with him completely shut off, leaving me feeling hollow and bleak on the inside. I didn't realize what a comfort it was having his presence inside my soul until he took it away. It saddened me, but above all else it pissed me off. He completely let his pride get in the way and let reasoning fly out the window, or in this case get carried off into the snowy wind.

Instead of going into his dwelling, he stalked down the stairs straight past me without even a sideways glance. "Where are you going?" I hollered from my frozen spot on the porch steps.

I wanted to run after him and demand he stop being an ass, except my pride kept me from doing that. Maybe we were alike in that instance. We both had extreme amounts of pride and neither one of us wanted to waver.

He kept walking and didn't even turn around to acknowledge me when he responded silently, *"It's midday and it is time for me to train with my warriors. Pick any room in my house that you want. I don't know when I'll be back."*

"Oh, that's comforting, guardian. I guess it's a good thing I can take care of myself then," I snapped.

"I guess so," he replied, and after that, the connection went silent.

Chapter Fourteen

Ariella

I WATCHED BRAYDEN walk away. With each passing moment it killed me not to chase after him and argue some sense into him, but I knew it wouldn't work. He wasn't like any other man I knew, and no amount of yelling or reasoning with him would work. However, there was a way I was going to get him to listen.

When I entered Brayden's dwelling, it wasn't what I expected. There were bookshelves along the side wall with hundreds of books stacked neatly on the shelves. Skimming a finger over the novels, they ranged from the everyday classics to history and philosophy. *Has he read all of these?* I wondered.

Several of my bags were tucked into a corner of the living room, so I grabbed the one I needed and headed up the stairs. I went into the first room I came to and threw my bag on the enormous bed sitting majestically in the middle of the room. The colors were almost the exact shades of blue and silver as my room in the Summer Court. It was almost uncanny how alike they were. Changing quickly into my armor—my Summer armor—I secured my breastplate and the laces of my vambraces on my arms. All I needed now was my sword and I'd be ready to go.

Once I had my sword, I set out on my way to find Brayden and his warriors. The snow stuck to my braid, making my bright blonde hair appear even whiter than what it already was. It didn't melt, but clung to it like a blanket of protection. I could feel the land calling me to complete the bond with Brayden. It was like a song I heard in my head over and over the moment I stepped inside the Winter Court boundary. I had overheard my sisters talk about the feeling they got when the land called to them. It was like a magnet pulling you in a direction that you knew you couldn't go to yet, and it took all I had to ignore it calling me.

Searching around the palace grounds, it didn't take me long to hear the clanging of swords, or the battle cries and grunts of the warriors as they fought against each other. I flattened myself against the side wall of the palace and slowly tilted my head around the corner so I could see them. Their training field was just as large as ours in Summer, except this one was covered in snow and adorned with hundreds of warriors in black and silver instead of brown and gold. I was going to be the odd one out. I watched quietly as Brayden gave his orders and directed them in a series of thrusts and dodges. I could tell he was a good leader just by the way he paid attention to his men and the determination in his eyes to make them better fighters.

Taking a deep breath, I left the cover of the wall and slowly sauntered out through the crowd with my head held high. The warriors halted in mid-motion, bowing as I walked past them heading toward Brayden. He hadn't turn to acknowledge me, but with the rigid stance and the tenseness in his muscles I knew he could feel I was there.

"What are you doing here?" Brayden asked, his voice bland and disinterested as he kept his back to me.

"I'm not going to answer that question until you turn to face me," I snapped. The warriors around us gasped and halted with their mouths wide open, staring back and forth at us.

Brayden crossed his arms over his chest and finally turned to face me. Yep, he was back to being the emotionless bastard that he was before. However, I was going to fix that problem … fast. Now that I had his attention I said, "Whether you like it or not I'm here to train. Either you can fight with me or I'll find one of these other handsome warriors to teach me a thing or two."

When all he did was clench his teeth, I backed away from him and pulled out my sword, turning around so I could address the warriors. "All right, since Prince Brayden won't answer me, who here wants to fight me and help me train?"

Several of the warriors smiled while others looked to Brayden for guidance. I heard one of them whispering to another, "I don't feel right about fighting his queen."

Brayden heard the fighter say it too because his gaze instantly found mine. "I'm not his queen," I announced, narrowing my eyes at him.

"She's right," he agreed. "She's not my queen. If she wants to fight then let's show her how we do it in the Winter Court."

The guys all hollered and resumed back to their fighting, except I caught several of them sneak glances my way to watch me battle. Brayden picked a couple of his warriors to stand back and join me, all circling me like I was their prey. With my sword gripped firmly in my right hand, I was ready. However, I couldn't stop myself from taunting Brayden just a little bit more. He was standing outside of the circle, watching on with a smirk on his face.

"What's wrong, Prince Brayden, afraid you might get your ass kicked?" I teased.

Brayden's smirk grew wider and he retorted back, "Not at all, Princess. I just have to see if *you* are worthy enough to fight me."

L. P. DOVER

"Asshole," I hissed in his mind, narrowing my eyes at him angrily. If he wanted worthy, I'd show him how worthy of a fighter I was.

Not waiting on the others to attack, I shifted on my feet and kicked the warrior's legs—who was standing in front of me—out from under him. He went down quickly, but then got right back up, snarling at me, "You are a sneaky one, aren't you?"

"That's what I've been known for," I chided.

He attacked this time along with two other warriors. I fought three of them at once while Brayden watched on curiously, keeping his gaze neutral. I took a few hits knowing my body was going to be sore afterwards, but it was worth it to make Brayden sweat. He finally began showing some emotion when one of the warriors started getting a little too close to me. His gaze grew hard and annoyed, and I could tell he'd had enough.

"Stop!" he yelled. He pulled out his sword and approached the four of us, keeping his eyes steadily on me. When he reached us, he quickly glanced at the three warriors and growled, "Back up, all of you. She's mine now."

The air around us turned electric, and it charged me with a newfound force. I was ready to fight him even though I'd been battling it out and using all my strength. The fire in his eyes let me know he wasn't going to take it easy on me, and I welcomed it.

"Let's see what you got," I said.

His wolfish smile was answer enough, but he silently added, *"Gladly."*

Brayden delivered the first blow by swinging his body around in a circle and swiping his sword against the armor on my stomach, except he didn't even touch me because I backed up just in time. Our swords clanged against each other, echoing across the field, as we fought. The other warriors had ceased their training and came to stand around us, watching intently as their prince fought the woman who was supposed to one day be his queen.

It wasn't just the warriors who crowded around; other Winter Fae had joined in the entertainment as well. I waited on him to use the moves that I knew he would use toward the end of the fight. Kamden had taught me the Winter warrior ways when I trained with him in the Spring Court. I was ready, but I knew Brayden didn't know I would use his moves against him.

Since we were putting on a show, I decided to spice it up just a bit. When Brayden lunged toward me, I called upon my wind magic and twisted him up in the air and then back down to the ground where he landed in a crouch. His lip tilted up ever so slightly and he raised an amused brow. "I see you have to cheat by using your magic. I knew I would be too much for you," he insisted slyly.

I scoffed and twirled the sword in my hand. "No, I don't have to cheat. I just want you to stop messing around and fight harder. I'm getting bored."

The crowd snickered, getting the rise out of Brayden that I needed. He snarled and lunged again, this time using the moves Kamden taught me. I dodged every single blow and he dodged mine, except I did manage to knick his arm with my blade. The blood dripped down his skin in rivulets, but he didn't seem to mind it. The opening I was waiting for finally came. However, I didn't expect him to deviate from his usual technique.

The crowd cheered as the fight came to a close, but it wasn't the sort of ending I was hoping for. Brayden and I faced each other with his blade at my neck and mine at his. It was a standoff, anyone's match. Breathing heavily, all it would take was one simple move and his sword would bite into my neck and the same for him. He gazed at me like he'd never seen me before, with awe and surprise, but most of all fascination. I didn't think he realized what he was up against when he took me on, just like I didn't realize he had an inner self that no one had seen other than me. He let his guard down with me and it was my turn to do the same.

"Do you want to know why I've hidden my thoughts from you?" I asked silently. Our blades were still at each other's throats, holding us captive. However, I wasn't ready to tell him everything, but I had to tell him how I felt. I owed him that much.

"Yes," he answered, *"Tell me."* His eyes had lost the fire and grew soft. In that moment, none of the people around us existed except him and me.

"It's because I'm scared," I admitted honestly. *"If you want to know how I feel, then I'll show you."* Closing my eyes, I let every single meeting with him play through my mind like he did with me. The first

day I met him about six years ago and how I thought he was mysterious but moody. The next time was in the Winter Court when I saw him staring at me and I deliberately wanted to make him jealous by dancing with another Winter Fae.

"I wanted you to notice me," I confessed.

"And I did."

Then I let things get a little more in depth. I let him feel the worry and angst I felt when I saw him ride up wounded after the battle to save Sorcha's friend and her guardian, and how I wanted to be the one to take care of him, but I couldn't. Then came the vision of him leaving me. I made him feel the anguish and rejection I felt as I watched him turn his back on me and also when he did the same thing during our time in the Summer Court. Lastly, I let him see the tears I cried while I was alone and no one was around. Tears for him, tears for our land, and most importantly tears for a love lost.

"Now you know," I whispered, trying to keep my voice from shaking.

I gradually lowered my sword and he did the same thing. Backing up slowly, I bowed my head to him before sheathing my blade. I turned on my heel and gave him one last glance before I took off through the crowd. Several of the Winter Fae congratulated me on besting Brayden while others just stared at me curiously, trying to figure out what was going on between me and their prince. Not everyone knew that Brayden was my guardian, but I was sure an announcement would be made at some point. Right now they were all kept in the dark with what happened between us, which was a good thing.

"Ariella, wait!" Brayden shouted in my mind.

As I came across the backside of the palace, I could feel Brayden's presence behind me, following me. I ducked into an alcove and concentrated hard on changing my appearance. I pictured one of the warriors in my mind with his long, brown hair and midnight blue eyes along with the black and silver armor of Winter. It was the first time in a while I had changed appearances, but I could feel it working as I imagined myself being one of the warriors I knew to be called Cyrus.

I smiled as I gazed down at my new body. Brayden charged around the corner, and when he saw me I froze. "Cyrus, did you see Princess Ariella pass by this way?" he asked quickly.

I shook my head and cleared my throat, hoping my voice would sound the same as Cyrus'. "I did, Your Highness. She ran up to the back entrance to the palace and went in that way," I lied, pointing in the direction I spoke of.

Brayden nodded and ran up the path to the back entrance. Leaning my head against the wall, I breathed a sigh of relief and closed my eyes. I wasn't ready to talk to Brayden, not after him being a douche bag and me breaking down and spilling my secrets. I needed to make him sweat a little bit more. Walking back into the crowd of people who were slowly dispersing, I couldn't help stopping the moment I heard my name come up. There was a group of warriors with a couple of fae women talking about the fight.

Slowly, I casually came in behind the group, trying to blend in, so I could hear what they were talking about. One of the warriors I fought was in the group and he was the one Brayden didn't like getting close to me. He was handsome with his curly, light brown hair and dark blue eyes, and you could tell he loved the women. There were three of them hanging all over him when he spoke, "There was definitely some tension there between the princess and Prince Brayden, wasn't there? Did all of you feel that?"

The group nodded in agreement with murmurs here and there. "Yes, there was," one of the fae women, who was holding onto his arm, said. She had long, wavy black hair and was very beautiful. By the dress she was wearing I would say she didn't come from the noble families. "I wonder what's going on with them," she uttered curiously.

"She said she wasn't his queen," another warrior cut in. "If I knew that was absolutely true I'd try to talk to her myself."

"Conner, she wouldn't give you the time of day," someone else said. "But we all know how our Prince gets when he trains hard." My ears perked up and I moved closer. The young warrior who just spoke turned his head and addressed a tall, brown haired female with supple breasts and curves to die for. "Taryn, since it's obvious the princess isn't going to work him out tonight, are you? You were the one he always wanted before."

What? I wanted to scream. Just the thought of Brayden with someone else made me sick and angry to the core. What made it worse was actually hearing about it.

The girl he called Taryn adjusted her dress and licked her lips seductively. "Of course he wanted me, Sage. How could he not?" *Because he has me you stupid bitch,* I thought. There was nothing redeeming about Taryn and I could tell it in the tone of her voice and the way she carried her body. She used sex to get what she wanted and it was clear as day that she used her body to work her way up the ladder to Brayden. *Not anymore.*

"When was the last time you were with him? Be careful because it might cause problems with the princess. I don't think you'd last in a fight against her," Sage said.

Taryn scoffed. "I'm not too worried about that, and besides, how is she going to know if I take her prince for a ride. I can be sneaky when I want to be."

So can I, I thought to myself. *You have no idea how sneaky I can be.*

When everyone dispersed and went their separate ways, I made sure to get a head start toward Brayden's dwelling. Hiding behind a tree so that no one could see, I glamoured myself back into my true form. Taryn strutted her way down the path, and when she came upon the tree I circled around, allowing her to see me. She froze where she stood and all the confidence I heard her spew just a few minutes ago evaporated.

"Your Highness, what are you doing out here?" she asked hesitantly.

Pushing off the tree, I walked up to her and smiled, even though I wanted to punch her in the face. She swallowed hard, but maintained her stance. "I'm waiting on you. You're not trying to be *sneaky* are you?" I said in a sweet voice. "Because sometimes being sneaky can get you into a lot of trouble. Do you understand where I'm going with this, or do I need to spell it out for you?"

She backed up and bowed her head before angrily answering with clenched teeth, "Yes, I understand, Your Highness."

My smile disappeared and I rested my hand casually on the hilt of my sword. "Good, I'm glad I didn't have to explain it to you. I think it's best that you turn around and go back to where you came from. Your services won't be needed again … ever."

Placing her hands on her hips, Taryn scoffed and stomped away. No one was going to be servicing Brayden ever again if he didn't pass the test I was going to throw him. I felt juvenile for playing these games, but it was up to me to keep my heart safe. It shouldn't come as a shock to anyone anyway. I was known for the tricks up my sleeve and I might as well do what I was good at.

Chapter Fifteen

Brayden

"ARIELLA, WHERE ARE you?" I hissed through our bond. I'd searched everywhere in the palace for her and nothing. No one had seen her since the fight and she wasn't answering me through our connection.

"Dammit, why aren't you answering me?"

I stormed through the castle halls angrily until I almost bumped into my mother coming out of the art room. She smiled at first, but then furrowed her brow, studying me. "Son, what's wrong? Why are you so angry?"

"Have you seen, Ariella?" I asked through clenched teeth.

With her eyes twinkling, she shook her head and tried to hold back her smile. "No, I haven't seen her, but I did hear about what happened this afternoon. I wish I could've seen it. Maybe we should get Ariella to train some of our females to fight."

That actually wasn't a bad idea. "I'll talk to her about it," I muttered, "but right now I need to find her. If you see her, tell her I'll be at our place waiting. Surely, she won't stay gone all night."

"Give her space, son. She'll be back when she's ready." She kissed me on the cheek and turned on her heel, but stopped abruptly and said, "Oh yeah, before I forget. Durin sent word that he's working on the dagger for the princesses. He will be delivering it in about three weeks."

Great, I thought. Three weeks of hell trying to keep Ariella safe from the sorcerer and from me. This foolishness was going to end tonight whether she liked it or not.

Closing my eyes, I sighed. "All right, three weeks. I'm sure we will manage somehow." I ambled away from my mother and out of the palace doors, running at a fast pace to my dwelling.

Slamming open the door, I called, "Ariella! Are you here?" There was no sound, only silence as I searched through the rooms of the house on the lower level. Running up the stairs, I searched through those rooms as well, but stopped when I saw her stuff in my bedroom. *Did she know this was my room?* I wondered.

Stripping out of my armor, I took a quick shower and wrapped a towel around my waist before heading to my closet. The wound on my arm had already healed from Ariella's sword slicing through my skin. It was only a surface scratch and I honestly didn't think she meant to do it. Before I could grab a set of clothes out of my closet a knock sounded at the door.

Hopefully, it was Ariella, but why would she knock on the door? Traipsing down the stairs, I could tell the figure on the other side of the door wasn't Ariella, but someone from my past, someone I had told I never wanted to see again.

When I opened the door she flung her arms around my shoulders and squealed, "Oh, Brayden, you fought amazing today. It got me all hot watching you and what's even better is looking at you in your towel. How about we go upstairs and reminisce on the good times we've had together."

What the ...

Appalled, I jerked out of her arms, tightened the towel around my waist, and snapped, "What the hell are you doing here, Taryn? I don't know what's going on with you, but you better leave this instant." Taryn and I had an arrangement of sorts a long time ago. There were no commitments or feelings involved ... just sex. That's all it was and that was all it ever would be, but I hadn't been with her in over a year.

Taryn pouted her lip, and moved closer. "But I thought we used to have fun together. Don't you want that again? I can tell you and your princess aren't getting along, so let me relieve some of that tension I know you have built up. It'll be fun."

"Enough," I shouted angrily. "Whatever is going on between me and your future queen is our business. You know very well that what we had between us was over a long time ago. I don't want you or anyone else for that matter. Now, if you don't mind I want you to leave … now."

Taryn narrowed her eyes and stood up straighter. "So what you're trying to tell me is if I got naked right now and asked you to fuck me that you wouldn't?"

"You're right, I wouldn't," I retorted truthfully. "There's only one person I want right now and it's not you."

Taryn laughed sarcastically. "So you're holding out for the princess who doesn't even want you? Why would you wait for her when you could have so many other women at your beck and call?"

Because I love her, I said to myself.

Taryn's eyes went wide, as if she'd heard me, and she whispered, "Please don't tell me that you love her? Is that what you're saying?"

I didn't have to think twice. "Yes," I said, "that's exactly what I'm saying. Now do me a favor and don't come back here again. I'm sure there are plenty of men out there that would be honored to have you, but it's not me."

Tears welled in her eyes as she backed up to the door and ran out of it, down the steps and into the night. Sighing, I shut the door and leaned against it.

"Ariella, please come home. I really need to talk to you."

I didn't expect to hear her reply, but it came through as a soft whisper, so unlike the Ariella from just a few hours ago. *"I'm on my way,"* she said. *"And Brayden?"*

"Yes, angel."

"I'm sorry."

I was sorry, too. Especially because I was going to have to explain to her what had just happened. Knowing Ariella and her fiery temper she'd blow up at the first mention of a woman trying to get me into bed. Honesty was something I lived by. Hopefully she'd respect that and listen to what I had to say. *I love her.*

It took me a while to figure out that was what I felt, but it was true. I loved her and I was going to tell her.

Chapter Sixteen

Ariella

I DIDN'T KNOW what to expect when I pretended to be Taryn, but hearing Brayden confess his love to me wasn't what I thought would happen. I felt guilty for tricking him and the weight of that guilt felt like a boulder pressing down against my chest. However, I didn't feel bad with confronting Taryn. She needed to be taken down a notch or two.

Taking a deep breath, I stared at the front door to Brayden's home for about five minutes before I had the courage to walk inside. As soon as I opened the door and shut it, I turned around and he was there. Brayden was dressed in a simple, fitted black T-shirt and jeans, and his hair was still damp from the shower. Just a few minutes ago when I was Taryn, I got to see him in nothing but a towel. My heart raced just looking at him sitting in one of his living room chairs; his legs crossed and resting over the table in front of him, a glass of faerie wine in his hands.

Another sparkling glass of wine waited on the kitchen counter and I assumed it was mine, so I smiled quickly at him and strolled over to the bar, gulping down the glittering blue liquid. It tingled in my belly and relaxed my muscles in an instant. I closed my eyes and sighed.

"I needed that," I breathed, sinking down into one of the chairs at the bar. "Thank you for pouring me a glass."

"You're welcome," he replied. I could hear him swallow down the rest of his wine and set the glass down on the table in front of him. My back was to him, but I could feel the presence of his body coming up behind me.

Now that the day was over and the excitement of the fight had died down, my body ached and my muscles were sore. I overdid it with Brayden this afternoon, but I wanted to push myself past any limit I had for myself. I had to do it. I put a hand on the back of my neck and began rubbing out the knots of tension.

Gently, Brayden moved my hand away and began working out the kinks in my muscles with his strong yet soothing fingers. Immediately, the tension ebbed and I liquefied under his touch. I couldn't stop the moan from escaping my lips or keep my eyes from rolling back because of how amazing his hands felt on my body.

"Can we talk?" he asked.

His hands moved from my neck down to my shoulders, kneading and rubbing. "I don't think I can talk with you touching me like that?" I moaned.

"You just did, Ariella," he murmured, a deep chuckle vibrating in his chest.

I groaned and lazily tilted my head to the side. If he kept it up, I was going to fall asleep. However, all thoughts of sleep were erased from my mind as I felt his firm, wet lips placed against my bare neck.

"What are you doing?" I whispered, tilting my head further to the side. The stubble on his chin tickled my neck and sent chills down my body, making me shudder.

Taking my hand, he pulled me off of the chair and leaned down to my ear. "Come with me," he commanded huskily.

With my hand in his, I followed him up the stairs to the room I had placed my bags in earlier. I needed to get out of my armor and into something more comfortable, and possibly sexier. Brayden shut the door behind us and leaned against it. "What are we doing in here?" I asked, lifting a curious brow. "You're not planning on seducing me, are you?"

He smiled and shook his head. "Not yet, angel. I thought you might like to change clothes and have dinner with me. We need to talk."

"About?" I inquired, even though I already knew.

My bags had all been moved, so I walked over to the closet to see if they were in there. When I opened the door my clothes had all been hung and placed neatly on one side, but the other side …

"Why are your clothes in here, too?" I asked. "I didn't know I was going to have to share."

Brayden chuckled and joined me. "You have it all wrong, angel. I didn't know *I* was going to have to share. You seem to have picked my room as yours."

What? There was no way the room could be his. "That's not possible," I shrieked. "How could someone like you have a room like this? It doesn't match your personality at all, and what's even weirder is that it's exactly like mine in the Summer Court."

"I know," he agreed. "I guess you and I have more things in common than you realized. Now get dressed and I'll have some food brought to us." He licked his lips while staring at mine, but he didn't follow through. Instead, he turned on his heel and looked back at me once before opening the bedroom door and leaving me to get dressed. *Were we going to share this room together?* I wondered.

Quickly, I picked out a dress, laid it on the bed, and rushed into the bathroom to take a hasty shower. By the time I got out, I used my wind magic to blow through my hair to make it dry and wrapped a towel around my body. I rushed into the bedroom to change, only to find Brayden standing in front of the open French style doors that led onto the balcony, staring out at the snowy night. There was a table out there with lit candles and two covered dishes that had steam billowing out into the cold air.

Brayden turned around and his eyes blazed with fire as he peered up and down my body. *"I don't think I'll ever get over how beautiful you are,"* he murmured in my mind. *"I'm really sorry with the way I acted earlier."*

"It's okay," I said with a smile. "I understand that guys don't think before they speak. I'm perfectly used to it." My gaze drifted over to my dress on the bed and back down to my body wrapped in the towel.

Brayden narrowed his eyes playfully and said, "Do you need help getting dressed, angel? I'll be glad to help."

Biting my lip, I shook my head and dropped the towel to the floor. "I think I can handle it," I muttered softly. He watched me from the doors as I carefully lifted the dress over my head and slowly lowered it down over my body. From the bulge in Brayden's jeans I could tell he wanted to do more than watch, but he kept his distance much to my dismay.

"I told you I was going to wait until you begged for it, didn't I?" he remarked, with a glint in his eye.

"That you did." There happened to be a problem with that scenario, though; I was never one to beg.

We ate dinner in silence and when we were done we stood on the balcony, side by side, and gazed out across the snowy landscape of the Winter Court. The sky was completely dark, but the snowflakes cascading down gave off its own light. The stark whiteness of it lit up the land so vibrantly that you would still be able to see your way through the dark. It was amazing.

Brayden broke the silence. "When I was out looking for you earlier I ran into my mother. She heard word from Durin that it'll be about three weeks before he can bring us the dagger."

"That long?" I gasped. "So much can happen in three weeks. If the sorcerer steals my power somehow there will be no way to stop him." I knew Durin couldn't make the dagger overnight, but I secretly hoped it wouldn't take that long. It felt like we were sitting on a ticking time bomb waiting to explode. The longer the dark sorcerer had, the more time he had to figure things out.

Brayden turned to me and took my hands, pulling me closer. "He's not going to get your power, angel," he murmured softly. "I know you want us to keep our distance when we are around the others, and now that I've thought about it I can live with that. I don't want to put you in harm's way. Therefore, all I'm asking is that when we are together away from the prying eyes of others that you open yourself up to me. You've seen and felt what I feel for you and you gave me a glimpse into what you feel for me. I want to go deeper, Ariella."

Closing my eyes, I released a shaky breath and lowered my gaze away from his heated stare. "How deep?" I asked.

He lifted my chin with his finger and slowly closed his lips over mine, gently. "As deep as you'll let me," he added. "But I have some things I need to tell you first."

And I knew what those things were going to be.

Chapter Seventeen

Ariella

WE MOVED INSIDE, shutting the glass doors to the balcony, and settled ourselves on the floor in front of the unlit fireplace. Brayden called upon his magic, and in an instant the flames leapt out of his hand and into the hearth. I never understood how someone from the Winter Court could have fire magic.

"You know, it's strange that a Winter Fae can wield fire. In a way, it makes no sense," I said, mesmerized by the flames warming the room. "One would think you'd melt." I snickered and I could feel Brayden shaking his head behind me.

"That might be why not that many Winter Fae have the ability for fire," he responded. "As far as I know my father and I are the only ones. So I guess it doesn't make sense."

Brayden grabbed a blanket off the chair behind him and wrapped it around us as he sidled up behind me, placing both of his legs on either side of me. It felt natural leaning up against him and having his arms around me, feeling his heartbeat against my back. He sighed loudly and I knew what he was getting ready to talk about. I could feel it through the bond how he was worried I'd get angry. It took him forever to explain about Taryn coming to visit him and all the while it took everything I had not to break down and laugh. I was thankful he couldn't see my face in that moment. I knew he was uncomfortable having to talk about it, but I already knew what happened … I was there. I waited on him to tell me the rest of the story about how he told Taryn he loved me, but that part of the conversation never came up.

"So you're not angry with me?" he asked.

"Why would I be angry? You told me nothing happened, even though you did answer the door in just a towel. Next time, don't do that. I don't think you would like it if I answered the door in a towel with one of your warriors standing out there."

He growled low in his chest. "Good point. I wouldn't like that at all, but I would love to see you in a towel again."

I laughed and turned to face him. "I'm sure you'll have plenty of chances to since I'm forced to live with you here," I teased.

Brayden lifted a brow and pulled me up on his lap, placing his hands on my thighs as I straddled his waist. "You know I'm not forcing you to stay here," he said in all seriousness. "You know I would never make you."

Resting my hands on his shoulders, I ran them over his back and up to his neck where I clasped them together firmly. "I want to be here, Brayden. I just wish our time together wasn't rushed. You're extremely good looking and trust me, my body is screaming for you to take me, and I can feel yours saying the same thing." Which was true, I could. The desire in his eyes along with his cock growing stiffer between my legs alerted me of that. "But you know I need more," I added softly.

He nodded. "I know that, and we're going to show each other more, but there's no harm in doing it in different ways is there?"

The look in his eyes was predatory as he bit his lip and wrapped his arms snuggly around my waist, holding me down on the hardness between his legs. I leaned down, our lips almost touching, when I whispered, "What did you have in mind?"

His hand tangled in my hair, gripping it tight, and pulling me down the rest of the way so our lips touched. "This, angel. This is what I had in *mind*. I know that it's a big step for us since our mating isn't like a normal faerie bond, but with our connection we can still do everything we want in our mind and share it together. All it takes is our imagination."

Intrigued, I bit my lip and sighed. "You know … I never thought about that. I think it could be kind of interesting, but I don't want everything to be strictly in our minds you know."

"Are you saying you want me to touch you like this?" he asked, sliding his hands up my bare thighs beneath my dress. "And like this?" he added, trailing his soft lips up my collarbone to my neck and jaw.

"Yes," I breathed. "That's exactly what I'm saying, but we can't let it get too far." Even as the words came out of my mouth I knew they were a lie. I wanted it to go further and I knew Brayden did, too. Unfortunately, I always made rash and irresponsible decisions in my life. For once, I wanted to do things slow and right.

Wrapping my legs around his waist, Brayden held me firmly and carried me over to the bed. "I'll only go as far as you let me, angel," he murmured gruffly, setting me down gently.

Lying down beside me, Brayden placed one of his legs in between mine and leaned over me, propping himself up on his elbow. His lip tilted up in an arrogant smirk as he lowered them to mine, crushing them to my lips in a possessive kiss. *"You taste so alive, angel. I never thought I could feel so much with anyone."*

"I never knew you could feel anything," I teased, but groaned when he growled and bit my lip.

"You're going to wish you didn't say that."

Rolling on top of me, he spread my legs with his knee and pushed his groin up against me. I bucked underneath him and moaned. I never had a chance to put on underwear, so the only thing between him and me were his jeans. The roughness of them teased my sensitive flesh as he rocked his hips back and forth, dipping and thrusting against my core.

"Touch me, Brayden," I demanded heatedly.

He stopped immediately and gazed down at me, grinning from ear to ear. "Are you actually begging me, angel?"

Grabbing him by the shoulders, I fisted my hands in his shirt and pulled him down to me. "Oh no, I'm not begging you …" I said, kissing him firmly on the lips, "… I'm telling you."

Brayden chuckled, but opened his mouth further, letting his tongue mingle with mine. *"Whenever the time comes for me to make love to you, Ariella, you will beg me. Of that I am certain."*

"I told you I'm not the begging type."

He chuckled again, and without breaking contact with my lips, he hooked a finger underneath the strap of my dress. He slowly glided it down my shoulder inch by inch until he freed my breast. Trailing his tongue down my chin to my neck, he carefully flicked my taut nipple with his tongue and closed his lips around my tender flesh, sucking greedily.

I moaned and arched my back into his touch, whispering his name. His hand removed the other strap of my dress and released the other breast. I ached for the feel of his skin on mine. Quickly, Brayden sat up and pulled off his shirt, throwing it to the floor. He gazed down at me with his hooded brown eyes and I up at him. His chest was hard and smooth with nothing except pure, lean muscle. My dress was bunched up at my waist, leaving me exposed and spread open to him as he watched me lying there beneath him, waiting. Waiting for what I had no clue.

Gently, Brayden trailed his fingers up my thighs, and when his thumb rubbed over my sensitive flesh I gasped. Lowering himself onto me again, he licked and sucked one of my nipples while circling his thumb across my clit. Only when he pushed a finger into my opening did I almost lose control. I was so close to begging, but I bit my tongue to keep my words silent. My breathing accelerated along with Brayden's. I was so deliciously close to the edge that when he pushed further inside me I lost it.

His fingers pumped relentlessly as I jerked and bucked against the bed, gripping onto the bed sheets. "Brayden," I shouted as the orgasm started to heighten.

"Let it go," he groaned. "I want you to let it go, angel."

Gliding his fingers in and out harder, I finally opened myself up and let the orgasm spill throughout my body. It felt like liquid fire as the tremors from my release spread to every nerve ending of my being. It felt amazing. Breathing hard, I closed my eyes while Brayden lay down beside me. When I opened them, I couldn't stop my gaze from wandering down to his waist where his cock bulged against his jeans.

Biting my lip, I started to unbutton his pants, but he stopped me by placing his hand on mine, halting me.

"You're playing a dangerous game, angel, by doing that. Are you sure you know what you're doing?" he asked.

"Trust me," I said, exposing his rigid cock, which lay heavy against his stomach. "I want you to close your eyes and concentrate on my thoughts. I'm going to show *you* a good time now."

Closing his eyes, he settled back onto the bed while I positioned myself beside him and took his penis into my grip. His body jerked as I stroked him gently at first, but then picked up my pace, squeezing him tightly. The images I sent from my mind to his were completely different. In my thoughts I was riding him hard, milking him for all he had. It was but a taste of what our life could be like if we just let it get to that point. Brayden groaned and thrust his hips with my movement just like he was in the thoughts I sent to him. Faster and faster I tortured him, wanting more than anything to straddle his body and make love to him the way I was in my thoughts. Brayden finally let go, groaning as his release came hot and swift. We both collapsed against the bed, breathing hard and satiated.

I kissed him on the lips and cuddled up beside him as he wrapped his arms around me. "That was very interesting, angel. I must say, you better be careful thinking those thoughts. I would hate for you to arouse me at the wrong time."

"Yeah, I don't think it would be good to be in the middle of addressing the court and suddenly have a complete hard on. I'll try to keep my thoughts to myself, but it might be kind of difficult," I admitted ruefully.

Brayden chuckled and nuzzled his nose into my hair, breathing me in. It was getting late and I was extremely tired. Moving to the Winter Court, fighting with Brayden, and then ending up in his bed was a lot to absorb in one day. Yawning, I reached down and pulled the covers over his body and mine.

"Goodnight, Brayden," I whispered in his mind.

"Goodnight, angel."

Brayden told me three weeks is what I had until Durin showed up. I had three weeks to enjoy my life before everything ended, and I was going to make sure I made the best of the days I had. Even if that included going against what I thought was right and finished what I started with Brayden. It was too late to go back, and it was too late to stop from jumping … I already leapt.

Chapter Eighteen

Ariella

THE SECOND MY eyes opened to the dawn I knew something was wrong. I could feel and smell the evil approaching like a distant plague threatening to spread its curse on our land. Brayden sensed my unease and immediately awoke beside me, his gaze alert and ready.

"What's wrong, angel?"

Sliding out of the bed we just spent the night together on, I quickly ran to the window and peered out. I couldn't see them, but I knew they were coming. Alasdair was almost there and he wasn't alone.

"Shit! He's coming, Brayden," I shouted, alarmed. "The sorcerer is almost here."

Brayden cursed angrily and quickly jumped out of bed to put on his armor and grab his sword. I did the same thing and had everything fastened except the vambraces on my arms. I was busy lacing them up when Brayden stopped in front of me with a scowl on his face. "I don't know what you think you're doing, but you're not going out there with me," he argued.

I huffed, "Don't start with me, Brayden. You know I'm a good fighter."

He walked past me out into the hall and down the steps with me following close behind. "Yes, I know you're a good fighter, but *you* are what the sorcerer wants and with your Summer armor on he'll find you in an instant. I don't want to keep you from defending our people, but this is the one time I need you to stay behind."

Before he could open the front door, we froze in place as the horns blared from one of the palace towers. The dark army was almost upon us. We both rushed out of the house and ran up the path to the palace. Warriors were everywhere, gearing up and forming lines in the front yard of the palace. The Winter Court gates were closed and locked, but with the sorcerer's power I had no idea if his army could get past the gates. Our gates were strong and the Land of the Fae infused its own magic to the protection of our courts. Alasdair was either extremely bold or extremely cocky to attack a whole court without his full power, or maybe he was testing us. Either way, we all knew what he wanted … me.

Brayden watched as his second in command, Coran, assembled the warriors. He was torn between his obligation to me and to his court, and I could see the turmoil in his eyes and feel it in his soul. He didn't want to let either one of us down.

Knowing I couldn't let our true feelings show, I kept my face blank while I talked to him silently, *"Brayden, go. It would be easier to fight alongside you, but I understand your reasoning. I'll be fine, I promise."*

He sighed. *"I'm going to hold you to that promise, Ariella. It is binding. If you break it you will face the consequences."*

"Yes, I know, caveman. That's why I said it. Just be careful out there."

He wanted to kiss me before he walked away, but we both knew he couldn't. I wasn't going to let him fight this battle on his own. I had my own plans and it didn't involve me sitting idly by and watch everyone fight because of me. However, those plans got sidetracked when Brayden grabbed a hold of Lukas, who happened to be one of his best warriors. Lukas had long, dark hair pulled back and wrapped with his thistleburch chord. Kalen would do the same thing with his instead of wearing it around his arm or wrist, and he was also the one who educated me about the special thistleburch trees. They only grew in the Winter Court, but they were perceived to give off strengthening powers. Every time I saw Brayden, and even now, he had his wrapped around his wrist. I was pretty sure he never took it off.

"Lukas, I need you to take the princess somewhere safe and guard her for me. Do not let anyone get to her, you understand?" Brayden ordered.

Great! Now how was I going to get away and glamour myself? I couldn't let Lukas see what I could do. He bowed to Brayden and said, "As you wish, Your Highness. Do you want me to take her to the king and queen?"

"No," I blurted out, drawing their attention. "If you take me there and for some reason the sorcerer finds me he will have us all. That's the last place you would want to take me."

"Very well," Brayden gave in, sighing. He glanced at me one last time before turning around and marching away. *"Don't you dare do anything stupid, angel. I know what you are capable of."*

"But that is part of my charm," I teased, hoping to break the tension. His shoulders tensed and he fisted his hands by his side, clearly not liking the joke. *"I'll be okay, Brayden. Just stay focused on defending your court and not worrying about me."*

"Not possible," he replied. *"But for you I'll try."*

That was as good of an answer as I was going to get from him. Lukas grasped my elbow lightly and turned me to face him. "We need to go, Your Highness," he said.

I nodded and followed him deep into the castle. I had explored it pretty thoroughly when I came here for the Winter Solstice Ball over a year ago. I was amazed with the architecture and the paintings they had in the halls. However, at this moment, I couldn't enjoy any of it because I was rushed down the corridors until I got to the end of one of the hallways. Lukas opened the heavy wooden door and ushered me inside. It was an old library filled with dusty books and scrolls.

"How do you know we will be safe in here?" I asked him.

He shut the door and locked it behind him. "I don't, but I figured it would be one of the last places someone would come looking for you."

"Or one of the first," I remarked, gazing at him warily. "Although one of the good things is that I can sense him when he's near. I'll know if he gets close."

Releasing a shaky breath, I ran my fingers over the ancient leather bound books stacked neatly on the shelves. I bet there was hundreds of year's worth of written knowledge from the fae and the mortal realm. I loved to read, but I was sure Calista would be ecstatic to explore this room for a while. I'd have to make sure to bring her here when she came to visit.

"How do you like being in the Winter Court?" Lukas asked. "I know it has to be a huge change coming from Summer."

"Oh, it has been a major change, but I had always been fascinated with the Winter Court. I think deep down I knew I was meant to be here," I said, leaning against one of the old wooden desks. Flipping through some of the books, I noticed that whoever inhabited this library loved the mortal classics.

"You fought well yesterday, Your Highness. I know the warriors were impressed with your ability to counter Prince Brayden. How did you know our technique?"

I smiled at him as I remembered the fun I had training with Kamden. "I had a friend in the Spring Court who taught me some Winter techniques. He used to be Winter until he followed Kalen to the Spring Court," I answered.

"Who was it?" Lukas inquired, furrowing his brow.

"His name is Kamden. Do you know who I'm talking about?"

He grinned and started to chuckle. "Ah, yes, I know who Kamden is. He's my younger brother. I wanted to come fight with him when we attacked to help Sorcha and your brother rescue her guardian and friend, except I was needed here. How is he by the way?"

Thinking of Kamden and Zanna made me miss them greatly. "He's doing really well. He and Zanna are going to bond soon," I informed him.

Lukas sighed happily and shook his head. "Well, it's about time they decided on it. Our parents will be happy to hear it."

Before I could say anything else, the feeling of unease and despair engulfed my body. I clutched my stomach and swallowed hard. Lukas noticed my hesitation and flew over to my side. "Are you ill, Princess?" he asked, taking my arm to steady me.

Without hesitating any further, I grabbed his hand and pulled him quickly to the door. "We have to get out of here, Lukas. He's coming and he's close," I told him. "I knew I should've stayed with everyone else. The sorcerer knew I wouldn't be with the army so he did the one thing that would ensure he could get to me easily."

Lukas unsheathed his sword and slowly opened the door, glancing back and forth down both sides of the hallway. "What do you suggest we do?" he whispered.

"We need to get to Brayden and the others. Once everyone realizes what's going on they'll all come back inside the palace, but until then we're stuck in here fighting our own battle. Let's try to get outside with everyone else."

"Let's go," Lukas agreed. With his sword poised in his grasp and mine held firmly in my hand, we both set out into the hallway and briskly walked toward the next corridor. The second we heard his voice we froze.

"Ariella, where are you?" he called out. However, his voice wasn't his normal one. It was one I knew well.

"It's Prince Brayden," Lukas muttered, starting toward him. I grabbed his arm and pulled him back.

"No, it's not. Trust me, it's not him. I would know if it was Brayden. Can you not feel the evil slithering around you?"

The stench of dark magic permeated all around me and I knew we were almost out of time. We had nowhere else to go except in a different room. Taking Lukas' hand, I pulled him through the door closest to us into the bedroom beyond and shut it quietly. I needed to think.

"How do I kill him?" he asked.

Turning to him, I sighed and shook my head. "You can't. We don't have a way to kill him right now. He can turn into his shadow self and disappear before a blade could even run him through."

Lukas grabbed my shoulders and squeezed, his blue gaze frantic yet determined. "I want you to hide, Princess. I'll distract the sorcerer so you can get away."

"No," I hissed quietly. "I'm not going to let you do this. I have an idea, but whatever you do don't freak out on me, okay?"

Impatiently, he furrowed his brows and started to protest, but then his mouth opened wide when he saw me change form right in front of his eyes. I was no longer Ariella, but a dark-haired, fair-skinned Winter Fae woman.

"Princess?" Lukas asked. "How did you do that?"

"I don't have time to explain. Just play along with what I do."

I flung myself into his arms and pressed my body against his like we were lovers trying to steal a few moments together. The door burst open, and standing in the doorway was the sorcerer pretending to be Brayden with a smirk on his face, thinking he caught me. When he realized it wasn't me in the room, his expression grew fierce, angry.

"Where is the princess?" he demanded. "I know she's here."

Lukas kept his expression blank and shook his head. In his hand he held his sword firmly, ready to strike. *Please don't let him do anything stupid.* The sorcerer moved into the room and lifted his head as if he was trying to sniff me out.

"She's not in here," Lukas said through clenched teeth.

"Where are you hiding her? I can sense she's near," he snapped. He pulled out a dagger from his belt and Lukas and I both tensed. It was the iron blade that could poison us and kill us within minutes. *Oh, no!*

"Ariella, what's wrong?" Brayden screamed in my mind.

"Lukas and I are in trouble. It was all a ruse. The sorcerer has been inside the palace trying to find me while all of you are out there guarding the gates," I told him quickly.

"She's not here," Lukas growled. "I would think, being her guardian, that you would know how to communicate with her."

The sorcerer laughed and used the tip of his iron dagger to scratch his chin. It was confusing seeing him as Brayden, but anyone could tell that it wasn't my prince in there. He lowered the dagger and said, "You know very well who I am so stop messing with me. I need to find her and you're going to tell me where she is. Or better yet, maybe your lover would be willing to tell me."

His dark eyes gleamed with anticipation as he approached me, but I stepped back and brought up my sword, ready to fight. Lukas blocked Alasdair from getting closer. "You are not going to touch her," he hissed.

Alasdair laughed evilly and shook his head incredulously. "I don't think you can stop me, warrior. Or better yet, you can always try." Everything after those words moved in slow motion. Lukas attacked at the same time I screamed for him to stop.

All it would take is one cut from that iron blade and it would be over. Being almost immortal in our land didn't mean anything against the poison in the sorcerer's blade. The sorcerer appeared and reappeared in a different location as Lukas tried hard to fight him off. However, I knew it was a losing battle even before I saw the sorcerer sweep his iron dagger toward Lukas' chest.

I lunged into the fray, sword swinging to knock the dagger out of Alasdair's hand, and immediately tried to push Lukas out of the way. I was too late. Lukas growled painfully as the iron blade grazed across his chest, and he fell to the floor, holding his hand over his wound.

"Lukas," I cried angrily, knowing he was two minutes away from dying.

I was mad with rage, with a burning fire in my gut that wanted blood and revenge … Alasdair's blood. Screaming out my fury, I swung my sword, blind to anything but the consuming hate. Lukas only wanted to protect me and now he was going to die. How many more people were going to lose their lives because of this atrocity of a man who wanted to steal our land?

The only thing I had was my sword, and I was up against his iron blade. One false move and everything could be lost, except I was angry and hurt, saddened by the fact that Lukas was lying there dying and was also the brother of my good friend. I was going to have to tell Kamden how I watched his brother die senselessly and how there was nothing I could do about it. I didn't want to feel that pain, I only wanted to think of the anger, the burning rage in my soul that demanded justice.

"Ariella!" Brayden shouted.

I couldn't respond to him. Instead, I screamed the loudest battle cry I could muster and thrust my sword into the sorcerer's chest. Even though he had taken the form of Brayden, I didn't let that sway me. He laughed as I pinned him up against the wall, my sword protruding out of his rib cage. My weapon was just a simple blade with no guardian qualities whatsoever, so I knew I didn't do any damage. Durin hadn't made my guardian sword yet for me to fight with, so I was stuck with nothing to defend myself with other than just a plain one. I could've wounded him if I only had what I needed.

"You are a feisty one," Alasdair taunted. "I think I could have fun playing around with you."

Thundering steps echoed down the hall and I knew it was Brayden and his warriors. The sorcerer slowly changed into his inky black form and escaped the clutches of my sword. "I'll be back for the princess, and when I do I'll come for you as well. I need someone who can keep up with me."

I scoffed, completely disgusted, and snarled angrily, "You make me sick, sorcerer. I would rather die than be anywhere near your clutches."

"That can be arranged, too," he bellowed, disappearing into the shadows. When I knew he was gone for sure, I used my glamour to turn my body back to its usual self. Dropping down to the floor beside Lukas, I pulled him into my lap. I tried to transfer some of my power to him, wishing that I could heal like Meliantha could, but it didn't work.

I inspected the gash across his chest and winced as his skin turned black with the spreading poison. "Lukas, please forgive me," I cried. "This wouldn't have happened if it weren't for me. I thought I could help you."

He swallowed hard and his voice came out raspy when he said, "You did help, Princess. You fought like a true warrior when you saw me in trouble. I am honored to die beside you."

I took his hands in mine and closed my eyes, my lip trembling because I knew what was about to happen. With tears streaming down my cheeks, I gazed down at him and kissed his forehead. "As am I," I whispered.

Lukas' body began to shake and I held him tighter. I could feel his soul slipping away to the Hereafter, but he gazed up into my eyes and mustered up the strength to say his last words, "Will you tell Kamden farewell for me? I've missed him so much."

I nodded fiercely and cried, "Of course I will, Lukas." Before his body turned to ash, he smiled and released a final breath. "Safe journey to the Hereafter, warrior. As long as I live you will never be forgotten here."

"Ariella," Brayden called, storming through the rooms frantically. When he reached the room I was in, he flung open the door and rushed to my side, followed by his warriors. He crouched down where Lukas' ashes lay helplessly on the floor and bowed his head. "I should've known," he expressed helplessly. "He knew I wouldn't want you out there fighting and he anticipated that." When his sorrowful gaze found mine, I wanted to cling to him and let the tears fall with no shame. Being strong and being a leader meant keeping your pain hidden, and for Brayden I could see it taking its toll.

Another life was lost, another soul taken because of the sorcerer's greed. Calling upon my wind, I closed my eyes and lifted my hands over Lukas' ashes. The window burst open and in gusted the cold, snowy breeze of Winter. It swirled around the ashes and gathered them up, carrying them out to the land.

"Take him somewhere special," I breathed across the wind.

Still gazing out the window, keeping my tear-stained face away from the warriors, I silently pleaded with Brayden, *We need to send word to everyone and let them know what's happened, especially Kamden. I didn't know Lukas was his brother until he told me.*

"I'll take care of it," Brayden uttered soothingly. *"Let's get you out of here."* He took my hand and helped me to my feet. The warriors bowed their heads solemnly and backed out of the room, leaving Brayden and I alone. Wrapping his arms around me tight, he held me up against his chest and said, "From now on, you are not leaving my sight. If we have to fight, we fight together. We are in this as one."

With my heart tired and bruised, I gazed up at him with a newfound strength. Maybe he wouldn't be too difficult to deal with after all. "And that's how it should be," I told him. "I will always fight for my people, for my court … and for you."

Always …

Chapter Nineteen

Ariella

THROUGHOUT THE EVENING, Brayden kept a contingent of warriors posted at the gates to keep lookout. There were times every now and again when we would see a scout scurrying along the forest line, keeping watch on our every movement. I couldn't feel the evil of the dark sorcerer, which was good, but what bothered me was that he had his people monitoring us. It almost seemed like we were being trapped somehow. How was Durin going to deliver the dagger without being attacked?

I watched as Brayden gave Coran his final commands before we could retire for the night. I had sat on the front steps of the palace for the past few hours, pondering how I was going to tell Kamden of his brother's death. I wondered if he was going to blame me.

Brayden approached me and reached out his hand. "He's not going to blame you, angel. Come on let's go home. You need your rest."

Taking his hand, I let him pull me up to lead me through the palace and out the back. The snow crunched beneath our feet as we somberly made our way to his dwelling, hand in hand. "How are Durin and everyone going to get here safely with Alasdair's scouts watching our every move? I know we can fight them if we have to, but I don't want to lose anyone else or put anyone in unnecessary danger," I said.

Nodding, he blew out a heavy sigh. "Right now I have an idea, and for the time being it's going to have to work. I sent our sprites with letters to go to each court, and even to Durin, to inform them of what happened here today. I also sent in a request to Calista asking if we could compensate Nixie somehow to get her to transport everyone here when the time comes, and to also get Elvena to figure out what it would take to put up a protection spell against the dark sorcerer. It's not safe for you anywhere if he can get to you."

Nixie was Calista's friend who helped rescue her from the dark sorcerer when she was in the Black Forest. She can port travel to anywhere in the Land of the Fae in a matter of seconds. Years ago, after the attack on Calista, Nixie was our only way of travelling safely and it appeared it was going to be that way again.

"When do you think we will hear back from everyone?" I asked.

"Most likely first thing in the morning, angel. Coran is going to keep watch for the rest of the night so I can be with you. There are some things I wanted to show you."

He let go of my hand and put his arm around my shoulders as we climbed up the stairs to his dwelling. "What did you need to show me?" I asked curiously, leaning my head on his shoulder.

"You'll see," he whispered. "You need something to get your mind off of things."

When we got inside, I took a shower and changed into one of my silky nightgowns. I was exhausted, and what I really wanted was to lay my head on Brayden's soft pillows and go to sleep. When I got back in the bedroom, Brayden was nowhere to be found. *"I'm down the hall, angel. It'll be your second door on the right."*

Opening the bedroom door, I found the hallway dark except for the sliver of light coming from the room two doors down. I slowly crept across the soft rugs on the hardwood floor and when I got to the crack in the door I peeked inside. What I saw had me completely taken by surprise. Gently pushing the door open, I ambled inside and gazed at the pictures on the walls in awe. Some were of places in the mortal realm, but most were of different landscapes in the Winter Court. I scanned each picture with appreciation, one after the other, until I came upon a couple of paintings on the opposite side of the wall. Gasping, I placed a hand over my mouth and gazed at them with tear-filled eyes.

"Brayden," I whispered. "Did you paint all of these?"

Brayden was behind the easel with a smirk on his face as his hands deftly moved up and down with the paintbrush. "I knew you would like them. My mother taught me how to draw when I was young, and over time I got really good at it. No one else knows I can do this other than her. I wanted to share something of me with you so you would know there is more to me than you realize."

I reached out to touch the face on the canvas before me … my face. It was like I was staring in a mirror it was that perfect. I murmured softly, "You know, your mother told me we had things in common and I thought she was crazy. I never once realized she could be right."

Brayden came up behind me and wrapped his arms around my waist, kissing me gently on the neck. "My mother is a smart woman most of the time, but do you want to know when I really started to see you differently?"

Turning around in his arms, I gazed up into his warm, brown eyes and nodded. "Tell me," I said.

He lowered his lips to mine, just a gentle brushing of his lips before he pulled back and explained, "It was when you were here with your family for the Winter Solstice Ball. I remember watching you get out of the carriage and thinking that it couldn't be you. You had changed so much in five years."

I laughed. "Five years is a long time for a female to grow up, Brayden. After everything that happened with Calista I had no choice but to see and do things differently."

"I know, angel, and it's definitely changed you for the better. However, I will never forget the day when I saw you playing with Merrick out in the snow. You were so carefree and everything I'd always wished I could be. The way you gazed at him with such love and adoration was an expression I'd never seen on anyone's face before, especially when they looked at me."

I cupped his face in my hands and smiled. "It's because I love him, Brayden. Do you really think no one has felt that way about you? I'm sure there are plenty of women here who have loved you."

"No, not like that," he admitted. He took my hands away from his face and walked me back to our bedroom where I took a seat on the bed. Leaving the room, he came back almost immediately with something hidden in the palm of his hand. "I do not know if this is the right time, but I need you to know where I stand in all of this. You could have been taken from me on several occasions, and I cannot begin to describe to you the way it made me feel to know that I could have lost you. I have never felt that way about anyone until you."

"What are you trying to say, Brayden?" I asked nervously.

My heart raced erratically to the point I could feel it pulsing throughout my body. I was sure Brayden could hear it and feel it through our bond. Through our connection I could feel how deep his emotions ran, and secretly I had hoped one day he would be able to tell me. No one had ever looked at me or loved me in the way I wanted, in the way I needed. We were the same in that aspect as well. My sisters had experienced love by other men, but I never had, even though I had taken lovers before.

Taking a deep breath, Brayden took my hand and opened his closed fist. In his palm lay a shiny silver and onyx band with a symbol engraved on it. I couldn't tell what the symbol was until he slid the band slowly down on my finger. However, it wasn't just a symbol, it was the crest of the Winter Court … our Court of Ice.

"How?" I whispered. *Did he really remember the symbol in our vision?*

"Yes, I did," he replied, giving me the answer to my silent question. "I can still see our vision clearly, right down to the way we made love by the fire. I remembered our crest on the wall in the room we were in, and it's been engraved in my mind ever since. I had Lukas make the ring for you."

"Lukas made this?" I cried, gazing down at the ring. "It's beautiful. I just wish I could tell him so."

Brayden lifted my chin with his finger and grazed my lips with his thumb. "He was a very talented man and a good friend of mine. I will miss him. I know it's not customary to exchange rings, but I wanted you to know that I am serious about us and about our court. We have so much to learn from each other, and by giving you this I am ready. I know you are not yet, and I am fine waiting for as long as you need me to, but I have faith in us. I've never believed in anything as much as I believe in you."

Staring at the man in front of me, I couldn't believe he was the same Brayden. Our time has been short together, but all along we both knew that we were the ones for each other. Deep down I knew I was ready to bond with him, except with everything going on I knew it wasn't the right time.

Kissing me gently on the lips, he whispered silently in my mind, *"Do you think you will ever love me the way I love you?"*

I stifled a gasp and let him deepen the kiss. He said he loved me. Tears sprang into my eyes as I melted in his arms, lying back against the bed. He covered my body with his while melding his tongue with mine, tasting me and claiming me, never taking his gaze away.

"I need to hear you say it, Brayden," I murmured tenderly.

He wiped away the tears in my eyes and whispered across my lips, "I love you, angel. No matter what happens and what challenges we face, I will always be there with you. In your mind, body, and soul, you will never be alone."

We stared at each other, him holding onto me as we lay together on the bed, and I knew without a doubt that I had fallen for him. The times he pissed me off and the times I thought he didn't care no longer mattered because I knew he did care ... all along he felt the same way about me that I had of him.

The ring on my finger was a symbol of everything I had to live for, but yet everything I was going to lose. I needed to live for the moment and I planned on doing that. With all the love and determination in my heart, I poured it all into Brayden as I gazed at him and said the words I knew he had always wanted to hear, "I know it's not easy for you to say these things to me, and I can't begin to tell you how much it means to hear them. I love you, Brayden. There may come a time in our lives when you doubt that, but I want you to understand that I will always love you. I will always do what I can to protect you and our court. I will never stop fighting for us."

After hours of kissing and consoling each other, I couldn't stop my exhausted body from giving out. Brayden held me tight as my eyes drifted close, and I was steadily carried away to the dream realm. I didn't, however, expect to find myself in the middle of a nightmare.

Chapter Twenty

Ariella

EVERYWHERE I TURNED it was dark and cold, devoid of any life except the heart that beat in my own chest. The stench of death was all I could smell, and judging by the black, oily looking trees I knew where I was ... the Black Forest. Chills crept up my spine because I knew I wasn't alone.

Alasdair's laugh echoed all around me, except I couldn't see him. He drifted around me in his shadow self, slithering across my skin, touching me. He couldn't physically harm me for real, but even in the dream realm a person could still feel pain or pleasure. I wasn't looking forward to this visit.

"You can't hide from me here, sweet princess," he taunted. *"I must say, I am very disappointed in you."*

"I don't care what you think of me," I snarled. *"You're just upset that you couldn't find me."*

Losing his humor, he revealed himself before me, taking his true form. He was tall with long, brown hair and glowing gray eyes. He appeared to be a little older than me, but I knew he was over a century old. He could almost pass for a fae warrior with the way he was dressed in a set of armor and leathers, but a warrior he was not.

Crossing my arms over my chest, I stood my ground and kept my gaze on his as he approached. "You think wrong, Your Highness. I am not upset, I'm disappointed. There's a big difference there. When I came for your sisters they challenged me and fought me with all they had, but you ..."He shook his head and clucked his tongue. "You just hid away letting others take the fall. All I needed was one simple thing from you and that would be it. I am not trying to steal you away, because frankly you are not worth it. I like strong women in my bed and from what I have seen of you, you would break too easily."

Gritting my teeth, it took all I had not to tell him that I was the one who fought him earlier and ran him through. If he would've been a normal man he would be dead. "I'm not going to give you what you want," I snapped.

He sidled up closer to me and circled me like a shark teasing its prey. I stood my ground, and wondered how long this nightmare was going to last. What kinds of things could he do to me while we were here? I knew one thing, I didn't want to find out and I sure as hell never wanted to sleep again if he was going to come to me every night.

Stopping behind me, he snaked his arm around my waist and slapped his hand across my neck, squeezing it tight. I couldn't take in a breath, so I clawed at his hand trying desperately to breathe. I bucked against his body hoping it would get him off of me, but all it did was entice him.

He laughed. "Keep fighting, Princess. It only turns me on more." When his grip loosened, I took in a ragged breath. Leaning down close to my ear, he whispered, "And I think you will give me what I want because if you don't I will bring my army over from the mortal realm and destroy everything and everyone you love."

I scoffed warily. "Isn't that your plan anyway? Even if I give you my power you're still going to bring them over. Why would I willingly give you what you want so you could destroy us? You must think I'm stupid."

He squeezed my neck again and I gasped for air. I knew I could fight him off, but it was best he thought I was really the weak princess he believed me to be. However, I didn't want to have to endure his toying with me and violating me. I tried to think of Brayden and if there was a way he could get me out of the dream. I screamed his name over and over, but I didn't know if he heard because there was no response in my mind.

"I am giving you until the next new moon, Princess. If you don't give me what I want before then, when I come for you I will have my army at your front gates to tear your world apart. You might as well face the realization that it's over. You have no way of defeating me, even if you and your prince complete the bond to form your court."

I struggled against his grasp, but I had had enough. Snapping my head back in a quick thrust, I bashed his nose and turned around to land a swift kick to his ribs. He doubled over but regained himself quickly, growling in anger. The dream realm shifted and began to shimmer. I could feel Brayden's influence slowly growing stronger; he was trying to get me out.

"It is not over," I spat. "There is still hope, and as long as that hope still lives I will not submit to you. I may appear weak, but there is more than meets the eyes with me." The pull on my soul began to get stronger and I could hear Brayden's frantic voice in my mind telling me to come back to him.

Before I disappeared, I stood my ground and glared at the sorcerer with all the anger and rage I had in my soul from the devastation he'd bestowed upon my people and our courts. Confident and without a doubt, I tilted my lip up in a snarling smirk and gave my final promise to him. "I can promise you this, Alasdair. On the day everything ends, I will be there to watch you fall. The hand that sends you to hell will be mine, and I will smile as I watch you and your evil be torn away from our land. I will be your demise."

It was strange … one minute I was standing in the Black Forest and the next I woke up in the bed with Brayden straddling my waist and his hands on both sides of my head. When he saw my eyes open, he breathed a sigh of relief and helped me sit up. His head was covered in sweat and the veins in his face and arms bulged as if he'd worked out for about ten hours.

"Are you okay?" he asked, wiping the sweat drenched hair off my forehead.

I nodded and rubbed my neck from where the sorcerer had cut off my air. Nothing was sore and that proved to me that he couldn't physically harm me in the reality sense, but in the dream it actually felt real. The room was still cloaked in darkness as the night sky filtered into our room. My eyes felt heavy, except I knew sleep wouldn't come easily for me now. Especially, knowing the sorcerer could come into my dreams and wreak havoc.

"I'm fine, Brayden. How did you know what was going on?" I questioned curiously. "I tried to scream your name in my mind but I didn't know if you'd hear me."

Gritting his teeth, he said, "I heard you, angel. When you screamed my name, I woke up not knowing what was going on. You were thrashing against the bed, and when I tried to calm you down you wouldn't wake up. I pushed into your mind as much as I could and that was when I could feel him there."

He pulled me into his arms and held me tight. I could hear his heart thumping erratically in his chest and through our bond I could feel his anxiety and anger about not being able to protect me. "You did protect me," I murmured gently. "You pulled me out of the dream."

"But I wasn't fast enough. I knew he hurt you in the dream because I could feel your pain. What did he do to you?" he demanded.

Sighing, I closed my eyes and reluctantly showed him what happened. "He's threatening to unleash his mortal army at our gates if I don't let him take my power. If they bring over mortal weapons from their realm we won't stand a chance. It'll poison our land and our people will die," I cried.

"Dammit," he hissed, running his hands angrily through his hair. He stormed out of bed and stalked over to the window, placing his hands on the cool, clear glass. The muscles in his back tensed and he lowered his head. "We're running out of time," he murmured regretfully.

I nodded even though he couldn't see me. "He said he would give me until the next new moon to give him my power. If not, then the war will begin."

"The next new moon," Brayden repeated incredulously. He turned around to face me with wide, concern-filled eyes. "That's only two weeks away."

Gazing down at the ring Brayden gave me to show his love, I knew in that moment what I had to do. It was a decision my heart had already made, but my stubbornness wanted me to take more time. However, time wasn't on our side. Slowly sliding out of bed, I ambled over to Brayden and took his face in my hands, running my fingers over his tensed muscles.

I opened my mind to him fully and let him feel what my heart desired and wanted. Groaning, he clutched me tight with his arms wrapped around my waist and lowered his forehead to mine. "Is that truly what you want?" he asked.

"Yes," I whispered across his lips. "I'll be ready when the time comes."

He leaned down and closed the distance between our lips, lingering for a few seconds while he responded silently to my reply, *So will I, angel. I have never been more ready for anything in my entire life. We will get through this.*

I had no doubt.

Chapter Twenty One

Ariella

MORNING CAME, AND Brayden and I had yet to fall back asleep after what had happened in my dreams. As soon as we approached the palace doors, Coran came ambling out holding a handful of letters. "These came for you, Your Highness," he said quickly, rushing toward us.

Brayden grabbed the papers and handed me half of them. The letters I held in my hands were from the Fall Court and Durin. I read over them quickly, and was happy to see that Durin was going to try to get the dagger finished within the week and bring it to us. I breathed a sigh of relief and smiled. Calista's letter was good news as well. Nixie had consented to help everyone travel here undetected, and Elvena believed she could find a spell to keep the dark sorcerer away from me for the time being. They were going to be arriving later in the day.

I held onto the letters while Brayden finished reading his. Sighing, he handed them to Coran and took my hand, leading me inside the palace. "What did yours say?" I asked inquisitively.

"Kalen said he's sending Kamden here today so we can tell him what happened. His family is going to want to spend some time with him while he's here, so he will probably stay for a while. Everyone else, including your parents, requested we send for them when it's time for Durin to arrive with the dagger. What news did Durin send?" Brayden inquired, gazing down at the letters in my hand.

I handed them to him so he could see for himself. When he read over the letters, he lifted his head and grinned. "This is just what we needed. If Elvena can buy us time with a protection spell for at least another week, we can get everyone here and formulate a strategy for attack." We stopped outside of the throne room doors and stared at each other. Brayden bit his lip and tucked a strand of my blonde hair behind my ear before asking softly, "Did you want to tell everyone what we decided to do?"

I smiled and shook my head. "I think it'll be fun to surprise them, don't you? They wouldn't expect anything less from me."

He narrowed his gaze, and smirked. "I'm starting to believe everything I had heard about you is true," he teased.

"Oh yeah, and what is that?" I asked incredulously.

He kissed me on the lips and chuckled. "That I am going to have my hands full when it comes to you."

I winked. "That may be true, but I think it goes both ways in this case. However, right now we have a hard day to get through, and I'm going to need your strength to do it."

"You will always have my strength, angel. We will get through the day together," Brayden murmured silently, before opening the throne room doors.

Queen Mab and King Madoc were waiting for us inside, so we informed them about everything that transpired during the night with the dream. Knowing there was nothing more that could be done at the moment, Brayden and I excused ourselves and decided to train together while we waited for Kamden to show up. My head wasn't into the fighting, but I tried to maneuver the best I could.

"You're fighting is terrible, Princess. Did you not learn anything that I taught you?" a voice called out.

Kamden's laugh echoed through the air as he rushed toward us and scooped me up in his arms, swinging me around. "Are you just being lazy, or do Prince Brayden and I need to show you how it's done?" he joked.

He set me down and all I could see were Lukas' eyes staring back at me. Kamden and Lukas had the same shaped eyes, cheek bones, and smile. *I can't believe I didn't notice the similarities earlier.*

Tears welled up behind my eyes and I couldn't stop my lips from turning down into a frown. Kamden narrowed his eyes and stepped back, unsure of what to do. "What's going on, Ariella? Why do you look like that?"

I gazed up at Brayden quickly before he nodded his head and pushed me gently toward Kamden. Taking Kamden's hands in mine, I squeezed them gently and looked up into his face. Wearily, I began, "Kam, there's something I need to tell you."

He kept his gaze strictly on me, never swaying, as I took a deep breath and let the tears fall from my eyes. "I hate we had to bring you here to tell you this, but I thought you deserved to hear it from me," I cried.

Kamden clenched his teeth and said, "Just tell me what happened, Ariella."

Lowering my head, I wrapped my arms around his waist, holding him tight, and laid my head on his chest. "It's about your brother ... Lukas," I told him.

"What about him?" he asked warily. His heart thundered against my ear and I could already feel the sadness creeping in around him. He knew what I was about to tell him.

"He's dead, Kam," I cried, my tears soaking through his shirt. "When the sorcerer came looking for me, Lukas was the one who guarded me. I tried to save him, but I failed. You have my promise that I will avenge him and all the others the sorcerer has taken away from us."

He stiffened in my arms and quickly pulled away from me. I tried to grab his arm to make him stay, but he jerked out of my grasp and left me standing there staring at his retreating form as he walked away. "Kamden," I shouted. "Kamden, wait!" I was about to run after him when Brayden caught my elbow in his grasp.

"Let him go, angel. He needs his space, but I know he'll come back," he assured me.

"He's going to blame me, isn't he?"

Brayden wrapped his arms around my shoulders and placed his chin on the top of my head. "He's not going to blame you, Ariella. He will, however, need you to be a friend and help him through it. He still has his parents that live in the village, but he and Lukas were really close. I can't imagine how it would feel to lose one of my brothers."

I watched Kamden disappear, and the farther he went the more it killed me to know that he was grieving alone. "I understand," I uttered sadly. "I'll ask Nixie if she'll fetch Zanna when she brings over Calista, Ryder, and Elvena this evening."

"I think that would be wise, angel. In the meantime, you need to focus. Coran told me we've had several of our fae women request to be trained, and I think it would be good for you to help them. They will need your guidance," he suggested warmly.

"Okay," I agreed. My heart wasn't into the training, but it was my duty to help the court. We hastily travelled to the training field, and when we got there I was amazed at all the women that were there ready to learn. Wide-eyed, my heart swelled with pride as I gazed at them in wonder. These women were willing to put their lives on the line for their people and their court. I wondered if soon there would be women in all the courts battling the front lines with their men. It was a new beginning for the Land of the Fae.

"This is amazing," I breathed in awe.

"Yes, it is angel. I know you will do right by them."

I searched over the women, but when I spied Taryn stretching and bending over in her tight black spandex outfit I groaned in annoyance. "Oh, I'll do right by them, but if any of your ex-lovers are on that training field, I can't promise they will make it through the first ten minutes."

Let the training begin ...

Training the women wasn't as easy as I thought it would be, but they were strong and they learned quickly. I was showing one of the women the proper way to hold a sword when a snowball smacked me against the back.

"Who the hell …" I growled, turning around to see who the instigator was. Brayden tried to hold in a laugh as my nephew, Merrick, balled up another snowball and pitched it at my head.

Laughing, I dodged the ball of snow as it flew past my head. I began to race toward the curly, blond haired little boy with the chubby cheeks. Merrick giggled and shrieked, "Ari! Ari!"

I scooped him up into my arms and twirled him around, loving the way his angelic laugh brought a smile to my face after the terrible day I'd had. "How's my little man doing?" I asked sweetly.

"Nixie brought me through the rainbow. It was fun," he exclaimed happily, bouncing in my arms. I had port travelled with Nixie a couple of times in the past, and when she took you from place to place the colors around you looked exactly like a shimmering rainbow. It was an amazing sight and feeling to be in one place one minute and then in a completely different one the next.

Merrick leaned closer to my ear and whispered, "Uncle Brayden made me throw the snowball at you."

"He did, did he?" I asked, pursing my lips at Brayden. "I think I might need to give a little payback to *Uncle* Brayden. Maybe later we can throw snowballs at him. He's never had a snowball fight before, you know."

L. P. DOVER

Merrick snickered and wrapped his arms around my neck. "Who told you to call him Uncle Brayden?" I asked quietly in his ear.

His whisper came out louder than I had hoped. "Mommy and Daddy told me to," he said.

When I glanced up at Brayden, he shrugged and commented silently, *"I will officially be his uncle soon, but I bet it was Ryder who put him up to it. It sounds like something my brother would do."*

By the time I set Merrick down, Calista made her way down the path to us, covered in a thick, long coat that billowed out in the wind. Her long, golden blonde hair matched little Merrick's and her Fall colored skin stood out amongst the brightness of the snow. I remembered having to bundle up when I was still a Summer Fae. It was amazing how things could change so drastically.

Calista's eyes went wide when she noticed all of the females training behind me. "You've been busy," she muttered in awe. "I think it's amazing what you're doing. Just imagine what it would be like if we had female warriors in all the courts."

"It'll soon be that way," I said. "Give it time and it will happen."

Calista hooked her arm through mine and lowered her voice when she asked, "Are you and Brayden finally getting along? He's completely different from the last time I saw you two together."

Brayden smirked and turned his head, trying to hide that he was listening. Rolling my eyes, I pulled on Calista's arm and held Merrick's hand as we ambled up toward the palace. "Yes, we are getting along. Now that we can hear each other's thoughts, things have gotten easier. I understand him, or at least I'm trying to."

"Do you think you would be where you are now if you didn't have the guardian bond?" Calista wondered.

That was a good question.

"Honestly," I started, "I don't think we would be where we are now without it. Eventually we would, but being able to see into his soul and feel his feelings has helped us to where we are now. He's changed, and I see it every day in how he opens up. All he needed was a push and he got it."

Calista smiled over at me. "I'm glad things are getting better. I was really worried about you and him. I know Sorcha was ready to kick his ass there for a moment."

We both laughed, and when I gazed back at Brayden following us, he rolled his eyes and shook his head. *"I was close to kicking your ass there for a moment,"* I said. *"You were a complete jerk to me."*

"Are you going to remind me of this every day for the rest of my life?"

For the rest of his life. In better terms it should be for the rest of my life, which wasn't going to be long. I didn't want to think about that, not when there was still happiness to be had. Brayden could feel my angst and uncertainty, so when he called out my name I let go of Calista and Merrick's hand and turned around.

"I'll see you in the throne room," I said over my shoulder to my sister. Smiling hesitantly, she glanced from me to Brayden, and took Merrick's hand. She led him away from us and toward the throne room where I knew everyone was waiting.

"Did I say something wrong?" Brayden asked.

"No," I lied, hating myself for keeping secrets from him. "I guess I just have so many things on my mind." Taking his hand, I gazed up into his soft, brown eyes. "Let's go see what kind of spell Elvena has cooked up for us. I'm pretty sure she found a way to protect the court."

"I sure hope so," Brayden remarked skeptically. "If not then we're going to have some major problems."

That was for certain.

Chapter Twenty Two

Ariella

RYDER WAS IN the throne room talking to Queen Mab and King Madoc when Brayden and I entered. Everything went silent as we approached the group, side by side. Elvena smiled and took my hands, pulling me down so she could kiss my forehead. "You look lovely, child. We were just discussing what we need to do to keep you safe from the sorcerer," she explained.

"What have you come up with?" I asked, looking from her to everyone in the room.

REGIN OF ICE (FOREVER FAE SERIES)

When Queen Mab and King Madoc joined the group on the floor, Elvena began, "Basically, what we need to do is perform a protection spell. The only problem is that we can't protect the whole expanse of the Winter Court. We can, however, protect the palace and extend it to your dwelling if need be." When Brayden and I both nodded, she continued, "When we do this, you will only be protected inside the walls. I know it'll feel like you're trapped, but this is the best I can do."

"Let's do it," Brayden insisted, gazing down at me. "We have to keep him away from you."

I hated feeling like a trapped animal, but I knew it was for the best. Sighing, I closed my eyes and blew out a frustrated breath. "All right, what do we have to do?" I muttered, giving in.

Elvena smiled sadly and said, "What we need is royal blood and a lot of it. We need enough to be able to scatter it around the palace and form a circle. It only needs to be a drop here and there around the walls. So now you can understand how we don't have the means to protect the entire grounds."

I nodded in understanding and so did everyone else. Queen Mab handed Elvena a bowl and immediately sliced her palm, letting her blood flow freely. "This is for you, my dear," Queen Mab murmured, gazing at me. King Madoc clapped Brayden on the shoulder before slicing his hand and mingling his blood with his queen's. Calista and Ryder joined in and gave their blood, along with Elvena who contributed some as well.

Brayden took out his guardian dagger and I casually held out my hand for him to slice open my skin. He lifted a brow, but I waved my hand at him. "Just do it," I scolded him playfully.

Slicing open my skin, Brayden immediately cut open his as well and we stood there staring at each other as our life essence joined in with the others. *"I wonder why everything involved with spells requires blood,"* I silently said to Brayden.

He smirked. *"Our blood is the strongest part of our bodies. It holds the key to everything."*

That actually made sense.

After our blood was taken, Elvena made her way outside and began to chant in the Old Fae language. In my spare time in the Summer Court, I had secretly been trying to learn the language of our elders. We never used it much, but in this case, with the spell it would've come in handy. We all watched and waited as Elvena disappeared around the side of the palace, pouring a thin trail of our blood in her wake.

When she was done, she came back inside with the empty bowl and breathed a sigh of relief. "It is done. The spell has been cast."

For the time being I was safe … just as long as I stayed within the boundaries.

❄❄❄

Nixie had taken Calista and everyone back to the Fall Court, and when she returned she had Zanna in tow.

L. P. DOVER

"Thank you, Nixie," I said softly. "I appreciate you doing this for me."

Nixie was a green imp with green hair and golden wings. She was a little smaller than a child, so she fluttered up to eye level with me and bowed her head, first to me and then to Brayden. "You're welcome, Your Highnesses. I will bring everyone back when the time comes."

Smiling, I took her small hand in mine. "If there's anything I can do to repay you I will gladly offer it," I promised.

"Just keep our land safe from the sorcerer. I was imprisoned by him for far too long and I can only imagine what his poison would do to our land."

Nodding somberly, I bowed my head to her and said, "I will keep our land safe. You have my word."

A sad smile passed across Nixie's face before she closed her eyes and disappeared almost immediately. Impatient, Zanna narrowed her eyes and crossed her arms over her chest while tapping her foot against the floor. "What's going on?" she asked quickly. "Where is Kamden? All I was told was that I had to come here as soon as possible."

Brayden squeezed my hand and muttered silently, *I'll give you some time with your friend, angel. There are some things I need to take care of.* He walked past me and placed a gentle hand on Zanna's shoulder before he left. Zanna's mouth dropped wide open and she became even more confused.

"Are you sure that's Prince Brayden, Ariella?" Zanna asked as she turned to watch him leave the room. "Because I swear he's not acting right."

"I promise it's him," I replied with a hesitant smile. "Things have changed since I've been here."

"Yeah, I can see that, but you never answered the question about Kamden. Where is he, Ariella? I have a bad feeling about this," she claimed.

Taking her hand, I led her to the window seat in my room and sat her down. Elvena'd had enough blood to extend the protection spell from the palace to Brayden's dwelling, so I had Nixie bring her here away from everyone else in the palace. Sitting beside her, I gazed out the window and wished I could answer her question. I had no clue where Kamden went or what he was doing. He left and hadn't come back.

"Lukas is dead," I whispered, my breath fogging up the glass. "We brought Kamden here to tell him about his brother."

Zanna gasped and covered her mouth with her hand. "Oh no," she cried. "He has to be devastated."

A tear escaped the corner of my eye, but I wiped it away quickly. "He is, which is why I needed you here. I don't know where he is, Zanna. After I told him, he left and I haven't seen him since. I figured you would be able to track him down."

Zanna sighed and wiped the moisture from her eyes. "I think I might know where he is. I'll find him and bring him back."

She squeezed my hand reassuringly and hastily got up, running out of the room to the front door. She wasn't the only one who had a bad feeling.

Chapter Twenty Three

Ariella

A WEEK HAD passed and there were no other attack attempts on the court or any bad dreams with Alasdair. The protection spell was working, but I only had a week to go before the new moon and before the threat of the upcoming battle. A battle we could definitely lose if we weren't strong enough. Durin had sent word saying that he would be arriving soon with the dagger, so we expected him to show up the following afternoon. Everyone else would be arriving as well.

"Are you coming to bed?" Brayden whispered gruffly in my ear, drawing me away from my thoughts. Brayden had hung one of his paintings in our room, and for the past hour I couldn't tear my eyes away from it. It was a picture of how our court was going to look when we completed the bond. At first, when everything came to light about my destiny, I didn't even want to complete the bond with him. Now I couldn't imagine not completing it.

Brayden wrapped his arms around my waist and slid his hands under my silky nightshirt to trace circles on my bare stomach. His touch sent tingles down my spine and it made me shiver. It was hard to imagine a Winter Fae getting chill bumps, but I did. His warm breath grazed across my neck as he chuckled and nipped my earlobe.

"I don't see how I can refuse with you tormenting me like this," I teased.

"It's not tormenting if I plan on doing something about it, angel."

Brayden kissed along down my neck to my collarbone while smoothing his hands up my bare skin to my breasts, cupping them gently. Tilting my head back, I rested against his chest as he kneaded and massaged them, rolling my nipples with the coldness of his fingers. For the past week we had explored each other's wants and needs, but tonight that was all over. I knew what he wanted and I knew what I needed.

"I'm ready, Brayden," I whispered, turning around so I could face him.

He brought his hands up and brushed a strand of hair off my forehead before cupping my cheeks in his hands. "There's no turning back, Ariella. Are you absolutely certain you're ready?" he inquired gently.

Smiling, I clutched the hem of my shirt and slowly lifted it over my head, exposing my breasts that ached for more of his touch. His gaze twinkled in the candlelight and his mouth tilted up in a tiny grin. I kissed his lips while pressing my bare chest against his and wrapping my arms around his neck.

"I want you to make love to me, Brayden. I'm ready to bond myself to you for the rest of my life, however long that may be," I vowed.

Brayden walked us back toward the bed and sat down on the edge with me standing between his legs. He looked up at me, his eyes glistening with unbound love and passion. "I love you, angel," he murmured wholeheartedly.

"And I love you," I cried, a lone tear sliding down my cheek.

Never taking his gaze off of mine, Brayden slid his fingers under the waist of my silky bottoms and slowly slid them down my legs, taking my underwear with them. He growled low in his chest and picked me up to set me on the bed. He was shirtless with only a pair of loose linen pants riding low on his hips, and when he untied them and let them fall to the floor, my insides trembled with the need to feel him inside me.

I moved back across the bed and propped myself up on my elbows as he stalked toward me. Starting with my ankles, he kissed his way up my calves to my knees, and then to the tender spot between my thighs. From there he trailed his tongue up my stomach to my breasts where he licked and sucked them generously. I arched off the bed and moaned as my body verged on the edge of climax. Before I could get there, Brayden chuckled and moved up to my neck, where he bit the soft, fleshy part of my shoulder.

"The next time you come it'll be with me inside you, angel," he whispered gruffly in my ear.

I groaned in protest, but he closed his lips over mine to cut off my cries. His tongue entangled with mine; he tasted so damn good I couldn't get enough of him. Pressing his body to mine, he separated my legs with his knee and rubbed the tip of his cock over my tender flesh. We needed to say the sacred words that would bind us together for eternity, but when Brayden opened his mouth to do just that, there was a loud knock on the front door.

It was late in the evening, too late for someone to be making a normal visit, which made us both wonder who it could be. Brayden lowered his forehead to mine and huffed angrily, "Someone better be attacking our palace, because if not then whoever is out there is dead."

Sighing, I rolled my eyes and shook my head. "It could be important, Brayden. There's no telling what could be going on." *All I know is that it* better *be important,* I thought to myself.

Reluctantly, he slid off of me and grabbed his pants off the floor, sliding them on. He reached over and took my hand, helping me up, and handed me my clothes as well. "I'll go see who it is," he grumbled. "And I promise not to kill whoever it is unless it's the sorcerer." He kissed me quickly and mumbled angrily the whole time he descended the stairs.

Quickly, I threw on my clothes and snatched my robe from the bathroom before I also headed down the stairs to see who it could be. I didn't hear any yelling or shouting, so I had no clue what was going on. I rounded the corner and saw Brayden standing there with his arms crossed, staring at Kamden who looked like he wanted to turn around and walk out the door.

"Kamden," I shrieked, rushing toward him. "Where have you been? I've been so worried about you."

As I approached, he opened his arms to me and gave me a sad smile. I took that as a sign that he wasn't mad at me, so I embraced him and held him tight. When he released me, his gaze glistened with unshed tears as he replied, "I'm sorry I left the way I did. I just needed some time to myself and time to spend with my family. My mother took it hard, but she's coming around."

"Do you blame me?" I whispered, lowering my gaze. I never liked to fail in anything I did, especially when it came to protecting my people. The weight of his death weighed heavily on my soul and it hurt even more knowing he was Kamden's brother.

Exasperated, he took me by the shoulders and bent his head to the side so he could see my face. "Ariella, no I don't blame you. Is that what you've been thinking this whole time?"

"Yes," Brayden interrupted, coming to my side. "I know you lost your brother and you are grieving, but in the future you don't just walk away from a royal when they are speaking to you."

"Brayden," I snapped. "He's my—"

He held up his hand to stop me and sighed. "You didn't let me finish, angel," he murmured out loud, but then finished silently, *"I know he's your friend, and with that being said he should've let you be there for him as a friend. He upset you and that's not acceptable."*

"You're such a caveman," I pointed out truthfully. *"You can't protect me from everything."*

"No," he admitted, *"but I can certainly try."*

He then leveled his stare at Kamden and continued, "I know Ariella is your friend, but you still have a duty to respect her as a royal. She was with him when he died, and she tried to save him. She's going through her own pain with his loss as well."

Kamden closed his eyes and bowed his head. "I know, and I'm sorry. Did he say anything before he died?"

A tear fell down my cheek at the remembrance of Lukas' last words. "Yes, he did, Kam. He told me to tell you farewell and that he missed you."

Kamden sighed and ran his hands through his messy, dark hair. "I can't believe he's gone. It doesn't feel real. I always thought he was invincible."

Brayden clapped him on the shoulder and smiled reassuringly. "Lukas was a friend of mine and one of my best warriors. He will never be forgotten."

Nodding, Kamden half-smiled and said, "I'm sorry to have bothered you tonight, but I honestly did feel bad about leaving you like that, Ariella. I appreciate you trying to be there for me, and I didn't like leaving with the way things ended with us."

Embracing him again, I squeezed him tight and breathed a sigh of relief. Hopefully, now I could rest knowing that he was safe and that he didn't blame me for his brother's death even though I wasn't strong enough to help him. That guilt would stay with me forever.

"You're welcome, Kam. That's why I sent for Zanna. I knew you needed someone to be there for you," I explained.

Kamden pulled away with wide eyes. "You sent for Zanna? Where is she?"

"What do you mean where is she?" I shrieked. "She was supposed to be with you. She got here a week ago, Kam. Are you trying to tell me you haven't seen her?"

"No," he expressed worriedly. "I spent some time with my family, but the rest of the time I spent going to all the places Lukas and I would go to when I was a kid."

I didn't want Kamden to hear what I was saying, so I looked to Brayden and said silently, *"What the hell, Brayden? You don't think anything has happened to her, do you?"*

He shrugged and furrowed his brows. *"I'm not sure, angel. She might be in the village at his parents dwelling. He said he didn't stay there the whole time. She could be there waiting on him."*

"Good point," I agreed. *"But if not then we're going to need to find her."*

Trying to shake off the uneasy feelings I knew he had plaguing his mind, Kamden spoke up, trying to sound optimistic, "You know, she's probably at my parents' house. I haven't been back there in a few days so she might be there. I'll go back and see if they've seen her."

Deep in my heart, I had a bad feeling that she wasn't going to be at his parents' house. *Please let it just be the worry and sadness of recent events making me paranoid,* I thought to myself.

Kamden opened the front door, but I caught his arm before he could leave. "If she's not there then we need to look for her. It's been a week, and the last thing she needs to do is go searching for you when the sorcerer will do anything to get to me. We have the palace and this place protected under a spell, but outside of the perimeter its fair game. Staying inside the protection spell is crucial," I stated adamantly.

He nodded and stepped out onto the front porch. "I'm sure I'll find her. Again, I'm sorry for disturbing you."

Brayden shut the door and ran his hands through his hair. "As much as I wanted to be angry at him for disturbing us, I guess it worked out for the best. At least now you won't be preoccupied with worrying about him."

Yawning, I collapsed onto the soft, leathery couch and leaned my head back on the cool fabric. "I'm just glad he doesn't hate me," I mumbled sleepily. "I hope he finds Zanna."

"He will," Brayden said. "Now come on and let's go to bed. You're tired and we have a big day tomorrow."

"What about …" I began, wondering if we were going to finish our bonding.

He shook his head and took my hand, pulling me off of the leathery chair. "We have tomorrow, and the next day, and the next. At least now I know you want to finish the bond with me. Once everyone leaves tomorrow we will have the night to do whatever it is you please."

I smiled and bit my lip. "Yes, we do, and I'm going to take full advantage when tomorrow night comes."

Brayden chuckled and I followed him up the stairs to our room. We both snuggled under the sheets on the bed and almost immediately my eyes grew heavy with sleep. He nuzzled my ear, kissed me on the neck, and stated, "I look forward to tomorrow night then, angel. Sweet dreams, my love."

As soon as my eyes closed, sweet dreams were what I had.

Chapter Twenty Four

Ariella

BRAYDEN AND I were the first ones in the throne room, followed by Queen Mab and King Madoc. The doors were locked so no one from the court could step into the room or overhear us in any way. If word got out about the dagger that could kill the sorcerer then our element of surprise would be gone.

Nixie appeared with Kalen and Meliantha first, and then with Sorcha and Drake. She also brought back Calista, Ryder, and Elvena, my mother and father, then lastly appearing with Durin who carried a large wooden box in his hands. The salvation of our land lay in that box.

Durin bowed, making sure to acknowledge us all with a quick glance and began, "Thank you for your patience, Your Highnesses. Constructing the dagger was interesting to say the least, except it appears it has a mind of its own."

"What do you mean by that?" I asked curiously.

He set the box on the table that had been placed in the middle of the room and we all gathered around it. Durin sighed, slowly opening the box, and said, "Well … everything was going fine until I added the vial of blood to the metal." His hands were covered in gloves, and when he removed them I realized what he was talking about. He held up his blistered and scorched palms for all of us to see.

He continued, "I do not know what happened, but when I grasped the handle after I added the blood it burned me. I can handle my fair share of pain or otherwise I wouldn't have lived so long, however, this kind of pain was none I had ever experienced before. You should've seen my hands yesterday."

Elvena approached the table and gazed inside the box cautiously while Meliantha stood in front of Durin and reached for his hands. Lightly grasping them, she turned them over and inspected them thoroughly, furrowing her brow the whole time. She closed her eyes and covered his wounded hands with hers while slowly moving her lips in a silent plea.

I could feel the power in the room heighten as her healing magic returned his hands to normal, with no trace of any wounds whatsoever. Durin sighed and bowed his head. "Thank you, Meliantha. Having healed hands will definitely make my life easier," he announced gratefully.

"You're welcome," my sister replied. "I wonder why the dagger would do that to you. You are the one who made it."

The box with the dagger lay open on the table, but inside the whole blade was surrounded by a black, velvet cover, concealing our view of the deadly weapon. Elvena was about to unwrap the material from around it, but I shouted, "Wait! Don't touch it!"

She stopped immediately and everyone turned to me, wide-eyed. "Let me do it," I insisted adamantly, glancing quickly at everyone.

If this was the weapon I was going to have to use to defeat the sorcerer then I needed to be able to touch it. The feeling in my gut had me thinking that only a certain few would be the ones allowed to touch it, and that certain few would be me, my sisters, and Sorcha.

Brayden came up behind me and squeezed my arms gently. "Are you sure you want to do this?" he asked quietly.

I nodded and blew out a shaky breath. "I have to," I whispered.

My sisters and Sorcha joined around the table, giving me reassuring smiles as I slowly unwrapped the black cloth from around the dagger. When the weapon was revealed, the others gasped and moved closer, staring at the one thing that was going to save us all. It was beautiful with its golden handle and silver blade that shone like the brightest sun. The handle had silver vines interlapping with the gold, and colored jewels signifying the color of our courts. However, it wasn't the jewels that caught my attention. Engraved in the center of the handle was a symbol that joined us all together. The crests of all our courts were combined into one.

"This is amazing," I breathed in awe. Not even thinking about the repercussions of touching the blade, I took hold of the dagger and lifted it up to my gaze. Brayden tensed behind me, but when it was clear it wasn't going to harm me, he loosened up.

"Let me try to hold it," Calista ordered, holding out her hand. Gently, I passed the dagger to her and she was rewarded with the ability to wield it as well. The same went for Meliantha and Sorcha just like I knew it would. The question was … could any of the others hold it?

Of course, my brother Drake was the first one to volunteer. The expression on his face was smug as he approached his queen and held out his hand, waiting on her to pass the dagger to him. The smile on her face was priceless as she set it down quickly in his hands. Drake growled as the skin of his palm sizzled under the power of the dagger.

"What the hell," he roared, passing it back to Sorcha immediately. "Why is it doing that?"

Out of the corner of my eye, I could see the hesitation in Elvena's gaze as she contemplated how to answer his question. None of them, other than Sorcha, knew that I was aware of what was supposed to happen, and even she looked uncomfortable with the question hanging in the air. It wasn't Elvena who spoke up with the answer; Queen Mab put it out there.

"Isn't it obvious?" she said, walking around our group. "The blade can only be touched by the power of the Four. It began with them and now it's going to end with them. It appears that one of you will need to kill the sorcerer."

My sisters stiffened and glanced at each other before turning their attention to Elvena, who gave them warning glares. Even now they still wanted to keep me in the dark.

Brayden slammed his hand on the table, and pierced his mother with a deadly stare. "That's not going to happen," he exclaimed. He then turned to his brothers and Drake, and addressed them, "What do you all have to say about this? I, for one, do not like the idea of sending in one of our mates to do this. I will do it before I let any one of them be thrown in the dark sorcerer's clutches."

Ryder and Kalen both gazed warily at Brayden, and when Ryder stole a glance at me that was when I realized … they already knew as well. Placing my hand on Brayden's arm, I sent a silent message to him, *"Calm down, Brayden. We will figure this all out, okay?"*

"I am not letting you go face to face with the sorcerer. I would rather die than let him get anywhere near you again," he argued.

If Brayden's outburst wasn't enough, my mother's sure was. She stalked up to Queen Mab and hissed in her face, "I don't know what you think you know, but Durin was able to still touch it after putting on his gloves. My daughters aren't going to be the ones laying their lives on the line for this. Haven't they been through enough already?"

Mab narrowed her eyes. I could see the anger and rage from the years past edging closer to the surface, ready to be unleashed, but she held it back for the sake of our courts. "I don't think it's up to you, Tatiana. Your girls are stronger than you will ever be and it's their decision. I believe in them and in whatever they do. Just because one of them has to wield the final blow doesn't mean they won't survive it."

I swallowed hard, waiting on someone to contradict her, but they never did. Elvena cleared her throat and tried to calm down the weary crowd. "Let's not get ahead of ourselves. We have the dagger, which means we can kill the sorcerer, and I personally think Ariella needs to be the one to carry it. She is the one Alasdair is after right now, and if he does happen to get to her she will be able to protect herself."

Sorcha passed me the dagger, so I took it carefully out of her hands and sheathed it in my belt. I wondered if anyone was going to ask who should keep it. Thankfully, I didn't have to worry about stealing it from one of the others.

Glancing back and forth from me to Brayden, Elvena reluctantly added, "There is, however, one element that we still need." She paused and cleared her throat. "Before we can attack we need to be at our strongest, and the only way we will be that is when the final Winter Court is formed. Until that happens, we need to send word to all of our allies and have them on alert and ready to join us when the time comes. According to the sorcerer, we have one more week before his threat to bring over his mortal army and their weapons comes a reality. We need to strike before he has that chance."

Brayden nudged me in side to get my attention. *"We need to tell them, angel. Look at their faces. We can't keep them in the dark on this."*

I could tell everyone was gazing at Brayden and I curiously, wondering how our relationship was going. I felt bad that we kept them in the dark, but we had to in the hopes of keeping Alasdair from coming at me full force.

Nodding, I smiled up at Brayden and murmured silently, *"I agree with you."*

Taking Brayden's hand, we both walked over to the dais and stood upon it so everyone would be able to see and hear us. Mouths dropped when they noticed Brayden's hand in mine and a smile on my face.

"Do you want to tell them or do you want me to?" I asked him.

He squeezed my hand and replied, *"I want to do it."*

I fully expected him to want me to do it since he always kept his feelings inside on personal matters, but having him take this step to speaking out to his family and to mine made me fall in love with him even more. He had changed so much and had given me so much of himself that I couldn't believe I never saw it in him before.

Brayden took a half step forward and cleared his throat before announcing, "Everyone, Ariella and I have something to say." The mood in the room lifted as it all became clear. Where there were worried frowns marring everyone's lips before, there were now happy smiles of joy. Brayden grinned down at me and back to our families. "Tonight things are going to change … we are going to change. We were going to surprise you all by completing the bond last night, but we got interrupted." He said the last part on a sigh and it earned us a few snickers from the crowd. "With that being said, we plan on completing the marriage bond tonight and sealing our fate … together."

Our families cheered, bursting out with laughter in celebration to the good news, except of course my mother who appeared sadder instead of joyful. From her actions and comments over the years I couldn't believe it took me so long to figure out what her problem was. She grew up having to hate the Winter Fae and even to this day she still did. It made me wonder if she hated me now that I'd turned.

"She doesn't hate you," Brayden expressed sadly, listening in on my thoughts. *"One of these days she might see things differently, but until then, you have me. Tonight nothing needs to be in your thoughts except you and me."*

Lifting up on my toes, I clasped my arms around his neck and tilted his head down so I could place my lips against his. He growled low in his chest and held me tighter with his hands pressed firmly on my lower back, pulling me toward him. *"You are all mine tonight, angel. Nothing is going to stand in our way this time."*

"I'm going to hold you to that," I teased, biting his lower lip.

Brayden licked the lip I just got through biting and took my face in his hands, gazing at me with his heat-filled eyes. *"After I take you back to my dwelling there's something I need to do afterward."*

"Like what?" I asked, narrowing my eyes.

He grinned mischievously and winked. *"I can't tell you, but it's something I had been thinking about all day. I'm going to need Calista's help to make it happen. I promise it won't take long. Then when I come back I'm going to make you my queen."*

"And then what are you going to do?"

Shivers raced across my skin as Brayden lowered his lips to my neck and kissed his way slowly up to my ear. His voice came out husky and full of need when he whispered in my ear, "And then, my sweet angel, I'm going to make love to you."

Chapter Twenty Five

Ariella

BRAYDEN HAD LEFT with Calista over an hour ago, along with Ryder and Kalen for protection purposes. The look on Calista's face was priceless when Brayden went to her and asked for her help. His brothers picked on him a little, and instead of getting mad like he did last time they picked on him, he joined in with the laughter and joked back. He wanted to escort me to his dwelling, but his mother requested some time with me before he took me away.

Sorcha also joined me, but held me back a few paces while we followed Queen Mab down the corridor to her side of the palace. Quietly, she whispered sarcastically in my ear, "What happened to all that mess about not getting attached and bonding with my brother?"

I rolled my eyes at her and sighed. "It was stupidity talking. I've been known to speak before I think sometimes. After everything that's happened I realized that by not bonding with him and forming our court that I would be putting you all at risk if I failed."

"I see," Sorcha remarked. "Is that the only reason why you're doing it?"

I smiled and shook my head. "No it's not, Sorcha. I love him."

We walked in silence the rest of the way until Queen Mab ushered us into one of her rooms and shut the door behind her. "Mother, what are you up to?" Sorcha asked. "I don't think Ariella is going to be interested in your hand me downs."

The room we were in looked like a huge closet that would put mine to shame any day. Queen Mab scoffed and dismissed Sorcha with a wave of her hand. "I didn't bring her here for a hand me down. I actually have something that I had made for her when she got here," she responded incredulously.

She disappeared into another room, and when she came back she had the most gorgeous white gown draped over her arm. She held it up to me and grinned. "When you came here and we had that talk, I knew you and Brayden would work things out. You will look like a true ice queen in this dress."

Sorcha snickered, "Why, because she's going to look like a snowflake? She's going to blend into the snow with that white dress, her bright blonde hair, and pale skin."

They bantered back and forth and I thought it was funny how they interacted with each other. My mother and I never talked like that or joked around, and it made me happy to know I was a part of something real. The dress was simply amazing, but what really made me smile was that I knew Brayden couldn't care less what I wore; it was what was underneath that counted.

❄ ❄ ❄

Brayden still wasn't back yet from doing whatever he and my sister had to do, but Coran was waiting for me by the back palace doors. "Did Brayden tell you to keep a watch over me or something?" I asked humorously.

He bowed his head and gave a slight grin. "Yes, he did, Your Highness. I was told to escort you to your home when you were done with the queen."

With my dress in hand, I was ready to go. Coran followed me closely as we ambled down the path to Brayden's home. It was hard to call it my home since once we formed our own court we wouldn't be living there anymore. It was strange to think that in just a matter of hours I would be queen of my own court. Up ahead, I could see Kamden waiting for me on the front porch steps with a worried frown marring his face. He was alone and that could only mean one thing … he hadn't found Zanna yet.

"Any luck whatsoever in figuring out where she could be?" I called out as Coran and I approached him.

He shook his head and threw his hands up in the air. "I've been looking, but I can't find her. I think something's wrong. This isn't like her to disappear like this."

"Hmmm …" I wondered. "I know she wouldn't have given up looking for you and went back to Spring, which means she's probably still here somewhere." I walked up the steps to my door and let Kamden and Coran follow me inside. Draping my dress over one of the chairs, I took a seat and tried to think. *Where could she be?*

Coran stationed himself by the front door while Kamden took the seat across from me. Frustrated, he ran his hands through his hair and grumbled, "What are we going to do if we don't find her? We've never been away from each other like this."

Reaching over, I placed a reassuring hand over his and squeezed. "We will find her, Kam. When Brayden gets back I'll get him to send some people out to look for her. It could be that you two just missed each other. Although, for some reason I have a feeling in my stomach that I don't see that as being the case here."

"I would say not," Coran interrupted angrily, gazing out the front window. He drew his sword and came to stand in front of me.

"What's going on?" I demanded, trying to see around him.

He pointed his sword to the window and said, "Look."

Kamden and I got to our feet, and I pushed past Coran to gaze out the window. "Oh, no," I wailed. "This can't be happening." What I saw made my blood run cold. At the edge of where Elvena put the protection spell stood Alasdair with Zanna in his grasp, and a huge smile on his face. Kamden stormed out of the house and raced down the steps, but stopped when I shouted, "Kamden, stop!"

I started to walk out the door, but Coran stepped in my path. "I can't let you go out there, Your Highness. You won't be protected if you go past the shield."

Zanna was terrified and trying her best to keep calm, except the iron blade at her throat wasn't helping. One tiny move and it would all be over; I refused to leave her at his mercy. I gazed up at Coran, my decision is final. "She's my friend, Coran. I can't just leave her out there."

I pushed past him and out the door, making sure I had a firm grasp on the dagger in my belt. Kamden moved closer to the border, with raw panic in his eyes, and roared, "Let her go!"

Alasdair laughed, the echo of it ringing menacingly in the air, and tightened his hold around Zanna's waist. The iron from the dagger was blistering her skin at the neck and I knew she had to be in great pain. What made everything worse was that not only did the sorcerer hold a fatal blade to her throat, she was also wearing the bloodstone talisman. It was the same necklace that could siphon a fae's energy and kill them within minutes. I could feel Kamden's fear for her and it broke my heart, but most importantly it made things more clear. I was ready to fight.

The sorcerer pointed his iron weapon at me and sneered, "If you want her bad enough you will step past your protective barrier and take the talisman off from around her neck. If not, then she will die here just like your friend I gutted the other day."

Those words were where I lost Kamden and his ability to restrain his anger. He leapt past the area of protection and attacked; all the while I screamed as I watched him make a fatal mistake. Zanna fell helplessly to the ground, blood oozing out in spurts from the cut through her neck by the iron blade. Her body thrashed as the poison spread and tried to invade her body.

"Coran!" I yelled. "Find Meliantha, and hurry. I'll be okay, just go now as fast as you can!"

I expected him to protest, but something must've shown on my face because he nodded and rushed off with impeccable speed up to the palace. Kamden attacked the sorcerer with everything he had and I knew he needed my help, but I had to save Zanna. Quickly, I ran past the safe zone, grabbed Zanna under the shoulders, and carried her back over to the protected side.

The bloodstone glowed an ominous red and I could see her getting weaker and fading by the minute. The cut on her throat was getting worse, her flesh slowly decaying as the poison seeped into her veins. "Dammit, Zanna, you better hold on and fight. Help is coming and I need you to stay strong," I pleaded.

I grabbed the talisman and tried to yank it from around her neck, but it burned me the second I touched it. It sizzled the skin on my hands as I tried to lift it over her head, but it was no use. It didn't budge.

"Shit," I hissed in pain. No wonder no one was capable of taking the talisman off of themselves.

It reminded me of the dagger Durin made for us. No one could touch it other than me and the others. *Was the sorcerer's talisman that same way?* Unsheathing the special dagger from my belt, I didn't know if what I was about to do would work, but I had to try. Sliding the blade under the golden chain, I jerked it up as fast as I could. I never expected it to be so easy, but it broke and fell to the ground.

I did it.

"Kamden!" I yelled, catching his attention briefly. When he saw I had Zanna on the safe side, he dodged another of the sorcerer's blows and immediately lunged back into the protection of

Elvena's spell. The second he was safe, he ran over to Zanna and picked her up in his arms.

"Zanna," he cried, holding her tight.

Meliantha raced toward us with Coran, Drake, and Sorcha trailing behind her. "Get her to Meliantha now!" I ordered him. With Zanna sputtering in his arms, he jogged up the path and collapsed in front of Meliantha, placing Zanna in front of her. Meliantha bent down, closed her eyes, and placed her hand on Zanna's throat. I prayed to the heavens that she would be okay.

Alasdair sheathed his iron dagger and smiled. "Well, that was fun, Princess. I was hoping to have some more dreams with you during this little reprieve, but again, you ran scared and had to have a protection spell to keep you safe. However, I knew you couldn't resist saving your friend," he taunted eagerly. His gaze found the talisman on the ground, and before I could secure it in my grasp, he extended his hand and chanted a few words in a language I didn't know. The necklace bolted off of the ground and back into his hands.

An uneasy feeling washed over me as he stared at me and smiled. "I must say this has been one of my simplest missions yet. I never thought it would be so easy to steal your power."

"What are you talking about? You haven't gotten my power," I snapped.

Alasdair dangled the necklace in his hand and chuckled menacingly. "Oh, Princess, that's where you're wrong. All it took was one simple touch to absorb your essence into the bloodstone and you've already done that. So thank you, Your Highness, for giving me what I needed."

My blood ran cold. What had I done? How could I have been so stupid as to touch it?

"You bastard," I hissed. Quickly, I shot to my feet and charged after him, heading for the border. Before I could get past the shield, I was knocked off my feet by the weight of someone tackling me to the ground. The breath whooshed out of me as the impact from the fall had me gasping for air. When I looked up, the sorcerer had disappeared and Brayden was on top of me, scowling and angry.

"Brayden, no!" I shouted, slamming my fist in his chest. "Why did you stop me?"

"I can't leave you alone for five minutes without you getting into trouble," he bellowed furiously. "What were you thinking?"

Defeated, I huffed and let my head fall back into the snow. I wanted to cry, scream, and demand that time rewind itself so I could finish this once and for all. I had a chance to end everything, and now the situation had made a turn for the worse. The sorcerer had my power, which meant he would be just as strong as us once he absorbed my essence.

Brayden was breathing hard and fuming when I glared up at him. "I had to save her, Brayden. I couldn't sit by and watch her die in front of my eyes. I could've killed him if you wouldn't have stopped me," I growled.

I waited on him to tell me how stupid I was for trying to charge after the sorcerer alone, but that never came. Instead, he stared at me, his eyes softening with understanding in his concerned, brown gaze as he helped me to my feet.

He brushed the hair out of my face before cupping my cheeks in his firm hands and placing a gentle kiss to my lips. "I know you're a good fighter, angel. It's just the thought of you fighting him sets me on edge. The last thing I want is to watch *you* die in front of *my* eyes."

"That's not going to happen," I whispered regretfully. He wasn't going to be around when I did what I had to do.

Peering over his shoulder, I could see Zanna still on the snow laden ground, unmoving, with Kamden and Meliantha hovering over her. "Oh no," I cried. Taking Brayden's hand, I ran as fast as I could to them and collapsed onto the ground by their sides. Meliantha's hand was covering Zanna's neck and she was rocking back and forth, her lips moving silently, with a sheen of sweat misting on her brow.

Kamden was devastated, tears streaming down his cheeks as he watched his one true love lying helpless on the ground. His pain tore through my heart and it killed me to know that Brayden was going to be in the same position soon, mourning my death. Deep in my heart, I felt stronger than I ever had in my entire life and in a way I did feel invincible. Maybe there would still be hope for me. When I faced off with the sorcerer I had no clue what was going to happen, but I had to have faith that things would work out the way they were supposed to. If I lived or died, I would at least know that I saved everyone I loved.

When Meliantha stopped chanting and opened her eyes, the whole world fell silent. She took a few deep breaths and a slow smile crept across her face. She removed her hand from Zanna's neck and spoke, "It's done. She'll be all right now. If I got to her later it would've been all over."

Kamden picked Zanna up in his arms and held her tight against his chest. "Thank you, thank you so much," he murmured over and over.

Meliantha smiled and squeezed his arm reassuringly. "She's a strong woman, Kamden. You're a very lucky man. She's going to need some rest, but she'll be as good as new in a couple of hours."

Kamden bowed and took Zanna up to the palace, followed by Coran. Now that Brayden was back with Calista and Ryder our whole group was complete. Meliantha placed her hands on her hips and scowled, "I would've given anything to be able to kill that son of a bitch. Seeing him again brought back everything he did to me and Kalen."

Out of all the princesses, Meliantha was the one who had been used and violated by Alasdair more than any of us. I could understand her desire and hunger to kill him. I ran my hands soothingly down her arm, but she caught them in her grasp and gasped. They were blistered from the talisman and I wasn't going to lie, they did hurt, but I knew they would heal soon. My sister, however, wasn't going to let me wait it out. The moment she sent her power flowing into my hands, it felt like a warm pair of gloves wrapping themselves around the blisters. Slowly, I could feel the pain ebbing away faster and faster until there was none left. When she let go of my hands, they were as good as new and perfectly unblemished. Breathing a sigh of relief, I pulled her to me and held her tight. Softly, I whispered in her ear, "Thank you, Mel. I would've given anything to have killed him for you. He will die soon, you have my word."

Somberly, I pulled back and addressed the rest of the group, "We have bigger problems now. We're going to need to call in our allies as soon as possible and get their help." Calista's eyes grew wide when I reluctantly met her gaze and nodded at her. She knew what I was getting ready to say … my power had been taken.

Drake interrupted with a wave of his hand, "I think we figured that out already judging by what he did here today. I'll make sure the Summer warriors are ready once you and Brayden..." He stopped mid-sentence, casting a mischievous glance in mine and Brayden's direction. Sorcha rolled her eyes, but nonchalantly he continued, "Never mind, I'm not going to finish that sentence. Anyway, I'll have my people ready."

He and Sorcha turned to leave, but I stopped them with my next words. "He took some of my power, Drake." With eyes wide, they both turned around and everyone stared at me, shocked. I nodded and continued, "Yeah, when I touched the talisman to get it off of Zanna's neck it siphoned some of my energy. I didn't realize it could do that without it being around my neck. So now his quest is complete. He's going to be stronger, and even with all of our courts combined it's going to be a devastating battle."

"Shit," he hissed, running his hands through his thick, red hair. "We need to get prepared quickly. I'll inform Mom and Dad and get the Summer warriors ready. This isn't going to be good." He and Sorcha rushed up to the palace and disappeared inside the walls.

"Meliantha," I said, turning toward her, "we're going to need the Tyvar and Redcaps in this. Is there any way to alert them and have them ready to fight?"

She nodded. "They will come. Bayleon and Bastian promised they would be ready when the time came. They won't let me down." Kalen scoffed and rolled his eyes. He didn't like the Tyvar much considering they wanted to make Meliantha their sex slave back when she was taken captive by them. Her power saved her from their clutches, and since they were enamored by her they let her free when they found out who she was. Bayleon and Bastian had kept in touch with Meliantha and would always send her gifts, which Kalen didn't like at all. Bayleon was the Tyvar leader, and Bastian was his brother and also one of the leaders who had taken an instant liking to me when I met them several months ago. I was out in the garden with Meliantha when they arrived one time, and ever since then I always made a point to be with her when they visited.

They weren't bad men at all, except for their utter lack of control when being around women they could seduce. One thing about being one of the powerful Four was that I couldn't be seduced by them … unless I wanted to. They weren't allowed inside the court grounds, so when they visited it had to be right outside the gate. When Bastian began to show more of an interest in me, he was warned by my sister that I could never be his. I think the appeal was that he could actually be around me and I wouldn't fall victim to his charms. He could have something real; he could have true love.

Kalen and Meliantha marched off, leaving only Brayden and me with Ryder and Calista. Ryder pulled Brayden to the side and they began discussing what they were going to do while Calista stayed beside me so she could talk to me alone. I couldn't keep my gaze off of Brayden, and deep in my heart I wondered how I was ever going to find the courage to leave him and break his heart.

"I can feel the weariness in you, Ariella," Calista whispered. "Care to talk to me about it?"

I really wanted to tell her how angry it made me that she deliberately kept me in the dark about things. It made me furious to be treated like I couldn't handle it, but being the person that Calista was I knew all she wanted was to protect me. I would probably do the same thing if I was in her position.

Sighing, I finally met her gaze and shrugged a shoulder saying, "I'm just ready for it all to be over. How are we going to get close enough to the sorcerer to kill him with the dagger? Not to mention one of us has to do it," I mentioned curiously, trying to see if she'd confide in me. I tried to keep my tone indifferent, but being that I was talking to Calista nothing ever seemed to get past her.

She started to speak, but stopped and narrowed her eyes at me, studying me. Pursing my lips, I stood there with my arms crossed, waiting and wondering what she was going to say now. Was she going to be honest or tell more lies? Cursing quietly, she groaned and closed her eyes. "Who told you? Was it Sorcha?"

"Now what would Sorcha have told me?" I asked sarcastically. "Is there something I should know?"

All she did was lift a brow and stare at me with that look on her face that said, 'Don't mess with me.'

Rolling my eyes, I answered, "Fine, I'll tell you and no, it wasn't Sorcha. I've known this whole time that it was I who had to kill the sorcerer. Although, Sorcha does know that I am aware of the situation. She came to me in a dream and I told her because I said I wasn't going to bond with Brayden. I didn't want him to suffer with my loss if I wasn't going to survive."

Her eyes misted with unshed tears, but the fierceness in her gaze was anything except sad. She grabbed me by the shoulders and leaned in close. "You listen to me, Ariella. I know how you are and so help me if you do something stupid I'm going to come after you and kill you myself, do you understand? We didn't come all this way and endure all of our losses for it to end this way. This whole mess started out with us, and it's going to end with *us*."

"Is everything okay?" Ryder asked, coming to Calista's side with a furrowed brow. Calista nodded quickly and smiled, but then turned her serious gaze to me.

"Yes, everything is fine," she assured him. "I just wanted to wish the best for my little sister on what will be one of the most magical nights of her life."

"Is that what you tell everyone ours was like?" Ryder teased, kissing her on the cheek.

"Of course," she agreed. "It *was* the most magical night of my life, and one I will never forget." Flinging her arms around my neck, she squeezed me tight and whispered in my ear, "You're going to make a wonderful queen, Ariella. I love you so much even though you are hard headed."

I laughed and squeezed her harder. "I get it from my oldest sister."

After we all said our good-byes, Brayden draped his arm protectively around my waist and held me close as we made our way back to his dwelling. I was curious as to why he needed my sister's help so I decided to ask. "Are you going to tell me what you and my sister were doing this whole time?"

With a gleam in his eye, he winked and grinned down at me. "No, but I am going to show you as soon as you get ready … that is, if you still want to do this after everything that just happened. I don't want us finishing this because we *need* to. I want to do this because we *want* to."

Sighing, I stopped him at the door before we could enter and whispered his name, "Brayden … nothing in this realm is going to stop us from being together tonight. I want you and need you more than the air I breathe, or even the heart that beats in my chest." My lips quivered when I kissed him on the lips. "I love you."

He smiled and cupped my cheek in his hand. "And I love you, angel. Now go and get ready so I can show you how much. You're probably going to be tired of me after the night is over." He opened the door and ushered me inside.

Grabbing the dress that I left draped over the chair, I rushed past him and up the steps to our room. *"There is no way that is ever going to happen,"* I said through our bond.

"You say that now, angel, but I don't think I'm going to be able to keep my hands off of you tonight."

That was definitely not a bad thing. The thought of his hands all over me all night made my insides clench and tighten with need. He wasn't the only one who was going to have a problem keeping their hands to themselves. I wanted desperately to feel him inside me and making love to me. Through the bond, I could feel his desire. It heightened when I opened up my own desire in his mind so he could feel how much I wanted him.

"If you plan on seducing me through our bond then you need to hurry up, my love. You have no idea what it's doing to me down here," Brayden teased. *"I am two seconds away from coming up there and taking you now."*

I washed up quickly and slid into the silky, white dress that Queen Mab gave me and strapped the all powerful dagger to the belt around my waist. The low, plunging v-neck was stunning and it sparkled like diamonds as I moved in the light. It was beautiful. Mab said I was going to look like a real ice queen in this dress, and after tonight it was certainly going to be true. My Winter Court was going to be formed with the man I loved, and together, even if only for one day, I was going to rule by his side in our court … our Court of Ice.

Chapter Twenty Six

Ariella

WHEN I WALKED down the stairs, Brayden was nowhere in sight, but there was a beautiful midnight blue cloak draped over one of the chairs with a note attached to it.

Meet me outside, angel. I'll

be waiting.

Brayden

Wrapping the cloak around my shoulders, I pulled the hood over my head and took a deep breath. *Here we go.* I opened the front door to find Brayden with his back to me, tightening the straps of my saddle to Lennox's back. Lennox whinnied when he saw me and Brayden immediately turned around, his gaze widening as he took me in.

"Ariella," he murmured, "you are so beautiful."

He never took his heated eyes off of me as I walked down the steps toward him. He helped me up onto my white stallion and then mounted his own horse, which happened to be an exquisite black mare. "Are we going far?" I asked.

Brayden smiled. "Not too far, but you will know where we are going very soon."

He winked at me before setting off down the snowy path toward the woods. I breathed in the cold, winter breeze as we raced through the trees, snow billowing out like white mist around us. The farther we got, the more the feeling in my gut grew stronger, pulling me faster to my destination. Yes, I knew exactly where we were going.

Brayden slowed his mare down with a tug of the reins; Lennox obediently complied to his command and slowed down as well. The moment Lennox stepped into the snowy meadow, the magic of the land grew stronger. I gasped as soon as we crossed over to the unclaimed land that would soon be mine and Brayden's. The power of the land was unreal.

Once the trees cleared, my breath was taken away at the vision before my eyes. The trees gave way to a small opening, and in the middle of that open meadow was a dwelling of sorts. It wasn't something I had ever seen before, but what made it special was that it was made of ice. It was but a taste of what my court would be like once it was formed.

"Brayden, it's amazing," I breathed. "Is this why you needed Calista?"

He dismounted from his mare and clutched my waist to help me slide off of Lennox. He nodded sheepishly and replied, "Yes, I had the vision in my head but I needed her to help make it come alive."

"It's beautiful."

Taking my hand, he led me to the door and followed me inside. The walls glowed and shimmered like diamonds from the fire, which cast its sensual light throughout the room. That was all the house of ice was, too. It was one huge room with windows peering out to the white abyss beyond and a crackling fireplace in the far wall with a mound of soft blankets in front of it. It reminded me so much of the vision we shared.

Brayden came up behind me and unclasped the cloak from around my shoulders and lowered the hood from my head, letting it fall to the floor. He moaned low in his throat and turned me around to face him.

"You are the one that's beautiful, angel," he claimed wholeheartedly. "I can't wait to make you mine forever." He lifted the hand with his ring adorning my finger and kissed it lightly. "Forever," he repeated.

Silently, he led me over to the fireplace and the bed of blankets on the floor. His heated gaze made me shiver as he pulled me closer and took my face in his hands. "I love you, Ariella. I know I may not be the kind of man who can tell you how I feel all the time, but with us being bonded the way we are, you will always be able to feel it. I have never let myself feel anything other than loyalty and duty for my court, but you have shown me a different way … a way to love."

He kissed me gently, but then deepened it by opening my lips with his tongue. I ran my hands through his hair and tugged him closer, tasting the sweet taste of Winter on his tongue and breathing in his heady scent of pure, fresh snow.

"Brayden," I murmured silently.

He gazed at me with his sensual brown eyes, filled with love and longing, and smiled down at me. The twinge in my heart grew deeper because I knew

REGIN OF ICE (FOREVER FAE SERIES)

that in the next day or so I would be leaving him. Bonding with him and the memory of it would be the only thing getting me through what I had to do. I was ready.

Smiling up at him, I decided to begin the first part of our bonding. It had to be said in the Old Fae language for it to be binding, and even though I didn't know much of that language I still knew what I needed to say.

"Brayden, no matter where I am or what happens in our world, you will always be with me … in here," I said, placing a hand over my heart. "I will be honored to be your mate, your queen, and … your wife. *Amin mela lle ilyamemie ar' ten' oio.* These words bond me to you, for always and forever."

I could feel the power of those words linking me to him in a stronger connection than the guardian bond. It was like an invisible chord that weaved its way around my heart and soul and connected me to his. My life was tethered to his now whether he completed his part of the bond or not.

Brayden smiled down at me and sighed, rubbing his thumb over my swollen lips from his kisses. "You will be my mate, my queen, and my wife and there's nothing in this realm that I want more than that. I bond myself to you, angel, and from here on out you will always be mine … forever and always. Freely and with no reservations, I give you my body, my soul, and most importantly my heart. *Amin mela lle ilyamemie ar' ten' oio.*"

The magic of our bond swirled between us like an invisible force tethering us together, bonding us. Brayden smoothed his fingers underneath the top of my dress and slowly lowered the white, silky fabric off my shoulders. He kept his gaze on mine as my dress slid down my arms, over my breasts, and the rest of the way to the floor.

Slowly, I unbuttoned each single button of his black shirt, exposing the smooth plains of his chest one inch at a time. He closed his eyes and groaned as I trailed my fingers teasingly over his pale, muscled skin. He grabbed my hand, stopping me, and brought my palm up to his lips. "I think we've had enough foreplay over the last few days to last us a lifetime, don't you think, angel?" he murmured huskily.

"Are you saying you didn't enjoy it?" I retorted.

Chuckling, he grabbed my hips and pressed me firmly against the hardness between his legs. "Oh, I have enjoyed every second of it, but I'm ready to make love to you. I've needed you too much to take things slow."

With hooded eyes, I lifted up on my toes and traced my tongue across his lips and whispered, "Then what are you waiting for?"

He didn't need to be told twice because in the next second we were both unclothed and wrapped in each other's arms on the soft bed of blankets on the floor. Brayden's face glowed in the firelight as he pushed my legs apart with his knee and brought his hands up to my breasts. He massaged them gently before lowering his lips to tease my nipples with his tongue.

I wrapped my legs around his waist and squeezed, bringing my hips up higher to his groin. Reaching my hand down between our legs, I stroked him gently at first, earning a strangled moan from his lips. He moved his hips along with my strokes, and the harder he sucked on my nipples the harder I squeezed along his cock.

"I thought you didn't want foreplay?" I teased in his mind.

He licked my nipple one last time and smirked down at me. Taking the hand that was wrapped around his erection, he pinned it above my head and replied gruffly, "You're right, I don't."

He teased me for a few more seconds by rubbing his hardness back and forth between my legs, and then entered me gently, thrusting in small strokes so I could get used to his fullness inside of me. I moaned and raked my fingernails down his back as he pushed in deep, as far as he could go. I could feel the magic of our bond growing and swirling around us as we made love, fueling our never ending need for each other. It reminded me of silver glitter the way it sparkled and shimmered in the room.

Taking my face in his hands, Brayden thrust harder between my legs and crushed his lips against mine, teasing and tasting greedily. I could feel my core tighten around him as my orgasm slowly began to build and build. With my breath coming out in pants, I dug my nails harder in his back and squeezed my legs tighter around his waist.

"Brayden," I cried out.

"Let it go, angel," he commanded. His brown eyes bore into mine, and I could tell he too was on the verge of losing control.

The harder and faster he pumped, the quicker my body let go. Closing my eyes, I shouted his name again, except he muffled those cries by closing his lips over mine as he released. He rocked his hips slowly as his cock pulsated and spilled every single drop of his seed inside me. The warmth of our love spread throughout my belly, and for the first time in my life I felt whole. Breathing hard, we both lay there silently, listening to the sounds of our hearts beating in tune to each other.

"Are you all right?" Brayden asked, wiping away the hair on my forehead.

I opened my eyes, and when I looked up at his face, I gasped. Now that our bond had been completed the changes in our bodies had taken place as well. What used to be just ordinary pale skin now shimmered with a silver glittery sheen. I gazed down at my own hand and it was the same. It was almost like Meliantha's skin where hers glittered with a golden hue, but ours glittered with a silver one. It was fascinating.

I nodded at him and replied, "Yes, I feel wonderful. This is all amazing."

The land beneath us began to shift and I knew it was changing into our court, into our land that would make the Land of the Fae stronger than any other force imaginable. I couldn't wait to see it. Brayden slowly pulled out of me and helped wrap a blanket around my body before wrapping one around his waist. He held out his hand and helped me to my feet.

"I think it is time we gaze upon our new court. How does that sound, my queen?" Brayden asked with a smile on his face.

"I think you just read my mind."

I didn't know how I was going to feel when I looked upon my court, but I knew it was going to take my breath away. As far as I could see past the trees, the land was smoothed over with ice, and as the snow flittered down from the sky to the ground it never showed up on the ice. It was like it disappeared before it touched the ground.

I could tell Brayden was as in awe with our court as I was when I looked up at him and saw him gazing out at our land. "I wonder how everyone is going to walk around on the ice without falling," I joked. Brayden chuckled by my ear, and wrapped his arms around my waist, pulling me up against his thickening cock.

"I'm sure they will get along just fine, but right now there are other things we need to worry about," he said, unwrapping the blanket from around my body.

"Like what?"

He cupped both of my bare breasts in his palms, rolling my nipples with his fingers, and answered, "Like going back to bed and letting me make love to you for the rest of the night. I promised that was what we were going to do and I have to live up to that promise."

His hand trailed down my stomach and I shivered when he rubbed his thumb across my clit and gently pushed a finger inside me. I moaned and leaned against him as his fingers worked their own magic on my body. "How can I say no to that?" I remarked breathlessly. "I can't let you go back on your word."

"No, you can't." He lifted me up in his arms and carried me back over to the fireplace where he laid me down gently on the thick, soft blankets. "Tonight is ours, angel, and nothing else should matter except me and you. Right now, nothing else exists except me and you. Put everything out of your mind and let's love each other like we will for the rest of our lives. Can you do that?"

My eyes welled with tears, but I nodded in reply. If this was our last night together I was going to do my utmost to fulfill his request. "Yes, Brayden. On this night nothing else exists, except you … and me."

The night was young and there was nowhere else I wanted to be than in Brayden's arms as we made love to each other. Hours upon hours our bodies and souls connected into one magnificent union, and what made it even better was that the magic of our court was strengthening our love. Out of every single gift in the world, love was the most powerful. I just wished it was strong enough to save the Land of the Fae.

Chapter Twenty Seven

Ariella

WHEN THE NIGHT ebbed off to bring the dawn, I watched Brayden sleep peacefully beside me. I wanted to fall asleep and relax in his arms, but the night was over, meaning that our world of nothing else existing didn't exist anymore. The evil was still there, lurking behind the corner and waiting to strike; I had to face it head on.

Dressing back in my white gown from the night before, I draped my blue cloak over my shoulders and quietly walked out of the house and out onto my land. The ice was smooth as I ambled across it, and I wondered what it would feel like to have ice skates and be able to dance and glide around on them. It didn't matter, though. All that mattered was that my court was strong and ready.

The sound of hooves beating across the ground vibrated through the trees, and when I glanced behind me, I was amazed to see a whole entourage of people headed our way. My whole family, now including Brayden's, trudged along on their horses along with Kamden and Zanna, and a contingent of warriors including Coran.

Brayden must have felt them coming because he walked out of the house, buttoning his shirt up in the process. "What are you doing out here?" Brayden asked softly. "I thought you would be in bed with me."

I smiled and kissed him on the cheek. "I couldn't sleep. Besides, we have company," I informed him, pointing at our approaching guests.

Calista reached us first and jumped off her horse, flinging her arms around me. "You look amazing, Ariella. So how does it feel to be the queen of your own court?"

"It feels great," I answered honestly. "Why are you all here?"

"Meliantha and I are here to help lend our magic to make your home, and the warriors are here because they choose to be allegiant to this Winter Court and follow Brayden. We also had a meeting last night about our plan of attack, and now that you and Brayden have completed the bond we wanted to discuss it all with you."

"What did you come up with?" I asked hesitantly.

She smiled and shook her head, but that smile didn't touch her eyes. "Let's talk about that later. Right now we need to get your home built. You don't want to stay in your little ice house forever do you? Where would you put all your kids?"

The thought did bring a smile to my face, imagining all the children Brayden and I would have, but it was just a dream and Calista knew it. Her eyes misted over, but I took her hand in mine and pulled her to the forest edge. "No tears, Calista, you understand me?" She nodded, but didn't say a word. "Let's use your magic and get this palace built." Meliantha came up on my other side and took my hand, leaving me in the middle of my sisters.

"You weren't planning on doing this without me were you?" Sorcha scolded playfully, taking Calista's other hand.

The moment we all four took hands, the magic between us exploded into the land. The ground rumbled and shook as everything began to shift and change. In my mind, I pictured a palace just like mine in the Summer Court, but this one with white stone bricks surrounded by glimmering sheens of ice. It sparkled just like mine and Brayden's little ice house in the woods and I loved it. Instead of gargoyles, like you would see on gothic castles across the world, I had angels protecting mine. If I couldn't be there for

Brayden, at least he would have his own guardian angels protecting our court. It all materialized in front of my eyes just as I imagined it.

"Thank you," I whispered to my sisters as I gazed out at my new home. "I have never seen anything more beautiful in my life."

They all looked over at me incredulously, and then to each other. "I didn't do anything," Calista admitted, letting go of my hand. "Once you grabbed a hold of my hand you took over somehow. I think that was all you. You didn't even tell me what you wanted, remember?"

I stared at her for a moment, brows furrowed, and then out to my new home. "You're right," I whispered with uncertainty. "I didn't tell you what I wanted."

It was strange, but it was true. I thought it up in my head, and the moment I grabbed everyone's hands it just appeared. It was weird, but then for some reason my whole body felt weird. *Did I get new powers when Brayden and I bonded?*

Things only got weirder when out of the corner of my eye I saw someone appear that I wasn't expecting to ever see again. I blinked a couple of times, thinking it was just from lack of sleep, but when he saw me looking at him, I knew then that he was actually there. He gazed at me uncertainly, not knowing if I was seeing him, but when I made full eye contact with him, he started to approach me slowly, cautiously.

I backed up quickly, thinking that I had to be going crazy. What was wrong with me? Brayden could immediately feel my panic and rushed over, taking my face in his hands and going on full alert.

"Ariella, what's wrong? You look like you've seen a ghost," he uttered worriedly, running his hands along my arms.

"I think I am," I told them.

Everyone gazed at me with concern in their eyes, but what was I supposed to say. I didn't understand what was happening, but even I couldn't deny what I was seeing. It wasn't an illusion, but there was some kind of magic at work that was making me see things.

It only became even more real when he spoke. "Ariella, can you see me?" he asked.

My eyes burned with unshed tears as I gazed upon the guy I looked up to as a child. I even had a silly crush on him when I was a little girl because he was always around my sister, Calista. Even in death he still followed her around. He still looked the same, all Summer Fae with golden tanned skin and blond hair that curled slightly over his ears and hung over his forehead. Merrick hadn't changed a bit in the six years he'd been gone to the Hereafter. The question was … why could I see him?

I nodded quickly and whispered, "Yes, I see you."

Brayden gently grasped my chin and turned my face toward him, his brows furrowed in confusion. "Are you all right? Who are you saying yes to?"

Standing by Calista, Merrick smiled and assured me, "I'm here, Ariella. Just tell them you see me. Maybe someone will know why you can. Elvena usually knows everything."

I glanced at Brayden and then over to Calista, letting the tears fall as I kept looking at them both and then to Merrick. Closing my eyes, I took a deep breath and opened them one more time ... only to see Merrick still there with a smirk on his face. "I'm still here," he teased.

"Oh, holy hell I am going crazy," I muttered, shaking my head. "I'm talking to a ghost."

"Who?" Brayden and Calista asked at the same time.

I glanced at them both and whispered, "Merrick."

❋ ❋ ❋

It turned out that Merrick wasn't the only deceased person I could see. Lukas happened to be one of them, too. It wasn't easy relaying his and Kamden's messages to each other. I spent the entire time crying, trying to talk to both of them. After a couple of hours of speculating and questions from Elvena and my family, the conclusion came down to my seeing ghosts being a case of delayed magical abilities. However, I knew it wasn't true, but how could I tell my family that it didn't feel right? I knew what my powers were and what I could do, but this gift didn't have anything to do with my own abilities. It was something else.

Everyone gathered in the throne room of mine and Brayden's newly built palace while he and I walked through the halls. I needed some time away; time to think. "I can't believe you can see Merrick and Lukas," Brayden announced. "I wonder why you can see them now and not before. Is it strange being able to see them?"

"Of course it is," I replied incredulously. "Especially with Merrick since I know how bad Calista misses him. Now that I can see him and she can't, it makes me feel bad for her. I know your sister helped her see him in her dreams, but I know it's not the same thing as what I can do."

He draped his arm across my shoulders and sighed. "I know it's not the same thing, but at least you have ties to him now in case she ever wanted to talk to him."

"Yeah, you're right."

"Are you ready to go back now?" he asked.

I glanced up at him and nodded. With my newfound powers my body felt odd and not like myself at all; it was strange. "Yeah, I'm ready to go in there. The sooner we do, the faster everyone will leave."

And the sooner I could get away and get to the dark sorcerer to kill him. The longer we waited the more time he had to get his mortal army into place. Brayden opened the giant heavy wooden doors with our Winter Court crest carved onto it and led the way into the room. Merrick and Lukas were still there, and with a nod I acknowledged them along with everyone else gathered around.

"What have you all discussed?" Brayden asked, glancing around the room.

I took a seat in the front of the room on the dais while Brayden gathered around everyone else on the floor. It was hard to participate in the strategy planning when I already knew what was going to happen. I was going to head out first thing tonight and make my way to the Black Forest.

Merrick lifted a brow and strolled up to me looking grim. "I hear that weapon you carry on your belt is what's going to save our land," he mentioned, taking a seat beside me.

"Yes, it is," I answered as quietly as I could.

Merrick pursed his lips and rubbed the back of his neck sheepishly. "Did you know they were thinking about taking it away from you?"

Immediately, I jerked my head in his direction and glared. "What?" I hissed, placing my hand protectively over the hilt of the dagger. "I don't think so."

"Why do you need it?"

I huffed, "Because I just do. I can't let them take it away from me."

He studied me for a moment and then lowered his head and groaned, running his hand through his blond hair. "Oh, baby girl, you haven't changed a bit. Always so fearless and strong, yet running head first into trouble any chance you got."

I rolled my eyes. "What is that supposed to mean?"

Merrick sighed. "It means that I know you're up to something. Have you forgotten already that I'd been a part of your family for years? I watched you grow up, Ariella, so I know what you're capable of. Calista told me to keep my eyes on you because she thinks the same thing."

"Is everyone going to always think I'm up to something?" I snapped halfheartedly, knowing very well everyone would always think that no matter how old or young I was.

He chuckled, showing off the dimples I used to love seeing on his face when he was alive. He said, "Yes, I think so. Look, whatever you have in your mind that you plan on doing, don't do it. I wasn't joking when I said they wanted to take your dagger, but if you have something up your sleeve you need to forget about it."

I scoffed and crossed my arms over my chest, glaring at him. "Even if I did have something up my sleeve there is nothing you could do to stop me. I'm a big girl now, Merrick, and I'm also queen of my own court. I think I know how to protect my people and keep them safe."

Standing from my chair, I didn't wait on him to reply. Instead, I joined into the group and went to stand by Brayden. "So what's the verdict?" I asked, peering at everyone and taking in their concerned gazes.

Leaning over the drawings of our land, Brayden straightened his shoulders and sighed. "We strike the day after tomorrow. It'll give us time to get everyone ready to fight and for our allies to join us."

I could deal with that because it would give me plenty of time to do what I had to do before anyone got hurt. The gloomy expressions on the faces of everyone around me, however, gave me pause. From the hesitation coming from Brayden through the bond I knew exactly what was going on; Merrick was right. They wanted the weapon.

"What else is going on?" I demanded, placing a protective hand on the dagger. The movement didn't go unnoticed, making the tension in the room elevate a hundred levels.

Brayden cleared his throat, his tone wary as he gazed at me and began, "I want you to let us have the dagger, angel. We all decided that since the sorcerer is not after you specifically anymore that it might be best for someone else to carry it into battle."

Fuming and eyes wide with rage, I hissed through gritted teeth, "Are you saying I'm not going to be fighting? Who else is going to carry it other than me? It's not like there are too many other choices of people who can touch it."

Taking a deep breath, he nodded sadly and closed his eyes. "You're right, there are not that many choices, but Elvena thinks we may have a way to where someone else can wield it other than you or the others. Also, I would never keep you from fighting, Ariella. You are an amazing warrior and no matter what I, or anyone else, says you will be out there with that sword in your hand."

"Who then?" I demanded, placing my hands on my hips, observing them all. "Which one of you is going to be the one to kill the sorcerer? I don't remember all of you letting me in on this decision."

I stood there waiting on someone to answer me, but all they did was either look away or send apologetic glances toward Brayden. Each second I didn't get an answer was a second closer I was to losing control. I couldn't take anymore.

"Who!" I shouted, my hands shaking with anger. The echo of my scream bounced off the walls with a deafening roar, making everyone flinch.

"It'll be me, angel," Brayden confessed softly. *"I have to know you're going to be safe,"* he finished silently.

My blood froze in my Winter veins and my heart tightened in my chest. Turning around slowly, I gazed at him in disbelief. There was no way in hell I was letting him sacrifice himself for me. He probably didn't even know that I was the one who *had* to do it. By the look in Elvena's eyes when I cast her a sideways glance I knew for a fact she hadn't told him the truth yet.

"Like hell you are," I exclaimed firmly with my head held high. To everyone, I said, "I am the one who is going to do this, not anyone else. It was destined for me and I've accepted that. Keeping me in the dark wasn't going to change anything."

Confused, Brayden furrowed his brows and spoke, "What are you talking about keeping you in the dark? Who kept you in the dark?"

My gaze found Elvena, my sisters, and Sorcha, but then I turned and focused just on Brayden. When I left this room it would be the last time I saw him, especially if he wanted to take the dagger from me. If he succeeded in that, our world would suffer the dire consequences, and I couldn't have that.

"Do you know what the scroll said?" I asked him.

He nodded quickly. "Yes, it told us what we needed to do as far as the weapon to kill the sorcerer."

"Is that it?"

"Yes, why?" he inquired hesitantly. "What else was there? Was there more?"

Sighing, and with tears beginning to blur my vision, I cupped his cheeks in my hand and kissed him one last time. If I explained to him what I knew he wouldn't let me out of his sight. I had to go now before he could stop me.

I poured all my love and soul into our final kiss and let my tears escape. *"I love you, Brayden. Whatever you do, don't forget that."*

He immediately pulled away from the kiss and narrowed his eyes. "Why are you saying that? What else was in the scroll? Tell me!"

Shaking my head, I wiped away the tears and forced myself to smile up at him even though I was breaking apart inside, knowing it was the last time I would ever set my eyes on him. As softly and calmly as I could, I cried, "It doesn't matter right now. All that matters is keeping our land safe and we're going to do that. If you don't mind I'm going to rest while you all finish up in here. If you need me I'll be in our room."

Frowning, he took my hand in his and lifted my chin with his other. "Do you want me to walk with you?" he asked, his tone laced with worry.

Shaking my head, I tried to keep my voice from trembling when I replied, "No, I'll be fine. Stay here with everyone and I'll see you when you get done. I just need to rest."

I kissed him one last time and turned away quickly so I could get out of the room before breaking down. My heart broke with each step I took toward the door, and it took all I had not to look back. I couldn't look back.

Good-bye, Brayden.

Chapter Twenty Eight

Brayden

"WHERE DID ARIELLA go?" Calista asked after Ariella left the room. Her gaze was wide and panicked as she rushed up to me.

Befuddled, I responded, "She said she was tired and needed to rest so she went to our room. Why does it matter?"

"She can't be alone right now," she muttered quickly. "She's up to something. I can feel it and it's not like her to just walk out of here calmly after we wanted to take the dagger away from her. Trust me, you need to go after her … now. We need to get the dagger before she goes and does something stupid."

"Tell me what's going on. Does this have to do with what the scroll said?" I demanded. "I'm not going anywhere until I get some damn answers."

Mumbling something about me being just like Ryder, Calista stepped aside so Elvena could come in and explain. When Calista told me to track down Ariella, I never knew the situation was as dire as they thought until Elvena said, "Brayden ... there are some things you don't know. Things that myself and the others kept from you and Ariella."

Clenching my fists at my sides, I started to fume but I had to hear what she had to say. "Go on," I snapped impatiently with a wave of my hand.

Elvena sighed and lowered her head. "The scroll not only told us how to defeat the sorcerer, but it also gave us an idea of who it would be that could defeat him ... and it's not any of you." She lifted her gaze and in it I saw nothing except sadness and regret. Immediately, my heart felt like it had been ripped out of my chest. I didn't need to hear her say who it was supposed to be because I already knew.

And if Ariella knew ...

Turning on my heel, I rushed out of the room, my heart beating like razor sharp drums in my chest. The only thing I could hear as I raced down the corridor to our room was the silent screams in my mind saying that I was too late. How could I have not known, or better yet, why the hell didn't anyone tell me?

"Ariella!" I shouted in her mind. I hoped I was wrong in my assumption that she had indeed decided

to take matters in her own hands. It wasn't until I fully concentrated on our connection that I could already tell she had me blocked out.

"Dammit," I growled, feeling as if I would explode.

The second I came to our bedroom door I kicked it open and rushed inside, already feeling the emptiness of her absence. The weight on my chest felt like a thousand tons crushing me to the floor as I struggled to breathe. After everything we had just gone through together, I couldn't begin to fathom that she would actually leave me … but she did. The harsh reality of it slammed me in the gut when I found the crisp, white letter lying on the bed with a lock of her hair beside it.

I picked up the bright blonde lock of hair and clutched it in my palm, squeezing it tight. "So help me, Ariella, when I get you home you're going to wish you didn't run away from me," I warned out loud to myself. The letter was folded over with a crease in the middle, but I could see her elegant handwriting inside. The ache in my chest grew deeper.

I opened it up slowly and read the words I'd been dreading.

Brayden,

By the time you read this, I'm sure you will already know the reasons why I had to leave. Please know that I love you and there's nothing I wouldn't do to keep you safe. When you said you were going to be the one to kill the sorcerer my heart ripped out of my chest. In that moment I fell in love with you even more and it made my decision even harder to face. In a way I wanted to be selfish and just stay with you, hoping that the scroll was wrong and that we would figure out another way ... but I knew it wasn't going to be so. There are so many things I need to ask your forgiveness on and I have no clue where to start. I need you to forgive me for leaving you. Trust me, it was the hardest thing I have ever had to do. Even as I write this I can't seem to get the tears to stop. I wanted to tell you about my fate, and that was the reason I kept closed off from you at the beginning. I didn't want you seeing the turmoil that warred within my body. I know that I can succeed in doing what I have planned because there are things I can do that you don't know about. "The one who can earn his trust will be the one to defeat him." That is the quote from the scroll. I have that ability, Brayden, and if I can save the lives of our people with the sacrifice of just mine then I'm going to do it. I know you would do the same thing if you could. Our time together and the love we share is the only thing keeping me going right now, and however long I have left I want you to know that I will love you always. We will never be apart, my love, because *you will always be in my heart and I will always be in yours ... forever.*

With all my love,

Your angel

I could feel the presence of someone behind me, and judging from the power level in the room it had to be Elvena. Holding the letter to my chest, I didn't even turn around when I asked the question I was too afraid to hear the answer to, "What's going to happen to her? Is she going to die?"

Elvena sniffled and cried, "I'm not sure, child. From what I'm gathering it looks like it'll be almost impossible for her to survive. No one could live through the magnitude of force the sorcerer's power will unleash once it's free."

It cannot end that way! I screamed in my mind. I couldn't believe that it would end that way ... I refused to.

Taking Ariella's letter, I folded it into a tiny square and placed it inside my armor belt. I wasn't going to let her die; I was going to find her and bring her home. If I couldn't find her tonight there was one person who could lead me to her … my sister. I just prayed to the heavens that I would find her before it was too late.

Chapter Twenty Nine

Ariella

I DIDN'T KNOW if I would have time to write Brayden the letter, but I did it anyway. I had to let him know how I felt and how sorry I was for leaving him. He was probably never going to forgive me, and if I did survive I was sure he would never let me live it down. Dressed in my warrior gear, I changed my appearance to make myself look like one of our warriors.

No sooner had I gotten out of the palace and almost into the stables when Coran stopped me.

"Saddle up your horse, lad. The queen has gone missing and we need to find her," he relayed quickly. "Meet the others at the gate." He didn't even wait for an answer, but ran off inside the palace.

That was quick, I thought to myself. I didn't expect them to search for me so soon. Lennox whinnied in his stall, and I knew he had to be confused. To him I smelled like Ariella, but I didn't look it. It was strange being a female and impersonating a male. It wasn't something I liked doing, but I had no choice.

Lennox sniffed me curiously as I rubbed his soft, white mane. I whispered in his ear, "It's me, Lennox, but I can't take you this time. I don't want anyone recognizing me."

I kissed him on the muzzle and saddled up the brown and white spotted mare beside him; I had no clue which warrior she belonged to.

"You are a beauty," I said to her.

She nuzzled me and blew out her breath. After I buckled everything down, I mounted her and rode quickly out of the stables. I immediately headed away from the palace, toward the front gate.

While trying to sneak out, I could feel Brayden's anguish like a knife to my chest. His pain was my pain and it felt terrible. I wanted to open my mind so I could speak to him, but if I did that I would probably lose my courage and go back. Coran's voice echoed against the wind as he updated the warriors' on my status. The sound of hoof beats thumped across the ground, and only seconds later they came into view thundering toward the gate. The doors opened and the riders blazed through like the speed of lightning. I joined in and followed them as we left the Winter Court and its protection behind.

No one even noticed they picked up a stray rider. Instead, they all kept their eyes on the forest and the surrounding foliage, looking for attackers while they searched for me. Without being noticed, I ambled off toward the woods and snuck away quietly. There were evil scouts that patrolled the forest so I knew I was bound to run into someone, but I didn't expect it to be the person who showed up … a person who was no longer a part of our realm and someone who had just recently become a pain in my ass.

"I knew you were up to no good," he said, pursing his lips. "And I must say that seeing you as a man is kind of weird. Does Brayden know you can do this?" Riding alongside me, or better yet, appearing right beside me, was Merrick on a majestic silver colored mare with eyes as black as coal.

"What are you doing here?" I hissed. "And how did you know it was me?"

Nonchalantly, he shrugged and rubbed the back of his neck with his hand, looking sheepish. "Well, let's see …" He paused for a minute and cleared his throat before admitting, "I was watching you, but not in a creepy sort of way. I followed you to your room and slipped inside without you noticing. Needless to say it was a shock when I saw you turn into a man. You don't actually …" He shuddered, glancing down at my waist and then back up to my eyes, lifting a curious brow.

"Really," I snapped, rolling my eyes. "Why are you going to ask me a question like that? No, I don't have man parts if that's what you're wondering. It's a glamour, Merrick. I don't go into all the fine details when it comes to certain parts of the body. I'm sure I could if I wanted to, but that's not really what I'm interested in."

He held his hands up in defeat. "Okay, I was just curious. So what is your plan exactly?"

We were only a quarter of the way through the Mystical Forest so we still had a good ride ahead of us before we would get to the sorcerer. I was hoping to get there before dawn, and if we rode hard it was a possibility.

Slowing our pace to a trot, I sighed and explained, "There's not much to tell really. I'm going to the Black Forest, and once I get close to Alasdair I'm going to kill him."

"Do you think it'll be that easy?" Merrick asked skeptically. "You're not going to get anywhere near him looking like that. You'll just be another worthless faerie in his army."

"I know that, Merrick. Believe it or not I have thought about this. I'm going to watch the sorcerer and find out who he trusts most. Once I figure that out, I'll glamour myself and get close to him that way. I know what I'm doing."

Groaning, Merrick nodded. "Well, then I guess it's a good thing I came along. I happen to know who the creature is that you seek. He was the one who helped Warren and Avery take Calista when the sorcerer was after her."

"Then it must be fate that brought you to me."

We rode for another couple of hours until the fatigue finally set in and I almost fell off my horse; I would have if Merrick didn't catch me in his arms. I was too tired to keep up the glamour, so I was back to my normal self, but what really shocked me was the feel of Merrick's skin against mine as he caught me.

"I didn't know you could touch me," I mumbled sleepily. "Can you touch Calista when you're around her?"

Merrick carried me over to a soft, patchy area of green grass and laid me down on a blanket he'd just spread out. Sadly, he shook his head and answered, "No, I can't touch her. The only time I can touch her is when Sorcha has us in the dream realm together."

"Then why can you touch me?" I wondered.

"I'm not sure. I didn't even know I could until I saw you falling off your horse. It's an amazing feeling to be able to touch someone other than in the Hereafter. It makes me almost feel alive."

"I'm glad," I murmured, my eyelids growing heavier. Merrick sat down beside me and put his arm around me.

"Go to sleep, Ariella. I'll watch over you tonight and wake you up if I hear someone coming."

Nodding, I snuggled into his side, and before I could reply I drifted off into an uneasy slumber. I should've known that sleep wouldn't keep my heart safe.

Chapter Thirty

Brayden

AS I WAITED on Sorcha to call Ariella into the dream realm, I paced along the snow and ice, contemplating what I was going to say to her. What the hell was I going to say? Come home?

"I've got her," Sorcha said as soon as she opened her eyes. "Don't be too hard on her, brother. She's only doing what the rest of us would've done. I'm sorry I didn't tell you that I knew. I told her I wouldn't unless she decided to do something like this."

She backed away and disappeared through the trees so I could have my time with Ariella. I wasn't happy knowing that my own family knew of Ariella's fate and I didn't.

Would I have handled things differently? Probably. However, nothing was going to stand in the way of me bonding with her. I would've spent the time I had trying to find ways to keep her safe and away from her fate.

I could feel her presence long before she actually appeared in the dream realm. Her long blonde hair hung loose around her shoulders, giving her face an ethereal look, and with her pale, glimmering skin there was no doubt that she could pass for a real angel ... she was my angel. When she turned around she wasn't surprised to see me.

Her eyes glistened with tears and her lips trembled when she cried, "Brayden, I'm so sorry. I didn't want to hurt you." Hearing her voice was all it took to tear me apart inside.

Rushing to her, I grabbed her around the waist and held her tight against me, so tight that I almost believed if I held on hard enough that she wouldn't be able to get away. "Please don't do this to me, Ariella. You don't have to do this alone," I pleaded.

She sobbed in my shoulder and held me almost as tight as I held her. "Yes, I do. I am the only one the sorcerer will trust, and if you come in and attack him we will lose. I will miss my chance. We might triumph in the end, but at what cost ... the lives of our people? We would risk and lose so much if we did that."

"I don't understand. How are you going to get the sorcerer to trust you?"

Before she could answer, the dream realm shifted and things started to fade. What was happening? Sorcha ran toward us and exclaimed, "She's waking up! She shouldn't be waking up now!"

"What?" I shouted.

That couldn't be so. We had only been in the dream realm for a matter of minutes. There was no way it could be over. Ariella closed her eyes and agreed, "She's right. I can feel myself trying to wake up. Merrick said he would wake me up if someone comes. There must be something going on."

"Wait ... Merrick is with you?" I asked angrily. "He better be glad he's a ghost because if I could hurt him right now I would."

"He's helping me," she claimed. "And at least I'm not alone."

Sighing, I breathed her in and crushed her lips with mine, tasting the sweetness of her Winter essence on her tongue. I took in the scent of her, my court in every fiber of her being. She was my lover, my queen, and ... my wife. I was never going to let her go, I couldn't.

"You will never be alone," I told her.

She gripped my arm, her eyes blazing. "Promise me you won't come for me, Brayden. Promise me!"

She began to fade, her body slowly disappearing before my eyes, while the grip she had on my arm started to loosen. I wish I could promise her, but that would be a lie.

"Promise me," she repeated more forcefully.

Shaking my head, I gazed into her tear-filled ice blue eyes and responded, "I can't promise that, angel. Can you honestly say you wouldn't come for me in this situation?"

She lowered her gaze and sighed, knowing very well that I knew her answer. When she lifted her head, the tears had streamed down her cheeks, and she was fading faster. Before she was completely taken out of the dream realm I did promise her one thing.

"I will always come for you, angel. That is what I promise you."

Then ... she was gone.

Chapter Thirty One

Ariella

"ARIELLA, WAKE UP," Merrick demanded, shaking me by the shoulders.

I gasped and opened my eyes. Immediately I wanted to go back into the dream realm to be with Brayden. Merrick breathed a sigh of relief and took my hand, lifting me up off the ground. "I tried waking you up for over a minute. It was like you were somewhere else, but you were crying."

"I *was* somewhere else," I said, wiping away the tears with the back of my hand. "I was in the dream realm with Brayden."

Merrick frowned and squeezed my hand. "I'm sorry I had to wake you and take you away from him, but we need to get out of here."

"What's going on? How long was I out?"

Quickly, he pulled me to our horses and lifted me up onto mine. "You only slept for about an hour when I started to hear noises out in the distance. I can hear someone coming and it's not just a couple of people I'm talking about. By the sounds of the vibrations on the ground we're looking at a whole army. I don't know if they are our allies or if it's the sorcerer's army, but I don't plan on sticking around to find out. Glamour yourself and let's get out of here."

Taking a deep breath, I concentrated on making myself look like a male Winter warrior and grabbed onto the reins. "Let's go," I ordered.

We set off at a brisk pace through the forest, going in the opposite direction from the unidentified army marching toward the courts. As long as our people stayed behind the gates they would be protected. At the moment, it wasn't them that needed protecting, but me. A quick glance behind me showed not only one, but two riders following our trail and gaining ground.

"Faster, Ariella," Merrick shouted. He couldn't be seen or heard by anyone other than me, so basically I was out in the woods alone with two riders chasing me down. I pushed my horse faster, but it was no use. The others were quicker and more agile than the horse I was on. If I was on Lennox there was no way anyone could ever catch me.

The second I heard the arrow zip through the air I knew it was over. My horse cried and bucked—throwing me off in the process—as the arrow stuck into her backside. She flung me up against a tree and the breath whooshed out of me, leaving me breathless and gasping as I fell to the ground with a hard thud. My traitorous horse whinnied and galloped away into the darkness, heading straight back home.

"Merrick," I choked out on a whisper. My head took a nasty hit and my vision was going from blurry to dark and back again. I tried to get up, but the pain in my head from hitting the tree was too much.

"You're losing your glamour, Ariella," Merrick growled impatiently, shaking me by the shoulders. "Dammit, wake up. I won't be able to fight them for you." I heard him getting angrier and cussing as my chasers dismounted their horses and took slow, curious steps toward me. The pain in my head pounded harder, but if these were minions of the dark sorcerer I was going to take them out no matter what.

Taking a few deep breaths, I grasped the handle of the dagger and slowly pulled it out of its sheath. It wasn't until I heard one of the riders speak that I realized who they were. My glamour was gone, and even from a distance I knew they would be able to tell who I was. Relaxing my hold on the dagger, I breathed a sigh of relief and let my head rest lightly on the ground.

"What are you doing?" Merrick hissed.

"It's okay," I whispered. "I know who they are. They aren't going to hurt me."

"Who are they?"

I couldn't reply because in the next instant, a pair of midnight blue eyes and stark, white blond hair came into my field of vision. The man above me had changed since the last time I saw him, but his angelic face had stayed the same. The hair that used to hang low down his back was now cut shorter and tousled in messy spikes on top of his head. It didn't take away from the ethereal beauty of his race; it made him more handsome.

He scooped me up off the ground and sighed heavily. "Holy hell, Your Highness, please forgive me. My eyes must have deceived me because I could have sworn I was chasing a warrior."

"You were," I told him groggily. I was exhausted and in pain, and I didn't want to lose consciousness … not yet.

Carrying me in his arms, he managed to mount his horse by pulling up on the saddle with one hand and keeping me balanced with the other. "Are you hurt?" he asked softly.

He touched the back of my head and I winced. "Just right there where you touched. My horse knocked me off when you shot her. I think you owe me big time after this."

"I don't know if I can ever make up for hurting you, Ariella. I was told you had gone missing so we've been trying to track you down. We need to get you home where you'll be safe. We were on our way there in hopes we could intercept you when one of my men scouted you out. He thought you were a traitor headed toward the Black Forest."

"You can't take me home," I pleaded, my eyes wide. "I will do whatever you want me to just please don't take me back. Everything I've done would be for nothing. Please, Bastian …"

Bastian groaned and closed his eyes. "You do realize how this will complicate things if Bayleon finds out I found you and didn't bring you back. Not only will I have his wrath, but your lover's as well. I think I need something in return for this favor," he decided.

"What happened to owing me?" I muttered incredulously.

"What happened to doing whatever I want just so I wouldn't take you back?" he countered mockingly.

Merrick smirked. "This guy is good. I guess with being what he is he perfected the art of manipulation over the years."

Narrowing my gaze, I huffed and pursed my lips at Bastian, ignoring Merrick's comment. "Fine, what do you want?"

Smiling, he pulled on the reins and we set off deeper into the woods. "I only want one night with you, Ariella. Now that you are queen, I know I will never get a night like this for as long as I live."

"What do you mean by one night with me, Bastian? You know I can't give you what you want," I murmured warily.

He sighed and rolled his eyes. "I know that and I would never ask that of you unless you came to me willingly. I can feel it in your soul how much you love your king and I know you would never betray that bond."

"Then what is it that you want?"

Bastian gazed up at the dark sky and then down to me. I was still clutched in his arms as we rode through the blackness of the Mystical Forest. "There are only a couple of hours left until dawn. All I want is for you to talk to me like you had before, like I was someone who was worthy of your time."

"But you are worthy, Bastian. You can't help the way you were born. I just wish there was a way I could break the curse on your people. I do want to see you happy," I uttered wholeheartedly.

He smiled and held me tighter. "Being with you tonight will make me happy. You have no idea how much. I promise to let you go at dawn."

"Thank you, Bastian. It means a lot," I said.

"Anything for you."

Chapter Thirty Two

Ariella

BASTIAN AND KRILL, the other Tyvar who had helped chase me down, built a small camp under the canopy of trees on the outskirts of the Mystical Forest. Merrick stayed with me the entire time, sitting in the corner of the little hut that Bastian and Krill made as our makeshift shelter. For the past couple of hours, I talked to him about many things ... normal things, and also the fact that I could see my sister's dead guardian and that he was accompanying us. I wasn't too sure if he believed me or not since I took a hard hit to the head.

Bastian wasn't accustomed to having a female around that could talk to him without wanting to rip his clothes off. You would think that would be any guy's dream to have naked women around you all the time, but I was wrong. I felt how lonely and sad he was not knowing what it would be like to have a normal life. He got a taste for it with Meliantha when she kissed him, and I could see it in his eyes that he wanted to feel it again.

"You never told me what you were doing out here, Ariella. I want to know why you don't want me to take you back to your king. Did he do something to you?" he asked, clenching his jaw.

"No," I cried, shaking my head. "Brayden would never do anything to harm me. You're not going to like what I tell you, but unfortunately, it's the way things have to be."

I swallowed down the last handful of berries and took a sip of water. I couldn't believe how hungry I was. Bastian already knew basically everything because of Meliantha. However, he didn't know about the scroll and what it said. Quickly, I told him about the dagger I carried and how I was the one who needed to kill the sorcerer. I skirted over the fact that I might not survive it.

"You're going to do what?" he demanded angrily, jumping to his feet. Merrick, fully alert now, got to his feet as well and stood above me. It was strange to think that I could see him in front of me, but Bastian couldn't. Bastian continued in a low growl, "If I would've known this was going to happen I wouldn't have agreed to let you go. From what you're telling me it sounds like you won't be making it home from the Black Forest. Is that what you're telling me?"

Still sitting on the ground, I gazed up at him and nodded. "Yes," I whispered. "That's why I had to leave. If Brayden knew he wouldn't have let me go." I got to my feet and faced him. "I have to do this, Bastian."

He shook his head and glared at me. "The only way you are going is if I go with you," he argued. "And if you refuse I'll tie you up and carry you back to the Winter Court. Trust me, you don't want me to do that."

"No," I exclaimed. "I don't care what you threaten me with, I'm not going to let you put yourself in danger. The whole reason why I'm doing this alone is so I can keep you all safe and protect you."

Bastian scoffed and began saddling up his horse while Krill saddled up his own as well. Merrick elbowed me in the side to get my attention. "I know you don't want to put him in harm's way, but he would be able to help you. Yes, I'm here with you, but there's nothing I can do to protect you. I can only touch *you* and no one else."

"I said no," I hissed quietly.

Merrick sighed and squeezed my shoulder sympathetically. "I'm sorry, Ariella, but you're not going to be able to make that decision for him." Unfortunately, I knew he was right, but it didn't make it any easier to deal with. Risking myself was one thing, but risking one of my friends was another.

When Bastian got done with his horse he stalked over to me and took me by the arms, holding me firm. "You do not have a choice in this, Ariella. Either you let me go with you or I take you back. It is all up to you."

"Why are you doing this? I told you that the chance of surviving is practically none," I told him.

Nonchalantly, he shrugged and lifted me up on his horse while Krill held the reins. Probably so I wouldn't run off. "Then we will die together, Your Highness," Bastian stated. "I would rather die honorably with you by my side than live centuries with the curse of my people. I am going with you whether you like it or not."

Bastian quickly mounted Krill's horse and called him over. Before sending him off on foot, he explained to him what he wanted him to relay back to his people, "Krill, when you find Bayleon tell him to send word to Meliantha that her sister is fine, and that I am with her. I'm not going to let her do this alone."

Krill frowned and bowed his head, replying solemnly, "As you wish, Bastian. Safe journey to you."

The farewell hung heavily in the air and immediately I regretted ever agreeing to let him come with me. Bastian wasn't just a normal Tyvar, he was one of their leaders with a brother who would miss him if he didn't make it back alive. The thought was like a knife in my gut, twisting and opening me up to more pain and death. I was hurting everyone by my decision to leave, and it killed me to know I was causing so much heartache and grief.

Bastian clasped Krill's forearm and said his good-bye, "Farewell, my brother. If I don't return then hopefully one day I will see you in the Hereafter. I can only pray that I am worthy enough to be set free."

Krill bowed to both of us and then set off at a brisk pace through the trees. I watched him disappear and imagined how angry Brayden and the others were going to be when they found out Bastian went against orders and didn't bring me in. If we survived this ordeal, the outcome wasn't going to be good.

"Why do you have that look on your face?" Bastian asked curiously. He sidled up to my right side while Merrick took up my left.

I blew out a heavy sigh and gave him a withering glance. "You better hope we don't survive this," I told him.

"And why is that?" he asked, lifting a curious brow.

"Because," I started, "once Brayden finds out you're with me and didn't take me back, he's going to be angry enough to kill. I fear of what he will do to you if we make it out alive."

Bastian scoffed, "I am not worried, Your Highness. If he feels the need to fight me then he can. I am not easy to take down."

Neither was he.

Chapter Thirty Three

Ariella

TRAIPSING ACROSS THE barren land to get to the Black Forest was ominous at best. Each step took us closer and closer to our doom and to the unknown. Merrick described what it was like on the way there, and I explained it all to Bastian as Merrick spoke. We were on the edge of the forest where the dark, oily trees stood high into the sky, filtering out all shades of sunlight. I shivered just gazing up at them.

"You might want to glamour yourself now," Merrick suggested.

I nodded and turned to him. "Good idea, but as what? We need to find this Gothin you spoke of and kill him. What is the best way to get to him?"

Bastian spoke up, "It is simple, Your Highness. No one could deny a beautiful female, especially if she's taken prisoner and entranced with the Tyvar curse. With me joining their side, I could offer you to him and that would get you close."

I groaned. "Okay, so female it is."

I knew the sorcerer liked the Summer Fae women more so than any others, so I glamoured myself to be golden skinned with a hint of red in a shade of golden blonde hair and green eyes. I took characteristics of my sisters and Sorcha and put them all into one. Merrick and Bastian both sucked in a sharp breath, their eyes wide.

"What do you think?" I asked, glancing back and forth to both of them.

Merrick smiled and reached over to touch my cheek. "You look so much like Calista right now."

He tenderly grazed my cheek and then pulled back when he realized what he was doing. My heart ached for him because I knew he wished Calista could see him and talk to him like I was doing. Seeing each other in the dream realm wasn't exactly the same as seeing each other in real time. Not to mention he couldn't touch her like he could touch me.

Bastian took a strand of my hair and rolled it through his fingers, smiling as he looked into my eyes. "I can see traces of Meliantha in you," he murmured. "She's a beautiful woman, but no one could ever be as beautiful as you. They aren't going to be able to resist when they see you."

"Thank you," I uttered kindly. I then turned to Merrick and said, "I think we're ready. Lead the way. I don't know where we're going."

He grunted. "Unfortunately, I do. Once we get to the middle of the forest we will come to a village. The sorcerer's dwelling is inside the massive tree you will see. You won't be able to miss it. The troll you want to find should be close by there. I'm sure someone will lead us to him."

Merrick took the lead while Bastian and I followed side by side behind him. As soon as we entered into the forest it was like all life had been sucked out of everything around us. The air smelled like death and decay, and everywhere I turned there was nothing except blackness. I guess it got its name for a reason.

I placed a hand on my dagger and took a deep breath. It felt so right in my hand that I knew I was meant for this, like it was made exactly for me. "Are you ready for this?" Merrick asked, turning his head so he could glance back at me.

I nodded, but I couldn't deny that I was a little nervous. *What if I failed?*

The whole time we rode through the forest I could hear the blood pounding in my ears and the shallowness of my breath as I tried to breathe. I had never been surrounded by so much evil and death, and hearing the erratic beating of my heart didn't help. Abruptly, Merrick came to a stop and held up his hand for us to halt. He pointed to an area up ahead where I could see the first sign of lights and hear the far away chatter of the sorcerer's army.

"We're almost there," Merrick informed us. "You might want to hide your dagger as well." I did as he said and hid it under my shirt behind my back. "When you get into the village, just get Bastian to ask someone how to find Gothin. I'm hoping that works, but if not I know what he looks like. Also, it might be good for you two to ride on the same horse going in."

"Why?" I asked incredulously.

Exasperated, Merrick rolled his eyes and said, "If you're supposed to be Bastian's sex slave, don't you think you would be a little bit closer to him than that. I thought the women who got enamored by them couldn't keep their hands away."

Groaning, I turned to look at Bastian who had a bewildered look on his face. "What's wrong?" he asked.

"Merrick thinks we should ride in on the same horse together since I'm supposed to be your sex slave and all," I answered matter-of-factly. Bastian tried to hold back his smile and failed. "Don't get any ideas," I snapped at him. "It will only add to Brayden's wrath if we make it out alive."

Bastian shook his head and slid back to make more room in front of him. He patted the saddle with his hand, a big smile on his face. "I would be foolish to not take advantage of this situation. *If* is the key word here, Your Highness. If I am going to die then why shouldn't I enjoy what little bit of joy I have left? I would gladly submit to the wrath of your lover just to be here with you."

Merrick lifted a brow and chuckled. "He has it bad for you, doesn't he? No wonder Kalen doesn't like it when Meliantha gets visits from him and his brother." I laughed and rolled my eyes knowing very well none of it was funny, but I had to find humor somewhere to get my mind off of what we were about to do. It was probably the last laugh I would have.

Slowly, I climbed down from my horse and took Bastian's hand so he could pull me up in front of him. He wrapped his arms around my waist with one across my stomach while the other held onto the reins. "Let's go, lover," he whispered jokingly in my ear.

"Keep it up, Bastian," I warned halfheartedly. He chuckled low in my ear and held me tighter just to mess with me.

As we approached the village there were guards stationed at the entrance. "Make sure you ask for Gothin," I told him quietly. Our time for joking was over.

I could feel him nod and tense behind me when the two giant Redcaps stopped us at the entrance. "Who are ye?" one of them said in a gruff voice. The blood from his cap ran in rivulets down the sides of his face. He smelled of raw meat and the metallic scent of the blood pulsing out of his cap.

"I am looking for Gothin," Bastian announced. "I was told he was the one I needed to find. I have a gift for the sorcerer."

The other Redcap approached from the other side and poked me in the leg with his pikestaff, piercing my skin through the leather pants I was wearing. The blood pooled by the wound and slowly drifted down my leg. Before the blood could fall to the ground, the Redcap took off his cap and soaked it up like a starved animal. Bastian growled low in his throat and held me tighter while I held my breath, hoping that it wouldn't come down to a fight.

When the Redcap placed the cap back on his head, he closed his eyes, releasing a contented sigh, and staggered forward as if he was drunk. "Aye, tis a nice gift ye have there," he said admiringly.

"So can we pass?" Bastian questioned impatiently through clenched teeth. I could feel the anger emanating off of him, and I knew that if they didn't let us pass he was going to attack.

The Redcap who took my blood immediately stepped aside and replied, "Aye, ye can pass." The other one glanced at us warily before slowly moving out of the way and letting us go.

Without wasting any time, Merrick, Bastian, and I entered on our horses and steadily made it through the camp. There were creatures everywhere: faeries, trolls, Redcaps, leprechauns, dwarves, and even some elves. They all stared at us like wolves as we sauntered past them, and I prayed that they wouldn't stop us. I couldn't believe the amount of people who had turned on our courts.

"Just keep going," Merrick assured us. "Do not stop until we get to Gothin. I know where he'll be."

We followed him until we got to the massive tree which stood as the sorcerer's private dwelling. Merrick had been in this exact same spot years ago when he and Ryder were waiting to save Calista. It was the same day he died, the same day my sister's heart broke. Bastian dismounted and inspected the wound on my leg from where the Redcap punctured me.

"Are you okay?" he asked.

I gazed down at my leg, and since we healed fast the wound had already started to close up. I nodded and answered him, "Yeah, I'm fine. It didn't hurt as much as it pissed me off. I was afraid we were going to fight."

"I thought so, too. I did not like what he did to you at all."

I smiled up at him. "I've had worse done. Believe me."

"All right, you two, let's go," Merrick called. "We need to find Gothin before the sorcerer finds *you*." He stared at various places in the village and then pointed to a building off to our right. "And I do believe we will find the troll in there."

"Why is that?" I asked, hooking a glance over my shoulder.

Oh, that's why. It didn't take me long to figure it out. The place looked like a dingy bar, all dark and disgusting, with nasty drunken men that you would see in the mortal realm. What made it even more like that were the trolls gathered around outside, toppling over each other with mugs of liquid in their hands. They were celebrating, and I knew why.

Bastian whispered in my ear, "I'm not going to hurt you, but go along with what I do. When we find Gothin we need to get him alone."

"And then kill him," I finished for him.

Taking my arm, he pulled me along behind him as we approached the building. Trolls were hideous creatures—with their warty faces, bad teeth, and various sized bodies—who probably never saw a bar of soap in their life. You could smell them from a mile away, and the ones here definitely didn't disappoint. Some of them were short and stocky while some were tall and lean. Out of all the creatures in the land it made me wonder how a disgusting creature like a troll could ever be the sorcerer's right hand man.

Ascending the steps, I followed behind Bastian and entered into the dank building that smelled of trolls and urine. The whole room fell silent as they spied us. "I'm looking for Gothin," Bastian called out.

All heads turned to the one troll at the back table who was sandwiched in by two faerie women. They looked worn and haggard, and immediately my hackles rose. An overwhelming sense of disgust swarmed through my body. I wanted to rip him in two and laugh while I did it. I wanted to save them, to get them out of this hell hole that they'd probably been living in for years with no hope of ever being saved.

Bastian gripped my hand tighter and shook his head. "Patience," he whispered. "We will get them out of here."

Gothin stood and eyed me curiously as we approached him. He had pointed, rotten teeth, and still smelled foul like the others, but also happened to be dressed better than them, too. "What do you want?" he grunted. "As you can see I am busy."

Bastian jerked me forward and pushed me toward the troll. "I have a gift for the sorcerer. I think he would find her to his satisfaction."

"Indeed," Gothin approved.

Dismissing the faerie women with a flick of his hand, he narrowed his gaze and ran his dark, beady eyes up and down my body like a vulture, while rubbing his scruffy chin. "Yes, I think she will do just fine. I can take her from here," he insisted greedily, licking his lips. "The master is not here for the time being, but she will be happy in my care until he returns."

Like hell I would be. Where the hell was the sorcerer?

The last thing we needed was to have to stay in the Black Forest longer than necessary. The longer we were there the harder it would be to keep our cover. Over Gothin's shoulder, Merrick shrugged and disappeared out of the bar with determination. Hopefully, he would find some answers or hear something somewhere about Alasdair's whereabouts. Gothin held out his hand, but Bastian didn't want to let loose of his hold on me, so he hesitated.

"I told you I can take her from here," Gothin snapped. "You brought her to me so now you can go."

I squeezed his hand reassuringly, hoping he would understand my message. *I'll be fine*, I wanted to say to him. Letting go of his hand, I circled around the table and sat down in the chair beside Gothin. I nodded quickly at Bastian and glanced at the door, hoping he would get the hint. He needed to leave before he drew too much attention to himself. Reluctantly, he turned on his heel and marched out the front door, never once looking back.

It was up to me now.

Chapter Thirty Four

Ariella

BASTIAN AND MERRICK were nowhere in sight when I left the trolls' meeting place with Gothin. Taking my arm in his slimy hand, Gothin quickly led me away from the curious onlookers. Pretending to be distressed, I gazed over at Gothin nervously and asked, "Where are we going?"

He grinned wolfishly at me with those rotten, pointy teeth. "I am taking you to my dwelling. A pretty little lass like yourself wouldn't last a night in the prison with my men."

The blood boiled in my veins as thoughts of helpless women without a way to protect themselves ran rampant through my mind. It sickened me to think that out of all the years the sorcerer had been here, there were probably thousands of women he'd had tortured and killed. Now that I was there it was going to stop.

I bit my tongue to keep from lashing out, and I clenched so hard I could taste the metallic essence of my blood going down my throat. I wanted to kill him and I wanted to kill Alasdair; I wanted to kill them all. I wanted them to suffer the way they'd made countless others suffer over the years, especially the people I loved.

Gothin's dwelling was a crappy little shack made from the oily black trees of the forest. I dreaded going inside, but I knew that I must. I took one last look around the village, hoping to catch a glimpse of Bastian or Merrick, but came up disappointed.

Where were they? I wondered.

Gothin pushed me inside and slammed the door behind me, barring it with a heavy wooden beam. There were no windows in his one room shack or even a bathroom, only a rickety old bed and some chairs. "Sit," he ordered, motioning toward the bed.

I could feel the dagger up against the bare skin of my back and I ached to have it in my hands and taking the life away from the worthless creature in front of me. I had never killed before, but I was ready. I was ready to show them once and for all that my people will triumph … we will save our land.

"When will the sorcerer be back?" I asked meekly.

Gothin grabbed a bundle of rope off of the floor and stalked over to me. He grabbed my legs and held them together while wrapping my ankles tightly with the rope. "The master will be back on the morrow. He is bringing over the mortals for the final battle."

"When does he plan on attacking?"

Gothin tightened the rope and it cut into my skin, drawing a line of blood. He glared at me and snarled impatiently, "You ask too many questions, lass. The only thing you need to be worried about is surviving tomorrow when the master has his way with you. Just sit tight and keep your mouth shut."

He got up to grab another bundle of rope, and turned his back away from me. That was a big mistake. Reaching behind my back, I slid the dagger out carefully and sliced it through the rope at my ankles. Quietly, I stalked over to Gothin and tapped him on the shoulder with the blade.

"See, that's the problem. I'm not the type of person to just sit tight and keep my mouth shut," I remarked.

With wide eyes, he turned around, glancing quickly from the tattered rope on the floor and then to me. "How did you …" he started, but then noticed the dagger in my hand. "Who are you?"

I smiled and grabbed him by the shoulders, forcing him up against the wall with the dagger at his throat. "You ask too many questions," I snarled in his face, repeating what he just said to me. "I think the only thing you need to be worried about is surviving the next few seconds. However, I will answer one question for you before you die."

The glamour I had shielding my true form slowly vanished, revealing who I really was … an Ice Queen. Gothin shook his head, his small beady eyes gazing at me first in disbelief, then to pure animosity. His breath stank of old, rotten meat when he teased, "I see you came into your power, Princess. It is a shame it won't be enough to defeat us."

I pressed the dagger into his skin and watched it sizzle and burn away like the iron blade does to our skin. His mouth flew open in panic, but before he could call for help I slapped my hand over his mouth and slammed his head against the wall.

"I'm not just a princess anymore you worthless sack of shit. I'm a queen," I hissed. "And judging by the way you look right now I would say that I have a pretty good chance at killing you … and him."

"How are you doing that?" he sneered, observing the dagger in my hand and trembling from pain. "This is impossible."

The skin around the puncture wound in his neck was slowly disintegrating and exposing the flesh and tendons underneath. I had never used the dagger on anyone before, so seeing it in action was interesting to say the least.

"Let's just say that things aren't always what they seem and leave it at that," I answered. "I hope you enjoy Hell because that's where you're going." Gripping the dagger firmly in my hands, I lifted it back and plunged it deep into Gothin's chest. He gasped for one quick second, his eyes wide and terrified, before he crumbled away into a dark pile of ash almost instantly. He was gone.

The first step had been accomplished. Unfortunately, the next stage in my plan required me to look like the hideous troll. Groaning, I concentrated on the gray skin, scraggly hair, and rotten teeth of the troll and willed my magic to do its work. As soon as I stepped outside the door of his rundown dwelling, a searing pain echoed throughout my head and I fell to my knees.

No, no, no ... this couldn't be happening! I screamed in my head. I knew what was going on, but I had to stop it. I couldn't let him in.

"Oh no," I said aloud, trying to keep my wall in place, but failing. When I glanced up, Merrick and Bastian were right there, cautiously approaching me but uncertain if it was me behind the glamour. "It's me," I whispered, cringing in pain.

Rushing to me, they helped me to my feet. "What's wrong?" they both asked at the same time.

In my mind, I could slowly see my protective wall crumbling piece by piece. There was nowhere to hide, nowhere to run, because once that wall came down I wouldn't be able to build it back up. It wasn't just his power tearing it down, but the power of the others.

"It's him," I wailed. "It's Brayden, and he's forcing himself into my mind. I don't think I can stop it." And I couldn't. Although the wall was barely hanging in there I could hear the tiniest echo of his voice calling my name.

"Ariella ..."

Chapter Thirty Five

Brayden

"WE'RE ALMOST THERE," I exclaimed triumphantly. Ariella had kept me blocked from her mind from the beginning of our bonding. She let me in a couple of times, but for the most part she refused to let me in. Not anymore. Forcing myself into her mind was not what I wanted to do, but she gave me no choice.

Her wall was strong, but Elvena had figured out a way to help break it down. We were standing in a circle; Elvena to my right, holding my hand, while Calista was on my left. All around the circle our families joined hands and lent me their power. The wall slowly began to disintegrate and I could feel Ariella behind it. She was alive, except the second our power pushed into her she felt it, and I could feel her heart break.

"Ariella ..." I waited for her to speak, but we hadn't gotten through to her yet. Just as we were about to break through the barrier, the door to the throne room burst open and Coran, my second in command, rushed in.

"Your Highness!" he shouted. When he saw my angry glare he continued quickly, "The Tyvar are here and they have word from the queen." Meliantha gasped, running out of the room, while Kalen and I followed behind her. "They are at the gate," Coran called out behind us.

Unfortunately, the Tyvar couldn't be allowed inside the walls because of their curse on women. I hated that we couldn't let them wander around our court, but it was too dangerous to put them near our faerie women. Meliantha reached the gate first and outside was the Tyvar leader, Bayleon, and a few of his men.

"Bayleon, what's going on?" Meliantha demanded breathlessly, grasping his hand through the gate.

Reluctantly, he smiled at her and kissed her hand, but didn't let it go. "I'm sorry to bring you this news, but—"

"But what?" I roared impatiently, catching his attention. "What do you know about my queen?"

Bayleon bowed his head and sighed regretfully. "It seems your queen has made it to the Black Forest, Your Highness."

No! She couldn't be there.

Never in my life had I succumbed to fear, but I couldn't stop it from tearing away at my soul. Ariella was there, alone, and surrounded by thousands of creatures, including the sorcerer who could tear her apart in seconds. "Did you see her? How do you know that?"

He hesitated for a second before responding, "No, I have not seen her. Apparently, my brother was the one who saw her and had sent one of our warriors to relay the message to me."

"Where is he now?" I demanded angrily. "I wish to speak to him." I had a feeling I knew where he would be, but I didn't want it to be so.

"Bastian went with her, Your Highness. He is sacrificing his life to keep her safe."

In that moment, I saw nothing but red. Bastian had found Ariella and didn't bring her back? If I ever saw him again I was going to kill him with my own bare hands. Shaking with pent up rage, I grabbed the bars of the gate and they bent under my grasp.

"Brother, calm down," Kalen said softly.

"Do not speak to me right now," I warned, glaring at him over my shoulder. Meliantha backed away and let go of Bayleon's hand as I took her place in front of him, eying him with nothing but fury in my gaze. "I am only going to say this once," I spat. Bayleon stared at me warily and nodded for me to continue. "Your brother better hopes he dies if anything happens to Ariella. If she dies and he survives he is going to have hell to pay, and in this case, death would be a lighter punishment compared to what I will do to him."

When all I got was silence, I turned on my heel and marched back into the palace. I wasn't going to sit idly by anymore. If no one was going to help me, I was going to go in alone. With my heart pounding, I pushed open the doors to the throne room and stood my ground.

"I'm going after her … now," I announced. "Even if I have to go alone, I'm going."

They all gaped at me uncertainly for a few seconds, but it didn't take long to get the approval I needed, and the help I wanted. Drake stepped forward and nodded. "I'm with you. They can't go up against the dragon," he said, grinning.

Sorcha snorted and glared at him. "I think you mean dragons," she retorted. Turning to me she said, "Besides, if you find out where she is we can fly in there quick and grab her. She's not going to be happy about that, though. She's risked her life to save us, and if we go in there it'll all be for nothing."

It was true, she had, but I was too selfish to let her go through with it alone. "I don't care," I argued. "She's my queen, and be that as it may we are supposed to make decisions together. She doesn't get the right to dictate how I am supposed to live out the rest of my life. I want her in it and I'll be damned if she throws it all away trying to save the world, not when we can help her."

Drake smirked and clapped me on the shoulder. "When will you ever learn that Ariella will do as she pleases? I've lived with her a lot longer than you and *nothing* ever stands in her way. The sooner you learn that, the better off you'll be. Now come on and let's go find her."

"I'm coming, too," Calista insisted, joining her brother's side. "I can ride on his back. He only flew with Ariella, so it'll be a first for me."

"And you can ride on mine," Sorcha added, elbowing me in the side.

"Thank you, to all of you. As soon as I get through to Ariella we leave," I announced.

As everyone fled the throne room, I stayed behind with Elvena. I needed her help to push through that last barrier to her. "Are you going to tell her you're coming for her?" she asked, taking my hands in hers.

Sighing, I shrugged my shoulders and said, "With how Ariella is I don't think it would be a good idea. She will just run away from me."

"She wouldn't be running away from you, child. That is the last thing she is doing."

I knew she wasn't running from me, but it sure didn't make it any easier with her blocking me out. Squeezing Elvena's hands, I closed my eyes and concentrated. Her power flowed through me and I could see it mingling with mine as we pushed against that barrier in Ariella's mind. When we first started it was like a thick slab of stone we had to push through, but now it was more like a pane of broken glass waiting for that last pebble to be thrown to make it shatter.

"We're almost there, child. Just keep concentrating," Elvena muttered.

The more we pushed, the more I could feel Ariella and her sadness. She knew what I was doing, but I wasn't going to back down. With as much force as I could muster, the barrier shook and shattered into a million pieces. I was in.

"Why?" she cried through the bond. *"Why are you making this harder on me?"*

"Because," I said, *"I love you and I am not ready to give you up."*

Chapter Thirty Six

Ariella

"ARE YOU OKAY? You're not hurt, are you?" Brayden asked.

Merrick and Bastian were both staring at me curiously, noses wrinkled in disgust. Since we were behind closed doors, I changed back into myself to make them feel more comfortable. It had to be strange knowing the grotesque creature in front of them was me.

"No, I'm not hurt physically, but emotionally is a different story."

"I'm sorry for what I did. I just had to know you were all right. Bayleon came to us today and told me about Bastian. Needless to say, I was not happy with what I heard."

"He's only trying to help me, and so is Merrick," I replied, feeling defeated.

"It should be me helping you!" I could feel the anger flowing off of him and pouring through our bond. He was close to losing it and it was all my fault.

Gently, Merrick tapped my arm and asked, "Are you talking to him now?"

Sighing, I nodded and hung my head. "Yes, and he's not happy with me, and especially, with Bastian."

"Brayden, I understand you're angry but I'm doing fine on my own. The sorcerer isn't even here right now. He's in the mortal realm getting his army. He's planning on bringing them over tomorrow. I have to be here to stop him before he gets them all here."

"What are you doing now?"

I glanced over at the corner where Gothin's ashes still remained on the dingy floor. *"If you must know, I'm staring at Gothin's ashes that are scattered on the floor."*

"Isn't that the sorcerer's right hand man? Did you kill him?"

"Yes," I assured him. *"I killed him with the dagger. It was strange because when I pierced him with it, it devoured his skin like iron does to ours. I had never seen anything like it."*

"Where are you now?"

"I'm in Gothin's home hiding out with Merrick and Bastian ... why?"

"That's all I needed to know," he said adamantly. His tone made me pause, and if it wasn't for the sinking feeling in my stomach I wouldn't think anything of it. However, something wasn't right and I could feel it as sure as I could feel my heart beating.

"Brayden, what's going on? I think the question right now is where are you? What the hell are you doing?" I waited for him to answer, but he never did.

My eyes went wide as Merrick jumped out of his seat and disappeared almost instantly. The air around us turned electric and hummed with the buzzing of power. Bastian felt it too and got to his feet immediately, rushing to the door. I glamoured myself to look like Gothin again and joined him.

"Can you feel it, Your Highness?" Bastian questioned, eyeing the people in the village. They were on full alert; they could feel it, too.

"He's coming ..."

As soon as I finished saying that, the forest lit up with the heat and blaze of a dragon's fire ... my brother's fire. *"Brayden! What are you doing?"* I screamed in his mind.

"I am getting you back, angel. You left me no choice. I told you I would always come for you and I am going to uphold that promise."

I grabbed Bastian's arm and pulled him out the door. "Let's go," I yelled, taking off toward one of the prisons.

It was the perfect time to get the prisoners out while the village was in disarray. The dragon roar from my brother sounded overhead, but then another battle cry screamed out in unison. It was Sorcha. They were getting ready to swoop and attack. Stopping outside of the prison doors, I turned to Bastian and said quickly, "Go to the horses and grab my bag. I need you to bring it here. Hurry!"

He nodded and took off through the village. Merrick finally appeared again and followed me into the prison. I noticed that most of the people in the cells were women, and they cowered away from me when I opened the doors. "You're free!" I shouted. "As soon as you get out of here run as fast as you can out of the forest. Help will come."

"They're scared of you, Ariella," Merrick said. "They see Gothin when they look at you."

Oh, no! Merrick was right; no wonder they were shaking and terrified. Dirty and starving, I could tell some of them were from the Summer Court and some of them were from Winter. *Will they ever recover from this?* I wondered.

"Who?" Brayden asked, interrupting my inner thought.

"These women in the prison," I said, frustrated. *"I'm freeing them. They are going to need help."*

Briskly, I transformed in front of their eyes and bent down to their level. I had no clue if they knew who I was or how long they had been there. They gasped and cried, but I cut them off, knowing we had to hurry. "Listen, I'm Ariella, former Princess of the Summer Court and now Queen of the Winter. Please, I need you to get up and get out of here."

"What about the sorcerer, and how did you come in here looking like that disgusting troll?" one of them asked, getting up on her shaky feet. I grabbed her hand and helped her, making sure she was settled before letting her go.

"One of my powers is the ability to shift into other people. I killed Gothin so I could get to the sorcerer and kill him. So hurry, I need you to get out of here," I ordered, pulling the others to their feet. They swiftly ran out of the cell and out the door, praising me with their thanks. I could only hope they made it to safety. It was a better chance than being locked away in the prison.

There was one woman, however, who wasn't moving nor was she conscious. She was a Winter fae, but with all the dirt and grime on her you could barely tell. I lifted her frail body in my arms and carried her to the door at the same time Bastian stormed in carrying my bag.

He dropped the bag and held out his arms. "Give her to me, Ariella. I'll carry her."

I passed her to him and bent down to open my bag. There was one thing I packed that could be used to my advantage, except the thought of deceiving the people I cared about almost made me not do it. The blue cloak from Brayden that I wore on our bonding night lay neatly bundled in my bag. I ran my fingers gently over its silky fabric as I remembered that night and how much I missed him.

Screams of death echoed outside and it brought me out of my thoughts. I grabbed the cloak and draped it over the woman in Bastian's arms. If she woke up she would need her eyes hidden away from him or she'd be under his spell forever. Bastian understood why I covered her face and nodded solemnly. However, it wasn't the only reason why I did it.

The ground shook like an earthquake was tearing our world apart, and then out of nowhere, my brother and Sorcha landed side by side in the middle of the village. That was also the moment when I saw … him. Sitting atop Sorcha's red dragon skin, fierce and in full control, Brayden had his sword drawn looking like an avenging angel in his black and silver armor.

I wanted to run to him and never let go, but the other part of me wanted to beat the shit out of him for putting himself in danger as well as the others. Calista and Ryder were both riding on Drake's back, using their magic to help fight off the sorcerer's army as they searched around the area. I knew who they were searching for … me.

The sound of arrows whizzing through the air made my blood run cold. One after the other, hundreds of arrows stuck through Drake and Sorcha's skin.

"No!" I screamed.

"Ariella, where are you?" Brayden demanded. *"We need to get out of here now!"*

Tears streamed down my face because doing what I was about to do hurt worse than an arrow piercing through my heart. Swallowing back the guilt, I leaned up against the wall, out of sight, and said, *"I'm in the prison with Bastian. We're coming out."*

Quickly wiping away the tears, I grabbed Bastian's arm and pushed him toward the door. "Go," I shouted. "Get her out of here and somewhere safe. I'll be right behind you."

"Why do I not believe you?" he asked, eyeing me with skepticism.

"Because you shouldn't," Merrick snorted, even though Bastian couldn't hear him. I ignored the jab and pushed Bastian out the door.

"Because you're an ass, now go!" I repeated with more force, glaring at Merrick and then to Bastian.

He took off without another question and headed straight for the woods, away from Sorcha and Drake. However, he didn't get very far. As soon as Sorcha and Brayden spotted him they did what I'd hoped they would do … they took him. Sorcha extended a giant claw and wrapped it around Bastian's body, securing him in her grasp. Back in Gothin form, I watched from the doorway as Drake and Sorcha prepared to take off into the black abyss, thinking I was the girl in Bastian's arms.

Glancing quickly my way, Bastian pounded against Sorcha's claw and yelled, "No, Ariella. Don't do this!" He kept fighting as Sorcha lifted up into the trees. I waved him good-bye and wished with all my heart that one day he would realize how sorry I was.

"We've got you, angel," Brayden murmured in my mind. I gave him one final glance as I watched him smile, thinking he had me in his grasp. Oh, how I would miss that smile. A smile he never let the world see until me. Would he ever smile again after this?

"Yes, you do," I cried. *"You will always have me."*

I watched as they took off into the trees and out of the inky blackness of my doom. They were gone in an instant, but at least it would give me the time I needed. The sorcerer would be back soon, and I had to make sure I ended him before he could strike back.

"I know that was hard," Merrick whispered, coming to my side.

I collapsed onto the muddy floor of the empty prison and covered my face with my hands. Merrick wrapped his arm around my shoulders and rocked me back and forth, murmuring that everything would be all right in my ear. There were no thoughts or words that could describe the agony I felt deceiving them the way I did … especially Brayden.

I was where I needed to be, and alone the way it should've been from the beginning. I just wished my heart would stop feeling like it would rip out of my chest. I would rather face death.

L. P. DOVER

Chapter Thirty Seven

Brayden

WE SUCCEEDED. I got her back.

It wasn't until nightfall that I saw the icy terrain of my court, the Winter Court. I breathed a sigh of relief and enjoyed the ride through the air on my sister's back as she flew majestically through the night sky. Her red dragon skin almost glowed in the moonlight along with Drake's green emerald glow right beside us.

Even though they took a few hits with the arrows, they still seemed to be going strong. Now that Ariella was back and all the secrets had been unveiled we could finally work together and fight together. This was the way it should've been from the beginning, but Ariella's hard headedness got in the way. If only I knew sooner what she was going through.

The horns blared as we approached the palace and down below I could see everyone coming out to see if we succeeded. Circling around and descending lower, Sorcha landed gracefully and so did Drake. I slid off of Sorcha's back and climbed the rest of the way down her body. My father and King Oberon, as well as Meliantha and Kalen, were crowded around Sorcha's claws where Bastian was slowly getting to his feet with Ariella in his arms. Calista and Ryder joined me almost immediately after they dismounted from Drake's scaly back.

"Give her to me," I snapped, glaring at Bastian and taking Ariella away from him. The cloak I gave her was draped over her face and body, and the moment I touched her skin I knew something was wrong.

"What the …" I started, but then stopped.

Immediately, I removed the cover from her face and my heart sank. It tore out of my chest and went right back to the Black Forest where I knew my angel was still in hell. She wasn't in my arms; she wasn't where she was supposed to be. She deceived me, and I had failed.

Coran was by my side in an instant and I passed the woman in my arms to him, glaring at Bastian the whole time. The air turned electric with both his and my power as we faced off at each other.

"What the hell is this?" I demanded angrily. "First, you defy my orders to bring Ariella back and instead you take her straight to the Black Forest. Second, you pull this stunt wanting me to believe you have her in your arms. If she didn't care about you, you would be dead at my feet right now."

"You are not the only one she deceived, Your Highness. I am just as angry as you are," he spat. "I did not know she was going to do what she did."

I scoffed. "Well, that makes us both fools."

Calista jumped between us and pushed us apart. "That's enough you two. There's nothing we can do about it now. I'm sure what Ariella did was just as hard on her as it was on you." She glared at us both before continuing, "It's late, and we need to rest up before tomorrow. We attack at dawn."

I turned away before I said or did something I'd regret and stormed into the palace. *"Ariella! Answer me, dammit!"* I exclaimed in her mind, my hands shaking with fury as I marched to our room. There was nothing but silence on the other end. She was still there because I could feel her, but in her mind there was nothing except floating colors and vague images. That could only mean one thing ... she was sleeping.

I knew just what to do.

Chapter
Thirty Eight

Ariella

I STRUGGLED TO stay awake as Merrick held me in his arms. I remembered him lifting me up off the prison floor and carrying me away into the dark destruction of the Black Forest. My brother and Sorcha did a lot of damage with their fire and frost, but it wasn't enough to deter the sorcerer's army. When Alasdair got back, there was going to be vengeance to pay. I would have to work quickly to stop him before he could attack.

Merrick laid me down gently on the bed in Gothin's home and knelt beside me on the floor. He wiped the tears away from my face and the hair from my eyes before whispering, "Sleep, Ariella. Tomorrow will be the day we take back what's ours."

Before falling into the peace that sleep would bring me, I smiled at him and held onto his hand. "At least I'm not alone," I cried.

"You will never be alone."

My eyes stung with fresh tears, but I closed them and shut myself off from the pain. Brayden said those same words to me not too long ago. Slowly, and with my eyes steadily falling shut, I slipped into the dream realm and envisioned my life back home.

The snowy cold was welcome against my skin as I walked through the forest toward the icy retreat I could see up ahead. It was the place where Brayden and I had completed our bond and became one; the place that would always stay with me for the rest of my life. Opening the heavy, icy door, I stepped inside to find it dark and lonely.

The fire that once burned in the fireplace was no more; Brayden wasn't there to lend his flame or to help heal my heart. I walked over to the blankets that were the same ones Brayden and I made love on, and carefully lowered onto them. I could smell his scent as I wrapped myself deeper into their warmth and laid my head down. I stared at the frozen fireplace as the tears began to freeze across my cheeks, except it wasn't long before everything changed and the room lit up with fire.

The fireplace exploded with the blazing heat of Brayden's fury and I knew it was his fire because I could feel it. His anger flowed through our connection to me and I could tell he was close ... so close. The second I stood from the floor was the second the door burst open.

My heart beat a thousand times a second as I gazed upon the man who was my mate, my lover, and my king. He stalked inside, never taking his eyes off of me, as he stormed his way to me, taking me by the shoulders.

"Why?" he demanded. "Why would you deceive me like that? I came there to take you back and you let me go thinking I had you in my grasp." His voice broke with those last words and it tore me down in the process.

Instead of saying how sorry I was or why I did it, I burst into tears and fell into his arms. He knew why I did it he just didn't understand. His emotions ran wild through my blood and mine were doing the same to him. He held me tight and kissed the top of my head as I sobbed against his chest.

"I had to do it," I cried. "I had to get you out of there before anyone got hurt."

He huffed, "I don't care if I get hurt, angel. I just want you home safe. As soon as the sun rises in the morning I will be back for you."

I shook my head and held him tighter. "It will all be over by then," I whispered.

He pulled me away and narrowed his eyes. "What do you mean it'll all be over? Why do you insist on doing this when I know there are other ways to defeat him ... together?"

Sadly, I smiled and took his face in my hands, saying softly, "Because there is no time. When the sorcerer comes back he's going to have his mortal army ready to attack. I have to kill him before he sends them to our doors. You won't make it here on time."

"So what am I supposed to do now? Just let you save the world and go on with my life? How am I going to do that without you in it?" he argued.

I couldn't argue with him on that because I wouldn't know what to do if the situation was turned. Also, I didn't want to spend what could be our last few moments together fighting. Taking Brayden's hand, I lifted it to my lips and kissed him softly on his palm. "You have me now, Brayden," I said soothingly, hoping to calm him down. "I'm here right now at this very moment with you. Whatever happens, I will always be by your side and in your heart." I paused and leaned up to kiss him. I missed the way his lips felt on mine and the way his hands would tenderly touch my skin. He tensed, his anger still coiled underneath the surface of his skin.

"Please, let me love you," I pleaded. "I need this, Brayden. I don't want to fight."

He sighed and leaned his forehead to mine, his muscles beginning to relax. "I don't want to fight either, but this feels too much like a good-bye," he whispered against my lips.

I shook my head and gazed into his soft, brown eyes. "There will never be a good-bye for us, my love. We are together, always and forever."

"Always and forever," he repeated quietly.

Knowing this was the last night I would spend in his arms and not knowing how long I had in the dream realm, I crushed myself to him and pulled him down to the floor. He ripped away my clothes, exposing my bare flesh, just as I did with him. There was no stopping us and there was no going slow. I needed him and he needed me. The weight of our fate loomed heavily in the air, but for one last time I wanted to feel his love ... I needed it.

He spread my legs and covered his body with mine. There was no going gentle tonight, there was no wasting time. It was just me and him, starved for each other's love. He lowered his lips to mine and claimed me with his mouth before pushing himself inside of me, taking my body. Never once did we stop tasting and making love to each other with our mouths and our bodies. I couldn't let go and I didn't want to miss a single moment.

He kept his eyes open, gazing into mine the whole time. I could see and feel the love and passion in his heart for me, but I could also feel the fear and rage below that. The fear was what got me. He was afraid for me, of what was going to happen to me without him being there to protect me. I didn't want to ruin the moment, so instead I let the tears fall down my cheeks as I let his feelings flow through my body.

Gripping me tighter, he pushed inside me harder until we were both gasping for air and on the verge of release. I felt him shudder and growl low in his throat as my body clenched around him and I called out his name, demanding that he not stop. We came together, him releasing his seed inside of me and me trembling in his arms as our love making came to a close. I had never felt so complete.

"Me either," he replied to my silent thought. "You make me feel complete."

We lay there, joined as one ... always as one. It wasn't until the dream realm started to fade that I panicked. It was over, and it was too soon. With wide, tear-filled eyes, Brayden held onto me tighter, almost bruising me as he shook his head and shouted, "No, this can't be happening. Stay with me, angel. Don't let go!"

It didn't matter about letting go because I had no choice. The hands I held to his face started to fade and disappear. I could no longer feel his Winter skin beneath my fingers or the beat of his heart against my chest. This was good-bye.

"I love you, Brayden," I murmured. I didn't know if he heard me because one minute I was staring up into brown eyes, hoping that I didn't have to let him go, and then the next ...

The ground trembled and shook, jolting me out of the dream and into the hell I had awoken to. Merrick ran to the window and I immediately scrambled to join him, gazing out at what could be the cause of the disturbance. What I saw was way worse than what I could have ever imagined.

Coming through a portal in the middle of the village were not just a few mere mortals, but hundreds; marching one after the other. When they all made it through, there was one person who had yet to enter. Alasdair stepped through with a grin on his face, but it swiftly disappeared the moment he saw his village and the destruction that lay within.

"Oh no," I whispered, horrified at the sight before me. "How am I going to do this?"

Merrick placed a gentle hand on my shoulder and turned me to face him. "I don't know, Ariella, but you're smart and cunning. You'll think of something. I have faith in you."

I had to think of something fast because the sorcerer was furious and angry … and he was headed toward Gothin's home. The place where I was standing.

Chapter Thirty Nine

Ariella

"DAMMIT," I HISSED quietly. "If he comes in here he might see Gothin's ashes. I can't let him come in here."

Dismally, Merrick sighed and nodded. "You're right, he can't."

Taking a deep breath, I knew what I had to do. Making sure my dagger was hidden at my back, I took the form of Gothin and headed for the door. Alasdair was coming closer because I could feel his anger pulsating all around him. Gripping the handle of the door with all my might, my fingers began to turn white and go numb. I could do this.

"I will be right there with you," Merrick promised. I nodded and took another deep breath before opening the door.

"Thank you," I whispered. I didn't look back at him, but kept my head held high as I walked toward the sorcerer. He was dressed in all black armor with his long brown hair pulled back at the nape and his iron blade secured in his belt. I had to stay away from it.

The snarl on his face and the fury in his eyes made me want to kill him right then, but with his mortal army gathered all around I wouldn't be able to strike. However, it didn't stop the sorcerer from striking me. I saw his hand flying, but I knew I had to take it. The pain from the blow to my face vibrated throughout my body as I collapsed onto the ground. Merrick yelled for me to keep focus, to concentrate on what I had to do and to keep my glamour. It was so hard to get past the pain, but I couldn't fail now.

"Ariella, what happened? I can feel your pain," Brayden shouted in my mind. *"Whatever is going on you better hold on. I am coming for you."*

I couldn't answer him yet because Alasdair grabbed me by the neck and hauled me to my feet. "What the fuck happened here?" he hissed in my face. Brayden's cries and shouts in my head were so loud I almost thought the sorcerer could hear him. All that came through our bond was my grunts of pain.

Gritting my teeth, I wiped the blood from my mouth and took a deep breath. Gothin wouldn't talk back to him, which meant I couldn't. Wincing at the pain, I held in my anger and replied, "We were attacked, Master. The dragons came in unexpectedly and destroyed everything."

He squeezed my neck, cutting off my air, and suddenly threw me back onto the ground. "Why didn't you summon me? I would have destroyed them all!"

Hanging my head, I pretended to be the obedient servant, but inside I was raging, ready to end his miserable existence by shoving my dagger in his chest and watching him die. "There was no time, Master. By the time we heard them coming it was too late," I informed him.

"Ariella!" Brayden called. *"Answer me!"* Over and over he yelled my name, but I forced myself to concentrate and block him out as best I could.

Merrick placed a calming hand on my shoulder and leaned down to whisper in my ear, "Calm down, Ariella. Patience …"

Alasdair pointed a finger at me and snarled, "Get the army prepared and ready to leave. This ends now." He turned on his heel and stalked off toward his dwelling. When I watched him disappear behind the door, I gazed out at the army as they salivated for the taste of blood.

"Yes, Alasdair, this ends now," I said to myself. Brayden and my people were coming; they were going to fight. I couldn't let that happen. There was going to be no more killing, no more destroying my land, and no more of his poisonous ways. The day for his evil to be stopped was now, and I was ready.

Storming my way to Alasdair's dwelling, I looked over at Merrick and told him, "Brayden and our people are on their way. I have to do this now or many will die. I can't let them come in here with all these mortals and their weapons."

He nodded solemnly and blew out a shaky breath. "I agree. Do you want me to come up there with you?"

I shook my head, trying desperately to keep the tears at bay and my voice from cracking when I said, "No, it's okay. I need to do this alone. Thank you for being here for me. I don't think I would have kept my sanity if it wasn't for you."

Sighing, he pulled me into his arms and held me tight. "You were always so brave, Ariella."

I laughed and squeezed him tight. "I honestly think I got it from Drake. He was the one who always pushed me to do the things I did. Without him I wouldn't have had the courage to do what I've done. My whole family has helped me be who I am today. They are all a part of me."

"Yes, they are," he stated honestly. "I can see all of them in you, or at least when you don't look like a troll."

I smiled and smacked him in the arm. "Leave it to you to make a joke in a time like this," I teased. He grinned back, but I knew our time was up. "I have to go," I said, backing away from him. "Tell them all I love them for me."

Merrick swallowed hard and nodded. "I will, Ariella. Be careful up there."

I opened the door to the sorcerer's dwelling and glanced back at Merrick with a smirk on my face. "I am never careful, Merrick. That's what makes me dangerous." Taking a deep breath, I waved him farewell and shut the door behind me.

Once I got inside I wasn't expecting to look up and find a mile long staircase winding its way to the top. I groaned and began climbing. One after the other I ascended the stairs, knowing I was one step closer to ending this.

"Brayden?"

"Please tell me you're not about to do anything foolish? I know that tone, angel."

I was up one flight of steps and had a few more to go. *"If you consider killing the sorcerer foolish then yes I am."*

"We will be there soon! Don't do this without me," he roared.

"And that is exactly the reason I'm going to do it. He brought over the whole mortal army, Brayden. We have magic, but all it would take is one hit by their bullets and it would be over."

"How are you even able to get around out there without someone recognizing you?" he asked.

"Because there are things about me you don't know, Brayden, and it might be best if I show you." I didn't want to do this, but I sent a mental picture of

Alasdair backhanding Gothin across the face, except it wasn't Gothin … it was me. It was time I came out and showed him what I could do. *"That was why you felt the pain,"* I cried.

I could feel his confusion when he said, *"I don't understand. Why did I feel the pain of that hit? It wasn't even you."*

I walked up a few more steps. *"Yes, it was, Brayden. I was the one who got hit. I am the troll in that image."*

"How is that possible?"

I shrugged my shoulders and then realized he couldn't even see me. We were so completely and utterly connected it was as if he was right there talking to me. I explained, *"I don't know how it's possible, but it is. On the day I turned twenty-one this ability came to me. I can shift to make myself look like anyone I please. I knew I could get close to the sorcerer if I could just shift into the one person he trusted most."*

"So that's how," he expressed warily. *"That's how you were able to leave the palace undetected, too, isn't it? It all makes sense."*

I had about two more flights of stairs to go. *"Yes, that was how I got away. I pretended to be one of the warriors."*

"What else have you done to trick me? Were there other times you did this?"

"Yes," I confessed sheepishly. I figured I might as well be honest with him since I had nothing else to

lose. *"On the night you had that visit from Taryn it wasn't exactly her coming on to you."*

"That was you?"

"Yes," I answered. *"I had to see what you would do. I heard of your reputation so I had to test you. I didn't mean to doubt, but I had to know."*

He sighed. *"And now you are in the shape of the troll to get close to the sorcerer?"*

"Yes, he trusts him."

"Where are you now?" he asked.

I had finally made it to the door of the sorcerer's dwelling so I leaned up against the wall and let out a heavy sigh. *"I am in your heart, Brayden. That's where I will always be."*

Even though he broke down my wall, I had regained enough strength to block him out, if only for short periods of time. It hurt, but I had to let him go; it was time.

Before knocking on the door, I changed into the form that got me in this place the first time. The hair of Meliantha mixed with Calista's golden blonde, green eyes like Sorcha's, and the face a mixture of all of us combined. I was dressed in my black leathers without the armor and with my dagger hidden behind my back under my top. It was easier to move around in the leather so I had to be prepared. Taking a deep breath, I knocked on the door and waited.

After a few minutes of waiting there was no answer, so instead of knocking again I slowly turned the handle and pushed open the door. Everything inside was pitch black, but I knew he was in there, hiding. I could smell the dark magic permeating the air and it slithered across my skin like it wanted to latch onto me and suck my essence dry.

Quietly, I reached behind my back to grab the dagger and crept into the lightless room. I only made it two steps before I felt him behind me, hovering. Even though I couldn't see, I knew where he would be. He grabbed me by the neck and I could feel the cold bite from the iron blade as he thrust it up against my flesh. However, much to his dismay, I wasn't the only one in the compromising position. I held him firm in my grasp with my dagger up against the beating vein in his neck, sizzling his skin. We were at a standstill.

"You must be really stupid to come in here uninvited and with a weapon ... interesting. Who are you and how the hell did you get in here?" he demanded, his voice a low growl.

Gritting my teeth, I bit back the pain from his dagger digging into my skin and snapped, "I opened the door and walked in you moron, and I happen to consider myself very smart, considering that I got in here undetected."

"You didn't answer my question. Who are you?"

"If you want to know who I am then turn on some damn lights," I countered impatiently. I was ready to get his dagger away from my neck and end this once and for all.

The room slowly began to fill up with a soft light, starting from the ground up. I couldn't see

Alasdair's face and he couldn't see mine, but when that light rose above my head …

His eyes went wide and I could see the confusion spreading across his face as he looked down at the dagger at his throat. "It can't be," he said, sounding uncertain.

"Yes, it can," I retorted, "because here I am, and with the weapon that's going to destroy you."

Chapter Forty

Ariella

"HOW DID YOU find the scroll? There's no way you could have found it," he roared. "I have it hidden and only I know where it's at."

"We never let it go," I told him, rolling my eyes. "If you would've been smart and looked at the paper Sorcha gave to you, you would see that it was a letter to Drake. So who is the foolish one now?"

Before either of us could make a move, the floor beneath us started to tremble and shake. The last time the land felt like that was when Alasdair brought over his mortal army. Not this time, though. My people were coming and they were getting close.

Alasdair laughed, still locked in my tight grasp and unmoving. "Ah, Ariella, the martyr. I bet your precious lover didn't take too well with you coming here, did he? How does it feel to know you sentenced them all to death? I'm sure that's why they have come … to get you. They will get a shock when they see what awaits them."

"They already know, but this will all be over before they get here," I spat. "It ends now."

He chuckled. "It will never end, Your Highness. No matter if I'm here or not, there will always be a part of me that will come back. Just wait and see," he remarked with an evil glint in his eye. "But you are more than welcome to try."

Gladly, I thought to myself.

I jammed my knee into his groin, and when he bent over in pain I backhanded him the way he did to me out in the middle of the village. "That's payback," I hissed. "It wasn't your troll you hit out there in front of everyone, it was me. You should thank me for putting him out of his misery."

Alasdair got to his feet and his chest heaved up and down with his rage. His eyes were no longer gray, but almost midnight black as he glared at me, ready to strike. His power magnified and pulsated throughout the room, and almost immediately I was thrust against the wall by an invisible force. I screamed as the dagger dropped out of my hand and I had to face the realization that I was trapped.

I tried to fight against the restraints but I couldn't. Alasdair chuckled and pointed the iron blade at my chest as he stalked closer. "Oh, what should I do first?" he wondered, tapping the iron blade against his palm. "Maybe I should take you outside and gut you in front of your people when they come. I think that would make an excellent show. The look on your lover's face would be priceless."

"You're a sick, pathetic bastard," I hissed. "When you die, this land will be rid of your filth. You're not going to win this."

Alasdair smirked and narrowed his eyes menacingly. Taking his iron dagger, he grazed it across my neck all the way down to the tops of my breasts. I gritted my teeth and squeezed my eyes shut against the pain. I would not scream … I refused to scream. My cold Winter blood oozed down my chest and dropped on the floor, staining the wood where it landed. My dagger glistened in the light, and as soon as my blood dripped onto its blade it lit up the room like a thousand suns.

Alasdair shied away from the light and covered his face with his arm. The beams coming from the dagger were beautiful, in all shades of color, and they didn't affect me at all. The invisible force holding me to the wall broke and I was free. Immediately, I bent down to grab the dagger and held it in my hands as the glow traveled across my body and surrounded me. It wasn't my magic doing this, but someone else's. There was someone else here helping me.

Who could it be?

The time had come to end it all. It was over and I knew it. I could feel the poison of the iron spreading through my body from the gash across my chest. When he cut me I didn't realize how deep it was. I didn't have long now. I opened up my mind and found Brayden right there, just behind the surface.

"Good-bye, my love," I whispered quickly in his mind. *"I love you. You will all be safe now."*

Alasdair pulled his arm away, and as he did he saw the exact moment I smiled and raised my dagger. "It's over," I growled. "I hope you rot in Hell."

The talisman gleamed around his neck so I took the dagger and plunged it into the bloodstone straight down through his heart. I had only one second to see the terror in his eyes and to know that I succeeded to end his evil existence when the end finally came. In a rush of light, it was over.

The blast from the power surge felt like a thousand sharp knives penetrating every surface of my skin as I was thrown into the sky. It almost felt like I was flying, but all too quickly I landed and tumbled on the ground below, breaking every single bone in my body.

I couldn't move and I could barely breathe. I did, however, know that I succeeded. Before I fell into darkness and away from everyone I loved, I got to at least see what my bravery and courage did for the land. Instead of being surrounded by inky black trees, it was instead open meadows of nothing except green grass. There was no trace of the Black Forest, Alasdair, or anyone in his army. It had all vanished.

"I did it," I whispered to myself. Tears fell down my cheeks, except I was too weak to wipe them away.

"Yes, you did," a voice called out, soft and angelic. It was a voice I didn't recognize. "And now it's time to take you home."

Yes ... home.

The land started to fade away, and instead of the darkness one would see when they fell asleep, I was seeing the brilliant shades of a light from a new land. It was beautiful, but it wasn't the bright shades of the snow or the icy court I belonged to. This was somewhere different. I had never seen this place before, but there was no mistaking where I was. From the glowing bright sun above to the ethereal glow of the land, there was no denying that I had crossed over to another realm, one that had always and forever been known as the heaven for my kind ... the Hereafter.

I was dead.

Chapter Forty One

Brayden

I DIDN'T KNOW how long I yelled her name or how the pain coming through the bond didn't kill me on the spot. All I knew was that Ariella was hurt, she was dying, and there was nothing I could do to save her. I yelled for Sorcha to go faster, to push harder, but when Ariella's life began to slip out of my hands my whole world was lost. I held onto our bond, our connection, trying to will my power into her body … to keep her alive.

"Dammit, you hang on," I shouted in her mind. She was still alive, but only barely. I had to get to her before I lost her for good.

I was riding in the air on Sorcha's back—my army and the others were riding on the ground below us—when the whole Land of the Fae lit up like a thousand suns. The blast from that exposed power blew us back into the air with its raw force, but Sorcha kept fighting, pushing her wings to the limit knowing we needed to keep going. I couldn't see a thing as we flew straight into the light.

Once the light slowly dimmed down and my eyes adjusted, it took a while to figure out what I was seeing. What was once the Black Forest below us with its dark oily trees and stench of death was now replaced with green meadows and a sense of life. There was no sign of the sorcerer or his army, or his evil for that matter. It all felt clean … and pure. However, there was something down there, something lying still in the grass.

"Sorcha, look!" I hollered, pointing down at the figure in the meadow.

Hope surged through my veins and each second we got closer to the ground, the more I could tell it was definitely my Ariella lying down there. As soon as Sorcha got close enough to the ground, I jumped off her back and ran straight to Ariella. With my heart racing and my lungs burning, I collapsed onto the ground beside her and scooped her into my arms.

"Ariella? I'm here, angel, open your eyes," I demanded.

Her body was so still, so broken. The gash across her chest was black with inky veins protruding from the wound, and as soon as I placed my hand against her heart, my world ended when all I got was silence. I could no longer feel her heart beating or the life that used to course through her blood.

She's gone.

"No!" I roared, holding her tight.

I yelled her name over and over, but she never opened her eyes; those same ice blue eyes that were the most beautiful shades of blue I'd ever seen and could see straight through my soul to the good. Never was there a time I let my emotions get to me, but the void in my heart from her loss was too much to bear. I couldn't hold it inside, the pain became too much. As I rocked her in my arms, I let the tears fall freely from my eyes.

"Brayden," a soft voice sounded behind me. I could barely hear it because of the pounding in my ears. I didn't want to hear anyone's voice other than Ariella's. Nothing else mattered.

A light hand touched my shoulder but I was too numb to actually feel it. Calista knelt down beside me, and with tears in her eyes she squeezed my arm that held Ariella tightly to my chest. "We need to get her home to Elvena, Brayden. There has to be hope since her body is still here and not into ash. It's time to go," she said softly.

Was there still hope? All I knew was there was no home without her, but I had to believe in something.

Getting to my feet, I carried Ariella over to Sorcha who was still in dragon form, hanging her head as I approached. I ignored all the pitying stares as I walked past my warriors and only concentrated on the angel I had in my arms, the angel who had also taken my heart. Sorcha held out her claw and I climbed up, never letting go of Ariella.

"Let's go," I called, holding on as Sorcha took off into the sky. We were followed by Drake, who roared and whimpered, gazing over at the sister he'd lost. "Please come back to me," I cried, wiping the tears angrily away from my eyes. I wanted to be furious at her for going against me and doing what she did on her own, except looking down at her angelic face I couldn't begin to feel anything except how much I loved her, and how empty and lonely my life was going to be without her.

The ride back to the Winter Court felt like an eternity, but if there was any hope left, I sure hoped Elvena could find it. If there was anyone who could it would be her. When Sorcha landed at the palace steps of my home, I jumped off and rushed Ariella inside.

As soon as I entered through the doors I yelled as loud as I could, "I need someone to find Elvena, now!"

Quickly, I carried Ariella to our room and kicked open the door. I gently laid her on the bed and sat down beside her, shaking from impatience. I wanted Elvena to hurry and say that she could find a way to save her. I wanted to hear those words come out of her mouth and know that everything would be okay.

"Hang on, Ariella. I'm going to bring you back," I cried, kissing her limp hand. It was the same hand that held my ring ... the ring I gave to her.

Shouts and shuffling feet echoed out in the hallway, but I couldn't focus on anything other than Ariella and her frozen body. By the time Elvena made it to the room and to my side, I hadn't realized that everyone had already joined in behind me. Tears were all I could see as I gazed at everyone's faces. Calista and Meliantha were holding onto each other as my brothers comforted them by their sides. My sister had Drake, my parents had each other, and so did Ariella's parents. I was the only one, standing alone, and doomed to live the rest of my life in misery.

How was that fair? Ariella sacrificed her life to save the Land of the Fae and this is what she got ... what we got. How could a land that loved its people so much not protect her when she had her own blood spilled to save it? If she didn't survive, I wasn't going to be a part of it anymore; I refused to be a part of it.

Elvena's chin trembled as she gazed upon Ariella with a hand over her mouth, trying to keep in her sobs. "How is she still here?" I asked. "She has to still be alive somehow, right?"

She swallowed hard and shook her head. "I don't know, child. I can't feel her presence, but she is still here. From the wound in her chest she should've been ashes a long time ago."

"What can we do?"

She sighed and hovered over Ariella, narrowing her eyes in concentration. "Let me take a look and see what I can find. There has to be an explanation somewhere."

I moved over so Elvena could get closer to her, watching as she placed her hands on Ariella's head. Closing her eyes, I could feel the energy spike in the room as Elvena mumbled a chant in the Old Fae language. I knew the language well, but even with my enhanced hearing I couldn't tell what she was saying.

She travelled her hands down Ariella's body, hovering about an inch above until she reached the place above her heart. She choked on a sob and sucked in a ragged breath before continuing on down. At that point I knew it was no use. The despair flowing off of Elvena was answer enough. Ariella's heart had died, and with it mine as well.

I couldn't take anymore.

I took one last look at my angel, my love, and my wife. Forever will she stay engraved in my mind, but there was only so much loss I could take. Turning on my heel, I dug my nails in my palm to keep my mind focused on the physical pain and not the pain of losing my love ripping my heart into shreds. I ignored everyone as I passed them, and for the first time ever, my brothers even knew to stay back.

Before I could get out the door, Elvena's command stopped me, "Brayden, wait!"

I turned around slowly and met her sorrowful brown eyes. My throat closed up and it felt like I couldn't breathe from the weight pressing down on me; I didn't want to breathe. By the look in her gaze I knew what she was about to say would only tear me apart more. I thought about just walking out, but I had to know.

"I know why she's still here," she uttered sadly, looking only at me.

She hung her head and took a deep breath before meeting my eyes again. The next words that came out of her mouth were not what I was expecting at all. The force of it slammed into my chest and took every ounce of happiness I had ever felt and shoved it into the pits of despair. Grief consumed me and I got lost in it, falling until I knew I would never find my way back.

I didn't want to find my way back.

Chapter Forty Two

Ariella

THERE WAS pain …

I was standing in the middle of a bright field with flowers as far as the eye could see. I was dressed in a beautiful white, flowing gown just like the dress I wore on mine and Brayden's bonding night. There were others here, some reading while lounging in the grass while others walked and picked flowers.

"Please tell me this isn't what I'm supposed to do while I'm here," I mumbled to myself.

L. P. DOVER

A deep, sad chuckle sounded from behind me so I turned around quickly and saw someone I wasn't expecting to see. He bowed his head and smiled. "You can do what you want here, Your Highness. I am not one for the flower picking either."

"Lukas!" I shrieked, taking hold of his hand. He felt so real … so alive. "What's going on? How long have I been gone?"

"Not long," he answered. "It's been about a day now."

"Where's Merrick?" I asked curiously. "I figured he would be here."

Sighing, Lukas shifted on his feet and hung his head. "No, he's not here. He wanted to be here when you crossed over, but Calista needed him more."

When his gaze lifted to mine, I could see the hesitance and sorrow in his eyes. "Oh no," I whispered, turning away. "I can't imagine what they must be going through right now."

Even though I didn't have a heart that beat, I could still feel the hurt and pain in knowing that everyone I loved was back home suffering.

"What's going on back home? Is Brayden all right?" I asked forlornly.

He opened his mouth to speak, but was interrupted by the same soft, angelic voice of the woman I remembered hearing when I died. I could feel her presence behind me. "They will all be fine, Ariella," she replied, placing a kind hand on my shoulder. "Losing someone you love is not an easy task to bear."

I think we all knew how that felt. Taking a deep breath, I turned around slowly and in front of me was the most beautiful creature I had ever seen. "What are you?" I breathed, taking in her whole appearance.

Her hair was like my own, appearing more white than blonde, while her body beamed in the bright light almost like a shimmering glow. She had wings behind her back, but they weren't feathery like you would imagine an angel to have. They were thin and iridescent, adding to the whole ethereal glow. I was amazed and in awe.

Smiling, she bowed her head and answered, "My name is Lailah, Your Highness. I am one of the keepers of the Hereafter. I have come to welcome you."

I tried hard to smile but failed. "Thank you, Lailah. However, I wish I could say that I was happy to be here. I mean, I'm glad I was given the privilege to be here, but my heart was left back in the Land of the Fae." I paused for a second and searched around again at all the people, noticing that none of them had wings except her. "So ..." I began. "With being a keeper of the Hereafter does that make you an angel?"

She laughed and reached down to take my hand. Her skin was warm and soft, but her grip was firm and strong. I could feel her power and the pureness in her soul, and never in my life or death had I ever felt that kind of power. "I guess you can say that," she said, "but my wings disappear when I leave the Hereafter and the moment I step back they appear."

"How is that possible?" I asked. "Did you have to earn them before you could become a Keeper?"

She shook her head. "No, I didn't earn them in the way you think. I was chosen."

"By whom?" I wondered. I had never heard of Keepers before.

"You ask a lot of questions, Your Highness," Lailah teased with a grin. "I will tell you all that you want to know, but there is somewhere we must go first."

She looked to Lukas, who had remained silent during our introduction, and bowed her head to him. "It was lovely to see you again, Lukas, as always."

"Same to you, Lailah," he responded warmly.

He backed away slowly as Lailah held my hand tighter and lifted us up into the sky. "Where are we going?" I asked, looking down at the ground disappearing beneath us. The land below us started to fade and I had to close my eyes to the bright light that glared all around us the farther we went.

"Just hold on tight, Ariella, and keep your eyes closed. All will be revealed soon."

Chapter Forty Three

Ariella

"OPEN YOUR EYES," Lailah commanded sweetly.

Before opening my eyes, it took only one second to know where I was. I was in the Land of the Fae, in the exact spot the life fled from my body. The green meadows flowed as far as the eye could see with no hint of evil anywhere, and where I had met my last minutes in our realm there was a bed of roses that grew where my body had lain. I picked a giant pink one and held it to my nose. It smelled so sweet and alive, and it reminded me so much of my home in Summer before I changed.

"Why did you bring me here?" I cried, kneeling down into the grass. "What purpose is it to remind me of what I left behind?"

Lailah knelt down beside me and placed her hands on the ground. "I didn't bring you here to make you upset, Your Highness. This is the first step to helping you understand."

"To understand what," I whispered.

She took my hand and placed it on the ground. "That this isn't the end," she claimed. "Concentrate on the land and tell me what you feel."

Closing my eyes, I connected with the land and searched deep within its depths. I knew what I was feeling because I had felt it before, before my court had been claimed. The land was waiting for someone to be worthy enough to claim it, to make it grow.

"It wants to be claimed," I told her, "but with all the four courts who is there left to claim it?"

Grinning from ear to ear, she held out her hand and smiled. "That is the right question, Your Highness. Come, we have somewhere else to go."

Instead of flying this time, the moment I took her hand the bright light that shone on us from before flashed all around us. I could hear the far away sound of voices off in the distance, and once the lights dimmed and we got closer, I knew who those voices belonged to. When the light disappeared, I immediately opened my eyes and gasped, clutching my chest. I could barely breathe from the sorrow and pain permeating the room ... mine and Brayden's room.

Merrick saw me and rushed over, taking me in his arms. "Oh, Ariella, I am so sorry I wasn't there to see you on the other side. I couldn't leave Calista ... she needed me."

"I understand," I whispered.

He raised a questioning brow at Lailah and she quickly shook her head in response. *I wonder what that's about.*

"How is Brayden?" I asked him. By the way he bit his lip and looked away, I knew something was wrong. I knew that look like the back of my hand. "Merrick, tell me," I pleaded.

He sighed and blew out a shaky breath. "He's not here, Ariella. After everything that happened he took it pretty hard. He said he was leaving."

"Leaving," I shrieked. "Leaving where?"

He shrugged. "No one knows."

"I have to find him," I exclaimed to Lailah, wanting to rush out the door. "Please, let me look for him." There was nothing I wanted more than to see him again, but then if he couldn't see me ...

Would he be able to feel my presence like Calista could with Merrick?

Lailah nodded sadly and brushed a gentle hand down my cheek. "You will have plenty of time to find your mate, Your Highness. However, there is something that you need to know before you do."

A lone tear escaped down my cheek and she wiped it away, smiling. She walked me over to my family and as we passed them I got a clear view of the bed. There—lying under the sheets—was my body, still and unmoving with my eyes closed and unseeing. But how was that possible? I was dead, so shouldn't my body have been turned to ash?

"Why am I lying there?" I asked nervously. "If I'm dead wouldn't my body be gone?"

Elvena was sitting on one side of the bed sobbing with her head lowered while my sisters and Sorcha sat on the other with their arms wrapped around each other, sniffling and wiping away their tears. Bayleon and Bastian were even in the room with their eyes downcast, probably to keep from looking at Queen Mab or my mother.

Ryder and Kalen both hung back, grieving to themselves, wanting to give Calista and Meliantha their space. Kamden and Zanna were in the corner, both holding onto each other for comfort. However, Drake was a different story. Never once had I seen him cry, but watching the tears fall down his cheeks at my absence ripped my soul into pieces.

"Don't despair, Ariella," Lailah murmured. She placed a hand on the forehead of my body lying in the bed and looked back at me. I had no idea what was going on or why my body was still whole, but I wanted answers … I needed them.

"Tell me what's going on," I cried.

Lailah sighed and explained, "As you already know, when one of the fae dies, the soul in your body leaves and travels to the Hereafter. Your soul is what keeps your body together, keeps it strong. Yours has crossed over, Ariella, and that is what I see when I look at you right now. However, there is something that keeps you tied to this world, something that keeps your body alive even though your soul is not a part of it."

"What could that be?" I whispered. "I have never heard of this happening before." Nothing she said was making sense. I had never known any of this to ever happen in the Land of the Fae. What could be keeping my body tethered to my realm?

Lailah smiled. "Of course you wouldn't have heard of this happening before. You are the first, Your Highness. The Keepers had known of your fate to defeat the sorcerer long before you even knew, except your destiny took an interesting turn that we didn't expect. It wasn't just something that saved you, but someone."

I felt the presence of someone else with me when I defeated the sorcerer, but I never understood who or what it was.

Lailah leaned over my body and placed a gentle hand on my stomach, smiling. I gasped and collapsed onto the bed beside my body, bursting into tears. "Are you saying I was pregnant?" I cried, my eyes wide. When she nodded my world came crashing down on me. How could I have been so stupid? I not only sacrificed my life, but the life of my unborn child.

"I didn't know," I sobbed, wiping the tears angrily away from my face. "I sacrificed myself when I had a baby growing inside of me. I will never be forgiven for that. Brayden will never forgive me for this, for leaving and sacrificing myself and his unborn child."

"He knows you didn't know, Ariella," Merrick spoke up softly. "Elvena told him there was no way you could've known so early if you weren't expecting it or looking for it to happen."

"It still doesn't change the fact that I'm gone and with it my child," I wailed.

Lailah knelt down and took my hands in hers, her amber eyes kind and full of life. "I am going to change that, Ariella," she revealed. "That's why I brought you here … to give you back your life."

"What? How?" I whispered hopefully.

She smiled and placed my own hand on my stomach. "The baby inside your womb is still alive, Ariella. She needs you and we need her. The night she was conceived she was marked to be a Keeper, and on that night she had already come into her power. That's why you were able to see Merrick and Lukas when you were here. Those are not your abilities, but your daughter's."

"I'm going to have a daughter?" I whispered, wrapping my arms around my stomach.

Tears of joy streamed down my face, but they were soon put on hold when I realized what Lailah just said. My daughter had been chosen to be a Keeper. How was that going to be possible with her alive?

"Wait," I exclaimed, grabbing her hand. "You said she's going to be a Keeper. To be a Keeper she will be in the Hereafter. Does that mean she has to die for that? I'm not going to let you take her!"

Lailah lifted a challenging brow. "I am not dead, Your Highness. Keepers are very much alive," she pointed out sternly. "And your daughter will be also. She will be able to travel from this realm to the Hereafter to assist those in crossing over. She will be able to see Merrick and Lukas or whoever she pleases anytime she wants. This is a very special gift that makes her a very important female in your realm, *and* in the mortal world. There are faeries not only here that she will be helping, but those that are lost in the mortal realm. That is why we are sending you back so you can bring her into your world and make her strong so she can fulfill her destiny. The Land of the Fae has not finished changing, and your daughter is going to be a part of it all."

I glanced down at my frozen body and then back to her. "So how do you put me back in my body exactly?"

She grinned, and about that time her body began to glow with a bright, beaming light. The brighter it got the more it felt like I was fading and being pulled in a new direction. "Getting you back is the easy part, Your Highness. I look forward to meeting your daughter when the time comes."

"So do I," I whispered with a smile. "So do I."

Closing my eyes, I succumbed to the pull on my soul and let it take me, deeper and deeper. I knew the moment I connected back with my body because I could feel it, I could feel her … my daughter. I could feel her life growing inside my belly and giving me the strength I had lost, but I could also feel Brayden's grief. It ripped through my chest like a thousand knives. I was home, I was safe, and I needed to find him … fast.

Chapter Forty Four

Ariella

WHEN I OPENED my eyes and took my first deep breath the whole room fell silent. I looked down at my chest where the gash from the iron blade had wounded me and I was surprised to see that there wasn't even a scar there; it had healed completely. I glanced around the room; they were all frozen in place, their eyes wide open in shock. I sat up slowly and cringed when my muscles stretched and popped

L. P. DOVER

with my movement. I guess being dead took its toll on my body.

"Ariella?" Calista cried, her eyes teary and wide. She was on the bed beside me, where she had been just a few minutes ago when I was still dead. She reached out a hand to touch me. "Please tell me I'm not seeing things."

"You're not seeing things," I assured her, taking her hand. "I'm here."

The room erupted in screams and shouts, and I had to close my ears because it was so deafening. Elvena took my face in her hands and closed her eyes, chanting in her usual way. She gasped and covered her mouth with her hands. "You've been touched by a Keeper," she sobbed. "They let you come back."

Smiling, I nodded and put a hand on my stomach. "Yes, they did. Apparently, I'm carrying something very important. How did you know about the Keepers?" I asked. "I never knew such a thing existed."

She waved me off. "Child, when you've lived as long as I have you see and hear things, and I am not surprised you didn't know anything about them because when it came to your studies you didn't listen very well," she scolded halfheartedly.

I chuckled lightly, but there was no time for that. I had to find Brayden. "I need to go," I blurted out. "Brayden needs me. I have to find him."

I got out of bed and embraced my family quickly, especially my brother, before turning back to

Calista. "Be honest," I said to her, "how bad did Brayden take it?"

She sighed and lowered her head. "It was bad," she answered softly. "Even Ryder and Kalen had never seen him explode like that. No one knows where he's at, and they're afraid he's going to try and leave for good."

I could feel our bond, strong as ever, but the grief had consumed him; it clouded his mind and all I could sense was emptiness coming from him. "That's not going to happen. I will find him," I promised.

I embraced her one last time before rushing to the door where Bastian waited patiently with his arms crossed at his chest. I tricked him in the Black Forest and it was something I didn't want to have to do, but I wanted to know he would be safe. It was the only thing I could think of to get him away unharmed.

"Are you mad at me?" I asked him.

He sighed and pulled me to him. "I was at first. However, now that you're alive I can't help but feel in awe of you right now. You were so brave, Ariella."

I leaned back and smiled. "Thank you, but I'm a little surprised to see you in the palace, though."

Lifting a brow, he rolled his eyes and laughed. "Your mate wanted to find a reason to kill me so he offered to let me come into the palace as long as I didn't enthrall any of your fae. The consequence would be death if I were to fail. I couldn't leave without seeing you one last time."

"There won't be a last time anymore. I'm back and I'm not going anywhere, except to find

Brayden," I stated adamantly. I looked back at everyone and they all smiled reassuringly at me before I left. As soon as I got out of the palace, I knew where I needed to go. Brayden's sorrow was like a beacon honing me to him and leading me the way. The closer I got to him the stronger I could feel his grief.

"Oh Brayden," I whispered to myself.

Glancing down at my flat belly, I rubbed a hand tenderly over my womb and sighed. "We're coming for you."

❄ ❄ ❄

The path to Brayden led me straight through the woods to the place where it all began. He was so close, but yet so far away. It was like my words would just float through his mind instead of him hearing them. *Please don't let me be too late to bring him back.*

Once our ice cottage came into view I couldn't wait any longer. Each second felt like an eternity and each step I took my heart raced even faster, a heart that could finally beat again. When I got to the door, I quickly burst through it expecting to see Brayden, but all I found was a dying flame and nothing except emptiness.

"No, no, no," I repeated over and over, rushing in. Where could he be? *I just felt him here.*

"Brayden!" I shouted, rummaging through the house for anything that might lead me to where he was. He was just there, but now he was gone; I couldn't feel him anymore. My heart sank when I realized I was too late. In the one second I couldn't make it here on time he was gone … to the mortal realm.

"Brayden, come back," I cried, shouting as loudly in his mind as I could. *"I'm here and I'm alive. Please come back to me."*

I felt nothing through our connection. He had shut off and he had me blocked. I had no clue where he went or how to find him. There was no telling how long it would take for me to locate him in the mortal realm, or if I would make it to him in time before he did something stupid.

Placing a hand on my stomach, I let the tears fall and murmured softly, "What am I going to do, little one? I have to find him somehow."

Before I could make it to the door, I gasped as something within my body began to pulse and come alive. There was magic blooming inside me and swirling around like butterflies in my stomach. I fell to my knees as all that energy built up and left my body in a huge rush of blinding light and colors that flew into the sky. Breathing hard, my chest heaving up and down from excitement, I slowly got to my feet and leaned against the door.

"I don't know what you did, little one, but it must have been something major for that amount of power. I say we go find your father now."

I was determined to find him no matter how long it took, but I prayed that it wouldn't take long. The longer it took, the worse his grief would consume him. When I opened the door and stepped out, I marched through the woods toward the palace. I didn't get too far; the sound of my name upon the wind had frozen me still.

"Ariella?"

I turned around slowly. My heart thumped wildly in my chest and the connection to Brayden suddenly surged back to life as I saw him standing there looking lost and unsure.

"You came back," I cried. "I was going to go to the mortal realm to find you."

"But you're gone, angel. Why would I want to be found without you by my side? You may have saved us, but you left me here when all I wanted to do was help you," he spat angrily.

"You did help me, Brayden," I exclaimed. "It may not have been you directly, but our daughter who *is* part of you brought me back, just like I'm assuming she brought you back to me just now."

"How is that possible? You're dead! I felt you, Ariella, and there was nothing left. You're probably not even here now, just a figment of my imagination."

"Why are you Winter men so stubborn?" I growled, stalking toward him. "You want me to prove I'm alive, well here it goes." The second I reached him, I grabbed his face in my hands and pulled him roughly down to my lips. *"Feel me, Brayden. Feel my touch and tell me I'm not alive,"* I muttered to him silently.

Groaning, he trailed his hands down my face, down my arms, and then down to my waist where he wrapped his arms around me, holding me tight. Ever so slowly, the sorrow and grief that consumed his soul from my loss began to disappear and wither away. He was coming back to me; he believed me.

Breathing hard, he released from the kiss and placed his forehead to mine. "You're really here," he breathed. "I can feel you."

"Yes," I whispered. "And so is our daughter." I took his hand and placed it on my belly. "She's in here and she's alive."

"How were you able to come back?"

I smiled and glanced down at his hand running circles across my stomach. "Originally, I wasn't supposed to come back, but our fate had taken a new turn and had given us our daughter. She's special, Brayden. I was sent back so I could bring her into the world. I don't know what is going to happen in the future, but I do know that she's going to play a huge part in it and she's going to need to be strong."

Brayden took my face in his hands, pressing his lips firmly to mine while never taking his eyes off of me. When he pulled back he said, "And we will make her strong … together. No more running away and trying to save the day by yourself. We are bonded for a reason, angel, and that is because we love and want to protect each other. What you did, sacrificing yourself like that, hurt worse than a thousand deaths."

I nodded and closed my eyes. "I know, and I will never forget the pain of that for as long as I live. I didn't know if you could ever forgive me for that."

He sighed, tilting up my chin. "I will on one condition."

When I opened my eyes, a tear escaped down my cheek and he wiped it away. As I gazed up into his soft, brown eyes I knew without a doubt that I would do anything to heal the wound I caused in his heart.

Softly, and with all the love in my being, I murmured, "I will do anything you wish, Brayden. Just name it."

Grazing my lips with his finger, he took a deep breath and let it out slowly. "I need you to promise me something. Promise me that no matter what happens in our future or how you think you are protecting me that you will never try to run off and save us again. We are one now ... a solid bond that will always be stronger together. I can't lose you again, angel. I don't want to ever know that kind of suffering again."

I nodded sadly, but it was my turn to wipe the tears away from his eyes. "You will never know how sorry I am for doing that to you. But I *can* tell you this ... I promise I will never do it again. You have my word, my oath, that from this day forward we will do everything as one. I will make it up to you for as long as I live."

Biting his lip, he turned his head toward our icy cottage with a mischievous grin on his face. "Well then, in that case you can start making it up to me now," he replied huskily. He reached down and lifted me up under my legs, making me giggle, and carried me the rest of the way to our little hideaway.

"And how would you like for me to make it up to you?"

Once inside, he shut the door and carried me over to the blankets, laying me down gently. He slowly lowered the straps of my dress off my shoulders, kissing along the way as he bared my naked flesh. "You're going to let me make love to you all night, angel, and then when we wake up tomorrow morning we are going to start all over again."

I smiled up at him and kissed him tenderly on the lips. "I think I like the sound of that," I cried softly. "It's the perfect start to a new beginning and a beginning that we will share together, just you and me … and our daughter."

For the rest of the night we made love to each other and basked in the joys of knowing that everything was going to be fine from now on, especially since we were together again and I was alive. There was no evil, there was no dark sorcerer … only us, our love, and our magic. The Land of the Fae had triumphed, we had won, and I was home.

My Winter of ice …

Epilogue

Ariella

Five Years Later

"DADDY, CAN YOU tell me the story again?" Ella chimed, jumping up and down. Brayden looked back at me and smiled, shaking his head incredulously.

He tucked our daughter into her small bed and we both took our place on each side of her. Brushing away the blonde hair out of her face, we both gazed down at her angelic, light brown eyes. Even though we knew the answer to the question, Brayden always asked it. "Do you not get tired of hearing the same story every night, little one?"

Ella beamed at us and shook her head. "Uh-uh, I love hearing how mommy saved us. I think the baby likes to hear the story, too."

"Actually, you saved us Ella," I said, tapping her nose playfully. "And the baby does like to hear the story. He wiggles around in my tummy when Daddy tells it."

Our son would be here any day now and I had Elvena on standby for when that time came. Brayden was excited to be welcoming a son into the family. He said he was going to go crazy with only females around him if we didn't add a son.

Ella giggled. "I know, because I can sense his happiness. But I still like to hear how brave you were, and also how fun it was to ride on Uncle Drake's back. Do you think he will let me ride on Aidan's back when he gets older?"

Brayden and I both chuckled. Aidan was Sorcha and Drake's newborn son, and a dragon as well. We all thought they weren't going to have any, but they surprised us a year ago with the news. It was very exciting considering it would be adding more dragons to our land.

To Ella, I said, "I'm sure once Aidan gets old enough you'll be able to, but it'll be a while considering he's only a baby right now. When you get older you will be able to fly as well when you get your wings. Don't forget that."

She nodded cheerfully. "I know," she squealed. "Lailah says she will teach me how to use my wings when I get them. I told Merrick I will fly him around."

"Is he here?" Brayden asked curiously.

She looked past Brayden's shoulder and snickered. "He's right behind you making faces," she replied.

Brayden rolled his eyes and in a serious voice he said, "Well, you tell Merrick that when you get older he's not going to be having these late night visits in your room. Make sure he understands that."

I put a hand over my mouth to cover my smile. Brayden was always the protective one, and I could just imagine Merrick rolling on the floor with laughter over that.

"He said okay," Ella announced, giggling again.

Now that Ella was born and separate from me, I had lost my ability to see those I loved in the Hereafter. I couldn't see Merrick and reminisce with him anymore nor could I see Lailah. When I was pregnant she had informed me of the changes Ella would go through once she got older, and also the amount of time she would need to spend in the Hereafter. The thought scared me at times, but I knew it was what she was destined to do.

The courts had grown stronger over the years with new life and new powers. Calista and Ryder had welcomed a daughter into their family and little Merrick adored her. He was her protector, or that was what he always said when we visited. Meliantha and

Kalen had their hands full with their twins, but fully expected to have more someday.

My friends Kamden and Zanna completed the marriage bond soon after I came back to life five years ago. They also had a daughter who was a little younger than Ella, and to this day both Ella and her were inseparable. When Kamden and Zanna would visit, Ella would relay messages back and forth between him and Lukas. To this day, years after, I still felt the guilt of his loss, but I was glad Kamden had a way to stay connected to his brother.

Yawning, Ella snuggled into her covers and smiled sleepily. "I'm ready for the story now, Daddy."

Smiling, Brayden reached over and took my hand. *"I love you, angel."*

"And I love you," I murmured back silently. *"Always ..."*

We both gazed down at our precious daughter, the one who brought me back, and the one who saved all our lives. Settling into place, Brayden kissed her cheek and began to tell the story that would forever be engrained in our minds and in our souls; the story of our lives.

"Once upon a time, in the Land of the Fae, there were four powerful princesses ..."

THE END

~Coming spring 2014~

REGIN OF ICE (FOREVER FAE SERIES)

The LAND OF THE FAE series
The journey continues in this all new spin off
series.

Other Books by L.P. Dover

Second Chances

Standalone

About the Author

L.P. Dover lives in the beautiful state of North Carolina with her husband and two wonderful daughters. She's an avid reader that loves her collection of books. Writing has always been her passion and she's delighted to share it with the world. L.P. Dover spent several years in college starting out with a major in Psychology and then switching to dental. She worked in the dental field for eight years and then decided to stay home with her two beautiful girls.

Her works consist of the Forever Fae series, the Second Chances series, and her standalone Love, Lies, and Deception. She's really excited to be able to experience writing in the different genres. Her reading used to consist of nothing but suspense thrillers, but now she can't get away from the paranormal/fantasy books. Now that she has started on her passion and began writing, you will not see her go anywhere without a notebook, pen, and her secret energy builder … chocolate.

L.P. Dover can be found at:

Facebook- https://www.facebook.com/pages/LP-Dover/318455714919114

Twitter- https://twitter.com/LPDover

Goodreads- http://www.goodreads.com/author/show/6526309.L_P_Dover

Website- http://authorlpdoverbooks.com/

**ALSO CHECK OUT THESE
EXTRAORDINARY AUTHORS & BOOKS:**

Alivia Anders ~ Illumine
Cambria Hebert ~ Recalled
Angela Orlowski Peart ~ Forged by Greed
Julia Crane ~ Freak of Nature
J.A. Huss ~ Tragic
Cameo Renae ~ Hidden Wings
A.J. Bennett ~ Now or Never
T.G. Ayer ~ Skin Deep
Tabatha Vargo ~ Playing Patience
Beth Balmanno ~ Set in Stone
Lizzy Ford ~ Zoey Rogue
Ella James ~ Selling Scarlett
Tara West ~ Say When
Heidi McLaughlin ~ Forever Your Girl
Melissa Andrea ~ The Edge of Darkness
Kelly Walker ~ No One's Angel
Komal Kant ~ Falling for Hadie
Melissa Pearl ~ Golden Blood
Alexia Purdy ~ Ever Shade (A Dark Faerie Tale #1)
Sarah M. Ross ~ Inhale, Exhale
Brina Courtney ~ Reveal
Amber Garza ~ Falling to Pieces
Anna Cruise ~ Maverick
Rebecca Ethington ~ Kiss of Fire

Sneak Peek of *CHARMED*

by Cambria Hebert

Chapter One

"Death Escort - an assassin employed by the Grim Reaper. Will kill a target by any means necessary. Including charm."

Charming

Present day

You would think being a Death Escort—a killer by trade—would make a man above getting a lecture from his boss. Apparently when you work for the Grim Reaper, the ultimate death dealer, it doesn't matter who you are, how many times you've killed, or how ruthless you might be because he is better.

After over ninety years of working for him, it's still annoying as hell.

And so are his lectures.

The fact is it gets old working for someone who is the be-all, end-all in life and death. So when I saw the chance to allow someone to get the best of him, I took it. I mean, it isn't every day when someone manages to get around the iron-clad rules of the Grim Reaper himself.

So yeah, I talked and wasted time. I "forgot" to mention that one of his new Escorts had figured out a way to break the call of death that was placed on a Target. Turns out in the eyes of the Reaper (who strangely looked a lot like Mr. Burns from that cartoon *The Simpsons*), that made me an accessory.

And now, after weeks of delaying the inevitable, I was getting my punishment.

Goody gumdrops.

Instead of listening to what a disappointment I was, how he should just Recall me right now and let me twist away in an eternity far worse than hell, blah, blah, blah, I turned my attention instead toward the floor-to-ceiling row of closets that lined the wall behind his massive desk.

The closets where he kept his bodies.

Some people collect coins, artifacts, or tools. G.R. collects bodies.

The doors were open, making me think he was displaying his collection to me for a certain reason. Shock value maybe? Though he must know that seeing a bunch of bodies wasn't something that would shock me. These bodies were all groomed and hanging in perfect rows. I was used to seeing bodies in… less than perfect condition.

Maybe it was to make me think that the very body I inhabited at this moment might end up back with the others and I would be nothing but the red mist that makes up my soul.

I scanned the bodies, my eyes looking for one that probably should have been familiar, but after so many years I wondered if it would be. I had done this occasionally through the years, but just like today, I didn't see it. I wondered what had become of my original body, the one I was born in. The one I died in. I couldn't imagine G.R. got rid of it; I mean, he was practically a body hoarder, yet in all my years of working as an escort, of rotating bodies, I hadn't seen it.

And I wasn't about to ask. Because asking would let him know I wondered; it would give him even more power over me... something he didn't need more of.

"I have a new Target for you," G.R. announced, effectively ending my thinking.

"A Target?" I asked, surprised, wondering if I somehow missed the punishment I was supposed to get.

"That is your job, is it not?" he mused, staring at me through narrowed eyes. His cheekbones jutted out and his wide forehead was further widened by the way he combed his dark hair back and away from his face. He wasn't a big man, but I guess when the merest touch could kill, muscles didn't really matter.

"I thought we were here to discuss the status of my job," I replied, looking right at him. I was careful to keep my posture bordering on lazy to give off the impression I could care less about whatever he dished out.

"Active," he said, irritation flashing through his eyes. "That's the status of your job. Like it or not, you're one of the best escorts I have."

I flashed a smile. I wasn't *one* of the best. I was *the* best. We both knew it. I guess that was the reason my punishment was lacking.

"Here," he said, holding out a file. I got up and took the folder, opening it up and staring down at the picture clipped to the front of the page. It was a young woman, in her twenties—long dark hair, brown eyes, and full lips. She was gorgeous, which could be considered a bonus. She had the bone structure of fine breeding and about four names, which spoke of old money.

She'd be dead by the end of the week.

I scanned the information, looking for her address, looking for the place I'd be flying off to next. Hopefully it was somewhere warm, with miles of beaches. Or perhaps the dessert where it seemed the sun always shined. I didn't really care as long as it wasn't here. Alaska sucked. I hoped I never came here again.

My eyes found the zip code and I stiffened. "Is this right?" I asked, turning to look at G.R.

"Have I ever given you faulty information?"

Here. The woman was here, in this godforsaken, cold, and dark town.

Something niggled at the back of my brain. I looked at her name again. *Rosalyn Elizabeth Kennedy Sinclair*. Her last name… I'd heard it before. I glanced down at the short paragraph on known information about the Target.

Daughter of Senator Jack Sinclair.

The file slapped my thigh when I jerked and spun around to look at G.R. "You've got to be kidding."

"I don't joke about business."

"She's the daughter of Jack Sinclair, the *Alaskan* senator. He's practically a celebrity around here," I said, thinking of all the times I watched the news or some show on TV. The press here loved him. They practically camped out on his lawn, just hoping for a glimpse of him.

"Yes. He is. His daughter is worth thirty million dollars."

"Money. So this Target is all about money," I said. I don't know why this irritated me, but it did. It certainly wasn't the first time I'd killed for money. It wouldn't be the last. In fact, I killed for money more than I killed for abilities because finding people with some sort of ability wasn't as easy as finding one with money.

"You have something against money, Charming?"

"No. But you have to know this girl has got to have security practically feeding her breakfast. Not to mention she probably has fifteen financial advisors and lawyers that will make actually getting to her money impossible."

"So are you saying you can't do this job? That you refuse?"

Ahhhh. And here it was.

Understanding dawned like the sun of a new day.

He was dolling out my punishment in the form of a job. He assigned me a Target that would practically guarantee failure. Failure would get me Recalled, would get my soul pulled out of my body and sent into an empty vast space of nothingness for all eternity. A place where I could hear the tortured wails of those lost around me, a place where I could think but feel nothing but pain, and a place where I would know no peace *ever*.

And if I refused this job?

Same thing. So here was an interesting dilemma. I could refuse and get Recalled. I could fail and get Recalled. Or I could pull off the most impossible kill in the history of escorting and I could make Mr. Death himself finally realize who he was attempting to mess with.

Really, there was no dilemma at all.

"You know this job is going to take longer. To infiltrate the camp of this woman, of this family… it isn't something I can do overnight."

G.R.'s eyes gleamed. "Yes, I'm aware. I'll give you six months."

I kept my face smooth, my posture relaxed as his timeline sucker punched me in the gut. *Six months?* That was insane. A job of this magnitude would take a year. I underestimated just how angry I had made him.

My eyes slid to the bowl of light-colored stones that sat on the corner of his desk. The stones that he always left in exchange for a life that he took. Once a stone was placed, the death—the end of a life—was sealed. There was no getting out of it.

Except for once.

Turns out if you can manage to break the stone, then you break the claim of the Grim Reaper. One of the new Escorts figured it out. It got him Recalled. It got me into this predicament.

"I want more than my usual cut," I said. Punishment or not, if I pulled this off I wanted what I earned. "Ten million."

"That's a lot of money," G.R. replied, leaning back in his chair as he appraised me. "You're in no position to be making demands."

I shrugged. "You're convinced I'll fail anyway. Who cares how much I ask for?"

Again, he rested chin atop his fingers. "Fine. Ten million."

I resisted the urge to smile.

"You get six months. Get into her life. Get into her bank accounts. Make sure when she is dead, it's all yours. And if you succeed…" He paused and looked at me. "Then I'll overlook your betrayal."

My betrayal? He acted like I was the one who broke his claim, who bested him. All I did was keep my mouth shut. If I had known I was going to be punished like this, then I would've made it worth it.

"Fine. I'll take the job." Like I really had a choice.

G.R. clapped his hands like a kid on Christmas morning. "Wonderful."

Yeah, great. Not only was I given the most impossible Target ever, but I was also being sentenced to this icy, dark prison that was Alaska.

I gripped the file and headed for the door. I was ready to go.

"Oh, Charming," G.R. called behind me.

34527071R00238

Made in the USA
Lexington, KY
11 August 2014